THE WRETCHED
The Kell Stone Prophecy
Book Two

Dana Trantham

Wayward Cat Publishing

The Wretched
A Fenn of the Wasteland Novel

Chapter One

1268 Autumn

Piercing screams echoed around him as Prince Welk of Michelruud startled awake in the darkness. He clambered up, for a moment unable to remember where he was. His tent had collapsed around him and he battled with it. *The tent.* Yes, the encampment on the grassy plain of Nergens between the Ruud and the ice realm—northeast of the lilac clover fields. He was in his nuptial tent, the morrow his wedding day when he would finally marry his beloved Rue, whose screams now terrified him into action.

Horse hooves pounded the ground around him, whinnies, shouts, and grunts filled the air as he struggled to free himself from the heavy tarp. It was still night, but as he found his opening, the campsite was lit in flames as the other tents burned.

"Rue-Anna," he screamed, and the reality of his terror shook him. His legs trembled violently as he climbed to his feet and darted toward the women's tent. Their screams had ceased. Only shouts of dark figures on foot and horseback thundered in the air—and the shrill cries of the felid folk child Frieden, who stood a few yards away, just outside his father's flaming tent.

"Rue-Anna," Welk cried out.

A rugged folk ran toward him, his hand raised above his head, a wooden mace locked in his fist. When he realized the man's prey was Frieden, Welk dove for the child, scooped him up and tumbled to the ground, shielding him from the swing of the club. A sharp, stabbing pain shot through his head; dazed, a blackness fell over him, even as he fought to hide the felid child from death, even as he realized his attacker was a soldier in his father's guard.

His own name on his brother's lips floated somewhere in Welk's pain-filled fog of sleep. Elrundt lived, and gently shook him into consciousness.

"Wake, brother," he was saying. "Hurry. Wake."

Welk reached for his throbbing head and forced himself to sit, fighting the waves of nausea rippling through his stomach. Fire raged somewhere near—the odor of burning flesh found him and brought him nearly to heaving. Morning had dawned. He squinted against the harsh summer sun.

"Rue," he whispered and winced.

There beside him was young Frieden, whimpering in his sleep.

"Who else lives, brother?" Welk closed his eyes against the sickening pain racking his body.

"None." There was a cold edge of rage to his brother's voice.

Elrundt helped him to his feet and led him through their burned encampment. Fifty yards east, against the backdrop of the snow-capped peaks of the ice realm, flames rose off a pyre and flumes of swirling black and gray smoke billowed into the clear blue morning sky. The eis had come to cremate their dead.

"No," Welk muttered and made toward them, but Elrundt pulled him back.

"They will not allow us. I have tried."

"They cannot be dead." He turned to Elrundt and let out a

choked cry. "They are not gone."

He reeled and looked back at the burned nuptial tents, heaps of ashes now. Belfen, the felid folk child's father, lay just outside the tent he shared with his brothers Quarn and Yew, bloodied and deathly still. Staggering, Welk made his way past him to where his betrothed's tent lay in a blackened clump. The tarp had burned away, exposing Vreni's charred remains, her arms stretched forward as if she'd tried to cover and protect another.

"All dead," Elrundt said following him. "Except the felidae Quarn and Yew. They watched as Belfen fought for his life and fled when he was killed. The eis arrived before I regained consciousness."

Welk remembered Frieden and turned back to see him still sleeping on the ground in the middle of the remains of their lives.

"Why didn't Belfen take his felid form?" Elrundt said.

"He and Vreni were bound by the old ways."

"He died for principle?"

"No, brother. Once they took the oath, they could not transform until Frieden was of a certain age. They were physically unable." Welk found his knees loosening and he let himself sit. "Quarn and Yew," he said. "They did nothing?"

"They might have fought valiantly and torn many of the guard apart," Elrundt said. "Before being shot... probably killed. But, they did nothing to stop this."

"It would be better to die fighting than live as cowards. The felidae would agree."

Elrundt shook his head, his eyes empty, his countenance dispirited.

"They cannot be dead," Welk muttered.

He remained on the ground for some time, his brother letting him have his silence; tears streamed down his face until he wiped them away and scowled.

"What happened? What did you see?" he asked Elrundt.

"I was just on the edge of sleep. They buckled the tents first and set the others on fire. I fought, but there were many. I watched Belfen carry Frieden out of his tent and try to get him to run while he fought off the guard. And I watched Quarn and Yew do nothing."

"Not our tents?"

"They knew our colors."

"And you were not harmed?"

"They cudgeled me. Same as you."

"It was Father's guard."

"And that is why we live." Elrundt nearly spat the words.

Welk stood and forced fresh air into his lungs, but it was tinged with the smoke of the bodies of their beloved eisen.

"Then we know what we must do now. We will go home. And kill him."

Elrundt stared at him, and Welk realized, sadness falling over him, that his brother had succumbed finally, to their father's ill will. He'd had his fill of abuse and it had hardened him. His dark eyes, instead of burning with rage, were dulled with pain.

"I will never return to the Ruud," Elrundt said. "I will never look upon our father again. Not even to murder him."

Tiny, muted cries startled them and they turned to see pale Frieden, sitting up and peering around him. Welk hurried to the child and lifted him into his arms.

He whimpered. "Mama."

"We have visitors," Elrundt said and turned to the west.

"From the south as well."

From the west came the felidae, dozens of them, padding through the tall plains grass into the camp in their svelte, black, feline forms—large, formidable beasts, who could kill a folk with a swipe of a paw. Without greeting, they sniffed out the bodies of Belfen and Vreni and several shifted into folk form to lift them.

"Quarn, you coward," Elrundt shouted and made for the group.

"No," Welk warned. "Now is not the time to break the troubled truce between us."

They watched as the party of felidae escorted their folk away with the bodies. But Quarn and Yew remained behind, turned to them, and transformed into frail, wan folk. Elrundt took a few steps toward them as they approached and Welk considered allowing him to take his vengeance on the felidae. But they would only have to shift back into their feline forms to rip him apart.

"Give us the child," Quarn said.

Welk's heart sank into his chest. Turn Belfen's son over to the felidae? "No."

Quarn let out a guttural growl and the pack of felidae stopped their march and turned, waiting.

"Give us the felid child. He does not belong with you."

"You will murder him," Elrundt said.

"That is none of your concern."

"It is," Welk said. "Belfen was my friend. He and Vreni pledged themselves to the old ways of your kind. You must honor them."

"He is mine now." Quarn stepped forward.

"Stop." One of the felidae in the pack had shifted into his folk form and his voice echoed in a loud penetrating hum all around them. "The prince speaks the truth. Our brothers left the forest to live among the folk. It was their wish."

Quarn turned to the felid. "But Frieden is my nephew. Now orphaned. He is my responsibility."

"Not if this folk will take him."

Looking back to Welk, Quarn's face twisted in fury. "I will not leave him in the hands of these vile creatures."

"You will do as I command," the felid folk behind him said.

Quarn's body shook with rage. He took two steps back,

shifted to his cat form, turned, and stalked away. He and Elrundt watched the felidae trod across the plain toward the snug villages of the Ruud miles distant, and their beast forest beyond.

Elrundt turned to him. "What do you intend to do with a young felid folk?"

Welk turned south where the old wissende's party made its way into the burned camp. There were five, all in their humble brown wissenry robes, tied at the waist with rope belts. It was unusual to find wissendes so far from the Ruud.

"What has happened here?" Father Britt said. He was a head shorter than Welk and twice as round. His straight brown hair sat about his head like a dirty bowl.

"Our party was attacked in the night," Welk said. "Eis and felidae were killed."

Father Britt stared at them, astonished. "But you live?"

"Yes, Father. And I have a charge for you." He handed the boy into the arms of the wissende.

"Orphaned?"

Welk nodded. "He is Frieden, named so because his parents wanted the freedom to live the felidae ways of old, when their young lived out their folk years as Mutterede intended."

"You wish the wissenry to raise a felid?"

"Indeed. You will find them not so much different from us."

Father Britt handed the child to one of his party and stepped into the camp. "But who did this?"

"What brings you here so far from the Cold Sea, Father?" Elrundt said.

"We look for Father Wold. Have you seen him? He is errant. Banished, but returned uninvited. We wish to see him settled for good in one of the wasteland villages. He was last seen heading north toward the ice realm. We fear for his sanity."

"You banished a wissende?"

"Indeed. Did you see him?"

They shook their heads, perplexed, then turned once more to the camp. Welk felt a great urge to let himself collapse to the ground, to stay there until he starved or died from thirst, to never leave his beloved Rue. But the eis had already claimed her—and they would not let him join her in their afterworld.

"May I offer you words of comfort, my young princes of the Ruud?" Father Britt said.

They shook their heads again.

"There is nothing to say," Elrundt said. "This is what is wrought by kings. My life as a prince of the Ruud is done."

1280 Autumn

King Welk paced the floor of the great hall an hour before dawn. Soon, the nobles of Michelruud Castle would gather for their breakfast, there would be noise and merriment, feasting and stories, before they'd all be off for horse races, hunting, or apple picking. Welk would allow them to go; the folk should not be alarmed as yet.

The threat from the ice realm in the northeast was merely percolating—a territorial dispute only. Why the eis were so adamant that no folk be allowed to settle in the hills abutting their realm was beyond him. If they weren't content to use the land, why keep it from others? Did they despise mortal folk so much?

The threat from the Hass of Emorah in the Great West was only brooding, as well. Their desire to retake the folk of the Ruud and abolish their self-rule was only rumor at this point. And as for the trouble with the bairn of prophecy, the guard alone could handle that. Although, Welk wondered at their prowess. They'd already let Fenn Foster run amok in the Ruud without one sighting. The devilish child broke into the great stone prison Steingefan and helped all the other children escape.

Welk thought the rumors of a bairn born in the wasteland,

following an old prophecy of the felidae, was nonsense. And yet the king's guard found the boy with a distinct mark. Could it be true? Was Fenn Foster, a wissenry orphan, fated to destroy the Ruud and kill him? A boy, kill a king? Destroy his homeland? No. It was ludicrous.

Back and forth before the large hearth on the western wall, Welk paced, stopping occasionally to look at the dirt in front of the smouldering fire, shuddering. He could still picture the mark, drawn by the young guard days ago after he'd seen it on young Fenn of the wissenry. He could still hear the oily Sorgood's curious voice, quivering with questions.

"What is it, Sire? What does it mean?"

But he'd refused to tell him anything. The mark of the faire was unknown to the folk. Welk himself had only learned of the design when he saw it for the first and only time on the upper arm of his beloved, Rue of the eis. She'd laughed at him playfully when he asked about it.

"I am special." She smiled and her eyes danced. He'd replied, "Of course you are," and the matter was settled.

Why would Fenn Foster bear that mark? Perhaps it was a mark typical of the eis. Welk had never found himself in a position to examine the arms of any other of the eis. His experience of them was limited to Rue and her sister Aliara—and he couldn't recall any such mark on *her*. If it *were* a mark distinctive of the eis, Welk was certain no one in the Ruud resembled the tall, pale folk of the frozen realm—certainly not Fenn Foster, though he couldn't place the boy's face in his memory.

Welk had turned to the guards who'd discovered Fenn and the stationer's daughter at the old prison, where they'd led the daring escape.

"What did he look like, this Fenn of the wissenry?"

They stared blankly at him.

"Was he tall? What were his features?"

"Tall?" Footman Wolf said. "No, Sire. Very small, for a boy

they say be twelve. Rather small for any sort of threat."

"Was he blond?"

"No, Sire, quite the opposite. Very dark of hair and eye. Like yourself, if you don't mind my saying. But very pale, very pale. Unlike you in that respect."

If he was not an eis, why did he have the mark? Now more than ever, Welk needed access to the stationer's library of tomes. He knew him to possess books on the beasts of the realm. There must be an explanation. And the stationer's daughter, raised surrounded by those books would have known, surely. And the innkeeper's son, who spent a lifetime listening to stories of the Ruud and beyond, who had teamed up with Fenn Foster, sporting his faire mark—perhaps he too had learned of its importance.

If this mark signified some connection to the beast, it would all make sense. His beast blood would give the boy the power and daring to rescue the imprisoned children from Steingefan. It would be no wonder, then, that the king's guard was unable to track him. He would be instinctively more cunning than other children.

Welk dragged his tired bones to his throne next to the fire. Though it was little more than a large chair covered in pelts of eleshag and rabbit atop a dais, he found it imposing and ridiculous; but he liked the height and watching the room as if a large bird. Here now, in the dim candle-lit silence of the great hall, he recalled his fear and awe as a small child in watching his father's great ceremony in taking the seat, and grimaced.

He could still see it. He could still smell the burnt hides and tents. He could not wipe from memory the bloodied body of his friend Belfen. The pyre on which his beloved burned. And Father Britt, gaping, horrified at the massacre, the felid boy clinging to him.

Turning on this throne to look again at the hearth where the mark of the faire had been made in the dirt, he shuddered. He should have killed his father as soon as he returned home. But he did not. Rue would not have borne it. He closed his eyes, waiting for day to dawn once more.

Chapter Two

Like a bubble rising from the bottom of a pond, Fenn came awake; he did not open his eyes, but lay still, allowing gentle sunlight to bath him in warmth. He was in the faire glade where the cold winds of autumn could not reach him. Grayson had told them the fairies abandoned the glade long ago, but Fenn remembered lying awake the night before—they came out of hiding and sang to him; and he understood their song. Sadie and Grayson would never believe him.

They were to have awakened at midnight to begin their journey across the boundary of the Ruud, escaping the king's guard into the hill country. Yet they had overslept; he could hear Sadie snoring not far away.

The night curse, yes, that was what woke him and his mother's charm was hot against his chest. He could hear her, a soft airy voice; in his vision, she grasped the robe of a wissende with her slender hand and said, "Keep him safe." He'd become accustomed to that image in his head.

But there had been more this time. "Tell him who he is." And those words startled him into pulling away from slumber. Was that truly a part of his vision, he wondered, or had he invented it himself, wishing she'd once said such a thing so he could confront the wissenry and demand to be told everything?

Darnit, the huntsman Rogget's brown bear, rustled his nose into someone's back pack. Jerky again?

"Darnit," Fenn said aloud, pulling his mother's charm from under his tunic to let his skin cool a bit. "Cut it out." But still he did not open his eyes until he heard the whisper of an unfamiliar voice.

"Gold."

Bolting upright, raising a hand to shield his eyes from the sun, Fenn startled to see a man standing over him, leering, his face pinched in a scowl. Three others dug through their supplies, tossing them about as if they were trash.

"Where did you get that?" The intruder reached out and lifted the charm from Fenn's chest.

"That's mine."

Grabbing Fenn's tunic, the grimy-haired folk lifted him in the air, giving him a shake.

"I said where did you get that?"

"It's mine, I tell you."

The man dropped Fenn and shoved him to the ground. Reaching out, he pulled Fenn's hemp rope from around his neck with a yank. Fenn tried to grab at it, but the thief batted him away as if he were a bug.

"That's mine," Fenn said. "Give it back. Grayson, Sadie!" He saw them startle awake.

"Now, now, let's not get excited," one of the others said.

"Tie them," the thief said.

The other men grabbed Sadie and Grayson.

"Give that back," Fenn demanded, but the folk sneered at him and pulled the hemp rope over his own head.

"You thieving little brat."

"Me? It's mine!"

Fenn jumped up and rushed at him, grabbing wildly for the rope, but the man seized him and held him and Fenn felt the cold blade of a knife scrape his neck. As Fenn's hands wrapped around the folk's thick arms, in a futile attempt to push him off, his first thought was of Darnit and Rogget. *Where were they?* Had the thieves killed them? Anger consumed him—then rage, hatred, and a lust for his gold charm. At first he directed it toward the sneering man holding him, pulling him to where Sadie and Grayson sat being tied up by the others. Then he felt as if he *were* the thief, as if he'd sunk down into the other man's clothes and *become* him—wanting the gold, wanting to kill Fenn, being held back by a confused feeling of remorse and hope buried deep within. As the folk pushed him to the ground beside Sadie, Fenn came back to himself, weak and trembling.

They huddled together, their hands tied behind their backs, watching as the thieves rifled through their supplies. Again, Fenn wondered where Rogget had gone.

"Look here, Clutch." One of the men, smaller and hunched, his face covered in dirt, limped toward him. "A pouch."

"Let me have it, Muck," the man who wore Fenn's charm growled, and the other tossed it at him. He opened it and smiled at the kids. "Coin." Closing the drawstring, he held the pouch up and shook it. "Thankee very much."

"Yo, Clutch." Muck returned to rooting in Sadie's knapsack. "What're they doing out here in the divide wood all 'lone, eh? It don't seem right."

"What do we care? Just get their valuables and let's head out. If we don't catch Grindelwell before his debtors do, we'll have to give him up for good."

"Aye, what's he worth anyway? What do we want with the likes o' him?"

"Eh, now. He's my brother." Stout and bald, this man tossed Grayson's belongings from his bag onto the ground.

"You don't see me begging special favors for *my* brother," Muck said.

"You ain't got one."

"Shut up, all o' you," Clutch yelled.

Grayson sucked in a deep breath and screamed, "Elrundt! I call on the spirit of Elrundt! Help us!"

Fenn winced and turned from him. "Do you have to yell?"

Clutch threw his head back and roared with laughter. He walked to where they sat, bound together on the ground, and leaned down to put his face very close to Grayson's.

"Elrundt's not going to help you today, boy."

"Are you sure?" one of Clutch's men said, turning in circles looking up at the sky. "Are you sure he ain't got a spirit helper?"

"It's only a legend, Gog. It isn't real."

"Wait a min'. I just thought o' something."

Clutch rolled his eyes. "What did I tell you about spouting off every stupid idea that pops into your noggin?"

"No, wait, Clutcher." He pulled a stationer's poster from his sack. "I got this here in Aaronland this morning as we passed through. They was posted all over the place."

Clutch shrugged. "So." He took the poster and glanced at it before handing it back to the other folk.

"So, it says here..."

"Oh, everybody stop stealing now." One of the others chuckled. "Goggle's planning on reading to us. Tell us a story now, Gog."

"Let him read it," Clutch said.

"It says these three kids be enemies of the king. The one in Michelruud, anyway."

"Three kids?"

"A girl, name of Sadie Pratt, daughter to the Path stationer; pale brown of hair and eye, with freckles."

"Freckles?" Sadie said. Grayson leaned into her with his shoulder to give her a nudge, frowning.

"A boy, Grayson Steppe, of the inn; dark in features—tall, scrawny."

Sadie giggled and once again, Grayson shoved at her.

"And a Fenn Foster of the wissenry—small, pale, but dark of hair and eye—who'll be havin' a mark on his right shoulder."

Clutch stared in amazement at the three of them crouched together at his feet. He stepped in front of Fenn and pulled at his tunic.

"That there's a mark right there." Muck said.

"You got him on the first try, Clutch!" Goggle said.

"Enemies of the king, eh?" Clutch said. "How much can we get for 'em?"

"It don't say how much. But it does say reward."

"A reward from the king?" Muck said.

"Aw, Clutch, no king's gonna give the likes of us no reward," the bald man said.

"The king of Michelruud will." Clutch nodded. "I think Grindelwell will have to be given up to his debtors, after all. Let's get these enemies to the king, eh? Goggle, you go on reading all you want. Don't nobody make fun of you anymore."

The crack of a tree branch echoed in the glade and Darnit burst into camp roaring and charging at the thieves. The folk scattered, shouting, running off in a panic. Darnit continued the chase into the wood as Rogget showed up with a few dead rabbits hanging by their back feet from a rope.

"Get up, get up." Rogget's thick fingers deftly worked the ties at their wrists, freeing them. "We need to move; they're likely to come back for you once they realize Darnit's got no bite nor sense of direction."

Chapter Three

The carriages stopped on the forest path to Michelruud and Leah looked up from her journal. She'd been remembering her trip so far with a heaviness that she attributed to homesickness. She was not enjoying herself in the Ruud as much as she'd expected.

Prenalin was kinder as the days wore on; he too must be longing for Ruhm and his family. Kirche was his usual hot and cold—one hour regaling her with stories of his childhood in the prestigious King's Chosen school back home, laughing at his own derogatory opinions on the folk of the Ruud, winking at her when he caught her staring at him—and the next moment sullen, brooding, quiet, and glaring.

Perhaps, she reasoned, Lord Kirche also missed home. Even the well-traveled must still wish for their own beds on occasion. That morning, Leah wished for any bed. They'd had the porters Gretchen and Zelda pack up their belongings for the short trip to Michelruud the night before and for some reason, probably known only to Rett himself, awoke before dawn to begin the trip without so much as a by your leave to King Arnot or his queen.

Only Cook was there to wave her a farewell after she'd

shoved a napkin full of breakfast tarts at her. Leah was grateful for both the tarts and the goodbye. She realized now, as the carriage horses danced in their harnesses, how much she'd written in her journal of her mother: her meals, her baked goods, her face, hands, and smile. But she most fondly remembered their long sessions in front of the looking glass as her mother brushed out Leah's long brown hair while singing ancient songs of Mutterede, long since forgotten by the followers of Rett.

"Why have we stopped?" She asked when Prenalin peered into her carriage, took her journal from her and set it on the opposite bench with a smile. He offered her his hand to help her to the ground outside. A fresh rush of autumn filled her nose and she breathed deeply. All about her, forest golds, reds, and yellows mingled with deep evergreens and brought a smile to her lips.

"Did I not tell you?" Prenalin said, watching her. "We are to go on a hunt before we go to Michelruud. We have quite an adventure planned."

"Oh."

"Are you not up for adventure?"

They followed Lord Kirche and his guards Alphonse and Redd, while Kipling remained at the carriage with the porters.

"My apologies, Prenalin. I'm afraid I'm too tired to appreciate it." She smiled at him.

"As soon as we make stop, we'll start a fire and heat up some kaff bitters. We hunt at mid-morning."

She nodded, tightened up the ribbon holding her hair behind her back, and followed along into the woods silently. There was a cold moistness in the air; the hair at the nape of her neck stuck to her skin. Heady aromas of pine and jasmine floated all around her and the damp ground was cold through her shoes and stockings to her feet. Leah couldn't keep the smile from her lips. Truly the Ruud and the eastern continent had beauty that rivaled the marble city of Ruhm. She so wished she could tell Prenalin, even Kirche, how much she felt at home in the forests of the Ruud, even on the streets of their villages among their folk. How often she'd thought she could stay here, if only her mother and father would join her. But she knew such comments bordered on blasphemy.

Ruhm was to be first in her heart, and certainly her loyalty. Ruhm was supreme on Kell. The most glorious city, the most noble Hass, the wisest High Preist, Kirche. All these things she'd been taught and knew deep in her soul.

But never at the Hass school did they tell her of the greens and golds of the east—they'd noshed Ruud apples, with pleasure, but were often told it was the trip across the sea to the Great West that turned them sweet.

Leah smiled to herself. Such silly stories only a child could believe. But believe them, they all did. Now she had to admit, the rich soil beneath her feet, the temperate weather, the freshness of the air, the clean, cold water in the streams—these were surely the necessary ingredients for the juiciest apples on Kell.

And never at the Hass school did they show pictures of the beauty of the landscape in the east. In Ruhm, once you left the city, you gazed upon a rocky, brown horizon to the far off mountains in the north—crags of rock that beckoned only outlaws and escaped beast folk. The Ruud, quite to the contrary was covered in succulent, colorful, fecund life.

Leah, smiling, took a deep breath and walked into Prenalin's back.

"Oh." She gasped and fell backward onto her bottom on the cold pine-covered ground.

Prenalin was there in an instant to help her to her feet. He chuckled but placed a finger to his lips. Leah realized they'd met up with a small group of folk. Prenalin stepped behind her to guide her forward, but they remained behind Kirche and were not introduced.

"This way." The slithering weasel waved a hand to lead them.

Leah walked on in stunned silence. They were now accompanied by the vile folk Lord Kirche had met with secretly in the woods a few nights before. There, he'd mentioned a hunt —a hunt for brownies. She shook off her nagging suspicion. She must have misheard him. For what purpose would one kill a brownie? Lord Kirche couldn't intend to eat one—the very idea was absurd.

"What do we hunt, Prenalin?"

He shrugged. "The usual, I would imagine. They have large pheasant in these woods, and boar. We will take gifts to Michelruud, no doubt."

Leah followed on, trying to remain behind Prenalin, hoping not to be noticed by the weasel. She feared her expression would make him suspicious, though she was certain he never saw her hiding in the woods listening in on his conversation with Kirche.

They found a small glade and Alphonse and Redd dug a fire pit and set up tender. Once the fire was ablaze and they had mugs of bitters, she relaxed on the blanket Prenalin gave her, resting her back against a stump.

"Michelruud is always the key," Kirche was saying to the weasel. "The others tolerate us very well. But King Evan was forever difficult."

"You will find his son no less so, I'm afraid."

"Were they close?"

"Far from it. And that may be to your disadvantage. The newly crowned King Welk will have things done his own way. He is not familiar with the Hass and its dealings with the Ruud."

"Perhaps I can work that to my advantage," Kirche said. "And now he has a little beast of a boy to deal with. Hass can help him with that problem."

"It would be best to rid us all of the little brat as soon as possible. The folk are beginning to speak out, to stand up to the guard and the king, out of their fear of the boy."

"If they truly believe he is prophesied, that will work well for us."

"I suppose, my Lord. You know best."

The vile man reached up to smooth the hair on the sides of his head, and tugged at his collar. Leah sucked in a tiny breath. His hands and neck were covered with tiny scars. She'd seen the like before. With a twitch, the weasel glared across the fire at her and she flinched.

"Your new aide is rather interested."

Kirche laughed. "You prefer your aides to pretend to be occupied, no doubt." He cast a glance at the two guardsmen who had accompanied their guest, now distant, standing alert and uninterested.

"Well, I certainly expect that they do not stare."

Leah lowered her gaze to the dark brew in her mug.

"Leah Hallowsing," Kirche said and she looked up again. "This is Sorgood. He is one of us."

"Is he?"

Kirche laughed again and Sorgood sneered.

"Insolence."

"My apoligies, Sorgood," Leah said. "I was surprised that is all. I thought you a folk of the Ruud. I meant no disrespect."

"He is indeed of the Ruud. We have some loyalists here, even in the east. Ruhm is their fatherland, after all. And Hass their mother church."

"Yes, sir. Of course. Do they teach about the Hass in the east?"

Leah glanced at Prenalin, sensing his disapproval at her outspoken nature, but his eyes were on his own mug of bitters.

"They do not," Sorgood said. "They have no schools in the Ruud and prefer to leave their folk in ignorance. Such is the legacy of the great wissendes of Ruhm."

"Then, if I may be so bold, sir, how did you learn of Hass?"

Sorgood chuckled and rolled his eyes. "From the annual visits of course."

"You will see when we arrive in Michelruud," Kirche said. "We have a small following there among some of the older children."

"Why only in Michelruud?"

"We concentrate our attention there. We—how shall I say it—recruit some of their young folk."

"But, again, why only Michelruud?"

Lord Kirche smiled at her. And though she was sure he was just as condescending as his friend Sorgood, it warmed her heart and her cheeks blushed.

"Because Michelruud is the key. Michelruud has always been the dominant kingdom of the Ruud and one day, soon, she will make a play to reunite all the kingdoms into one, as they were in the beginning. Michelruud is where the power concentrates. We do not want to train the youth of Aaronland and Damon Wall only to have them fight between themselves when the time comes. No, Michelruud will take the entire Ruud, and our recruits there will be ready."

"I see."

Both men smiled at her as if she were a child and went on in conversation between them. Leah turned again to Prenalin. He sipped his bitters and looked about him, avoiding her gaze. The kaff took root in her blood and she was energized. Leah stood and brushed imaginary soil from her skirt.

"Yes." Kirche also stood. "Let us be on the hunt. Alphonse and Redd will remain here with our things. We need only our firearms and bows."

"Surely, I am to remain behind as well," Leah said.

"Oh, no, no," Kirche said. "You must join us. I insist."

"I have no practice with the firearm, Lord."

"But you do with a bow, no doubt. I hear the archery classes at the Hass school are superb."

"Yes, of course."

Reluctantly, Leah took the bow and quiver she was offered. As they walked on, away from the warmth of the fire, she tested her string and examined her bow.

"And what will you be hunting today, Leah?" Prenalin smiled at her.

"I've bagged my share of squirrel and hundrat. But I do not think the king of Michelruud would be much impressed by them."

"Agreed. It's boars and elchen for a king's table."

"We won't find elchen in these woods, will we?"

"Quiet down," Sorgood said, glaring at the two of them. "From here out, we are silent. Even in our footsteps."

"I confess," Prenalin whispered in her ear, his right arm pulling at her right shoulder, drawing her close so that she could feel his breath on her neck. "I myself am not a hunter."

He let her go and moved a few paces in front of her, but looked back at her with a smile. They trod quietly as they could, with Sorgood and Kirche occasionally turning back to them with annoyed expressions or fingers to their lips. Sorgood led the way through the dense wood that grew darker as they walked; moistness now hung heavy in the air as fog just at their torsos and rising up past their heads. They could see through the mist only as if through a ratty worn bed sheet and thus snuck ever so slowly through the forest.

On occasion, Sorgood would stop, raise a hand, lower himself to the ground to peer beneath the fog, then stand, and motion for them to continue. While Leah felt out of place with the hunting party, the feel, the smell, the deep green of her surroundings lulled her into a fantasy dream in which she was on a great exploration in a foreign land, searching for the lost treasure of Ruhm.

Once again, Sorgood's arm popped up; they halted and waited. Sorgood knelt and peered through the wood under the fog. He stood and motioned for them to move on.

"Perhaps," Prenalin whispered again in her ear, "we should make our way on our hands and knees to better see whatever it is we look for."

Leah slapped her hand against her mouth and turned from the group, trying to hold in her laughter. Bent over and forcing herself to think upsetting thoughts of brownies fleeing their bows for their lives, she sucked in several deep breaths through her fingers. When she turned, Kirche and Sorgood were glaring at her. She could do nothing more than slug Prenalin in the shoulder, still smiling.

Sorgood held up his hand, turned and knelt. He stood again and beckoned them move forward. The fog eased as they hiked, lifted higher and higher as they crept behind Sorgood and Kirche. Leah's nose tickled at a familiar smell.

She turned to Prenalin; her face broke into a smile. Kettering's roses. The forest there was abloom. She could not see them, but she smelled the heady perfume, just as she did while passing Kettering's cart in the town square back home. Roses, like the ones that lined the gardens at the grand Hall of Hass. Prenalin turned to her, and smiled in response to hers, but she said nothing, not wanting another scolding form Sorgood.

Their steps slowed, the fog now lifted, and the forest opened into a clearing. Beyond, at the base of an enormous pine, a brownie rooted in the dirt. He dug a tiny hole only to replace the dirt, patted the ground with both hands, sniffed about, dug, refilled, and patted again, then bounced against the earth as if tamping it. Leah's heart sank. Without thinking, she shook her head and grimaced. So it was true.

Kirche raised his firearm and aimed, squinting into the sight. A shot shattered the woods, echoing in waves into the distance. Birds shrieked and flitted all around, fighting for the sky. Other beasts, unseen, darted away from them through the trees and shrubs. And the brownie, writhing on the mossy ground, began

24

to scream.

Leah's gut churned and pushed against her throat as Kirche moved forward toward the poor creature and raised his firearm once more.

Chapter Four

The early morning mist tingled at his face as Lucas hiked through the woods of Timber on his way to Michelruud Castle. He'd dug his wissende's cloak out of his pack and wrapped himself in it, now pulling the hood over his head for extra warmth. Quarn and the eis assassin followed him—sometimes behind, sometimes to the left or right. Their scents mingled with the pine and honeysuckle. Lucas reached for the grip of Father Treacher's firearm at his hip, reassured.

In his last encounter with Quarn, Father had taken an arrow meant for him. His chest swelled with indignation at the thought that Father might have lost his life. But he was merely shot through the arm; Father Britt assured him Treacher would heal fully in a month or two.

"I am grateful for Father Treacher's bravery and sacrifice," he told Britt. "And I am glad I don't have to avenge his death."

"Avenge him?" Britt had sputtered. "We do not advocate such actions. They lead only to more death and strife."

"And a clear conscience."

"A clear conscience, my boy? Live long enough, and you will realize there is no such thing."

Lucas chuckled to himself. Perhaps Fenn Foster was right

after all. The wissendes say much...and yet very little. A twig broke nearby and he stopped his trek. The hair on the back of his neck, and on his arms, stood erect. Slowly, he turned to find the frail Quarn and the taller eis hunter standing four yards distant among the trees.

"Come into the clearing," he told them and watched, every nerve in his body aquiver, as they made their way forward to greet him.

"And so you would still have me murdered, Quarn."

"You belittle our ways by remaining in that disgusting form."

"And yet you stand before me the same."

Quarn moved forward, his lips curled into a scowl. "You know not of what you speak, young felid. Once you are turned, you will see that this form is weak. It is vile. And only used when necessary."

Lucas' gaze was focused behind Quarn on the eis readying his bow.

"Has he paid you?" he asked him, his right hand finding Father Treacher's firearm.

The eis looked puzzled.

"He won't pay you," Lucas said. He pulled the gun from its holster and pointed it at the eis.

"That won't do enough harm to stop me from killing you." The eis chuckled. "Even should your aim be true, I would have your throat slit before I succumb."

"Then I will shoot Quarn." Lucas aimed the gun at his uncle. "As I said, he won't pay you."

"You would murder your uncle?" Quarn said.

"You would have me murdered. What's the difference?"

"Life itself is the difference, you fool."

"Exactly," Lucas said. "I choose to live my life as folk. You have no right to deny me that."

Lucas sensed motion behind him; Quarn and the eis hunter

stepped back several paces and the eis lowered his weapon. Quarn, threatened, shuddered into his feline form. Lucas turned to see Red Lichen and three other centaurs standing behind him.

"What have we here?" Lichen said, his front hoofs pounding the earth.

Quarn shook and trembled, his enormous head rocked back and forth in agitation, until he reformed as a felid folk.

"You have no right to interfere," he growled.

"You speak of rights?" Lucas said. "He means to have me murdered by this eis."

The eis stepped back another pace, shouldered his bow and raised his hands as if in surrender. Being trampled by powerful centaurs was not in his plans.

Lichen gazed upon the scene for a moment before speaking again.

"Do you wish an overthrow of Dag Voorspeld?" he asked Quarn. "Or do you attempt this for Lucas' sake only?"

"His name is not Lucas. His name is Frieden; he is my nephew and my responsibility."

"Your responsibility was severed when he was given up to the folk. Your actions now will be brought to the attention of the lord."

A low, guttural growl rolled from Quarn and he slunk back into his cat form, turned and padded away. The eis assassin bowed low.

"My apologies for offending you, Red Lichen."

"Stay away from Lucas."

"Of course." The eis smirked and turned to follow Quarn.

Lucas let himself breathe again and turned to Lichen and the others.

"What were you going to do?" Lichen said. "Shoot Quarn?"

Lucas tilted his head and smiled. "I had few choices."

"You need a guard. The eis will not defer from this challenge simply because we defended you this time. He would find pleasure in killing you. And he knows we are confined to the forest."

"And yet I find you here, out of the forest, in the Timber woods."

"The brownies and fairies alerted us. Being followed by an eis hunter, they said. I am surprised to find they were telling the truth."

"Well, you're most likely right about the eis continuing in this adventure. But why does he not snipe at me from a distance? Why does he show himself first?"

"It is not sporting to kill a folk by stealth. A guard will prevent him from approaching you."

"I intend to find myself a guard of sorts."

"See that you do. We will escort you to the edge of the wood. Stay in the open until you are with others."

Lucas felt like a lost lamb with his escort; but he couldn't deny the wisdom of it.

Chapter Five

They gathered their discarded sacks and returned to them all that the thieves had no use for—their second pair of clothes and Sadie's book of maps which they hadn't even opened. All their food was gone, Sadie's money and Fenn's charm—in the hands of thieves.

"Hurry." Rogget herded them out of the faire glade.

"What about Darnit?" Fenn said.

"He'll find us, come on."

Sadie stopped to spin around in a circle, getting her last look then turned to follow them.

"Grayson," she whispered. "What was all that about Elrundt? Huh?" And she giggled.

"What's so funny?"

"Nothing. I just didn't know you were the superstitious type."

"I don't believe in Elrundt, okay? I'd have been calling on him plenty of times before this if I did."

"Then why *did* you call him?"

"I was calling Rogget, you dope."

"Then why did you say Elrundt?"

"And let those thugs know we had someone else with us?

Sometimes you think too much like a girl, Sadie."

"Well...well, I am a girl. And what does being a girl have to do with it? Honestly, Grayson, sometimes—"

"Hush," Rogget said in a loud whisper.

As they headed east toward the hill country, Fenn remembered the anger and hatred he'd felt when he grabbed Clutch; and when, for a moment he felt like he *was* Clutch, and filled with the pain of loss and fear. Clutch wanted the gold charm desperately; was it from hunger or just greed? And when Fenn felt he'd become himself again and lost the feelings of Clutch, it was still there, a deep connection with the gold charm and a strong desire for it. When Clutch had tossed him to the ground he felt something draw him thin as if he were far from the thing he needed most: the charm.

Strange as it was to feel he had become Clutch, he was more confused that their feelings had been so similar. Had he that much in common with a filthy criminal? He wished he could talk to Father Treacher about it. He would explain what had happened. Maybe it had something to do with being trained as a wissende. But Father Treacher, he remembered, while teaching him a great deal, had failed to explain the most important things to him. He'd probably say something nonsensical about skills and not worrying. Why were they trying to keep him in the dark?

Suddenly, he remembered the fairies in the trees and their song of the early morning, and he stopped walking; but Rogget continued ahead of him.

"We're going the wrong way." They all stopped and turned to look at him.

"The border's that way," Rogget said pointing behind him. "Through the divide wood."

"We've lost all our supplies. We have no food left."

Grayson and Sadie nodded.

"We need to go north, through Aaronland. We'll get supplies and head to the north border instead."

"But that will take us into the wasteland."

"Not exactly," Grayson said. "Let me see your maps." He'd pulled Sadie's pack from her back before she could agree and rifled through it for her book of maps.

"Why don't you just keep them," Sadie said, "if you're going to want to look at them every five minutes."

"Look here." Grayson pointed at the map of the northern outskirts of the Ruud. "If we cross the border north of the Waverly wissenry, we'll be at the northwestern edge of the hill country."

Fenn studied the map. The rapid river they'd crossed again and again in the last two weeks wove between the wasteland and the hill country just north of the Ruud, before disappearing off the map. There was a bridge several miles out. That was where he would cross into the wasteland.

"From there," Grayson said, "we can make our way farther in and to the east, if you want, before turning north toward the cold lands."

"I think the farther we can get from the Ruud the better," Sadie said.

Rogget shook his head. "It's dangerous to try for Aaronland. The guard's on the lookout for you now; all of the guard—even King Arnot's."

"What choice do we have? We need food and supplies," Fenn said.

"Really, Rogget." Sadie put her hands on her hips and frowned at him. "They even took our blankets."

"But," Rogget stammered. "You'll have to cross the plains of Aaron. Wide open."

"Maybe we'll be less conspicuous out in the open. They'd be expecting us to hide," Grayson said.

"And there won't be thieves out in the open either." Sadie's eyes pleaded with Rogget to see reason.

"You'll be finding worse in the hill country, so you best be prepared."

"We'll need weapons then," Fenn said. "Do you have any money?"

Rogget nodded. "I do."

After a pause and a careful study of the map, Rogget shrugged. "All right then. We pass through Town Village for supplies and make our way across the border to the north."

And so they plodded on in silence, only their footsteps on the forest floor thudding against the cold morning air. Fenn struggled again with his feelings of being Clutch, until the quiet boomed heavy in his ears. Why were they all so silent? Rogget, he could understand. As guide, he carried the safety of them all on his shoulders. Grayson seemed to have a new determination about him for their quest, while Sadie acted as if adventure was more than she'd bargained for.

"Freckles," she mumbled. "I bet it was that Jeopard Link who printed up the flyer. He knows how I feel about freckles."

"You have freckles on your nose, Sadie," Grayson said. "You can't deny it."

"But he didn't have to put it on a flyer."

"What's wrong with freckles?" Fenn smiled at her. "I think they're cute."

"You do?" Sadie said.

"Sure, they dabble across your nose and on top of your cheeks like...like a little patch of wild flowers."

Grayson let out a chortle and Sadie frowned at him.

"Maybe my freckles aren't so bad." She smiled.

Grayson turned to Fenn with a glare and they trod on without speaking for some time. When the silence was too much for Fenn and he felt the need to speak, Rogget put out a hand to stop their hike.

Muttering, cursing, and occasional whomps, echoed through the wood, as if someone were trying to chop a tree with his boot. Motioning them forward, Rogget peered around a thick pine. Fenn approached the other side of the tree and looked into a small clearing where a folk was spinning about thwacking trunks, stammering, and whining.

Chapter Six

Leah turned and darted from the scene, through the woods, back into the fog, branches and shrubs tearing at her face and arms, pulling at her hair. She heard the second shot and the brownie's piercing cries fell silent. A knotty vine reached up and tripped her ankles, sending her sprawling on the needle-covered earth. Scrambling to her knees, she crawled to a large rotwood trunk, nearly three times as wide as she was, and leaned against it. Pulling her knees to her chest, she buried her face there to quiet her wailing. Now the smell of Kettering's red roses smothered and nauseated her. Her stomach lurched and she turned to lie across the ground, but nothing came of it. Still, she lay there, her cheek cold on the earth of Kell, settling her breath and her mind.

When footsteps startled her, she sat up and found Prenalin settling himself against the tree beside her. His face was drawn and concerned, but he did not look at her. Prenalin was quite the opposite of Kirche, she thought, taking the opportunity of a long look. His was a rugged and timeworn appearance, while Kirche's skin was soft, almost delicate. And Prenalin's dark eyes could not pierce her thoughts as Kirche's pale gaze did; instead, they only brought confusion and mystery when he frowned at her.

"We must go back," he said.

She shook her head stubbornly, even as she knew she must do as she was told.

"He did not bring you along to upset you. I assure you."

Now Leah stared ahead of her and slightly nodded. Of course Kirche did not do such a thing. But what could he have been thinking?

"He thought I would enjoy the spectacle," she said.

"Yes."

Here she put her face in her hands and began to weep again. "But the poor creature. It is not to be eaten; why would he kill it?"

She wiped at her eyes and turned again to Prenalin, but he still would not look at her and gave no response.

"Tell me," she said. "He does not mean to eat it?"

He sighed and shook his head. "No, of course not. It is a trophy."

"A living, sentient being."

Now he turned to her, anger ablaze in his eyes. "You blaspheme."

Leah shuddered and returned his glare for a second or two, before breathing in an erratic gasp of air to calm her tears. "Of course, you are right. Forgive me."

"Leah, Leah," he said. "It is all he's been raised to believe. They are not equals. They have no spirit that lives on. And they do not worship Rett. They are therefore expendable."

"Of course."

"You cannot pretend to me to believe it. You are not alone. But you must keep your thoughts to yourself. They are zoo animals, nothing more."

A heavy silence hung between them while they looked at each other. It was the first time Leah felt understood in his presence and a light smile touched her lips even through her disgust at the hunt.

"How old are you, Pren?" she said, without thinking.

He smiled. "Twenty-seven."

"I always thought you much older. You behave much older than your years."

"As do you, Leah."

She stood, brushing the dirt and pine from her clothes and he rose as well.

"Understand," he said. Kirche's voice sounded their names several yards distant. "He meant to impress you."

"Impress me? Why would he want to do that?"

"For the same reason any young folk would want to impress a charming girl."

Prenalin had lost his smile, though what he said was certainly a joke.

"Come," he reached for her hand. "They are near."

They rounded the large rotwood and found their way toward Kirche's voice. He and Sorgood emerged from the wood, beaming, Sorgood's bloody sword still in his hand.

Kirche held up a burlap sack soaked in blood. "I have my trophy," he said. "Shall we try for another?"

Leah was startled first by Kirche's face, lit with joy and animation as she'd never seen it before, and then by the bag which she surmised contained the head of the poor brownie.

"Oh, no, Lord Kirche," Sorgood said. "We've certainly been spotted by the felidae already. We've lost the surprise for the rest of the trip, I'm afraid. There will be a next time. When their sense of security returns."

Undeterred in his triumph, Kirche shrugged. "Leah, you won't mind having my prize on your carriage. I'm sure there's no room on mine."

Leah belched and vomited her breakfast tarts at Kirche's feet.

Chapter Seven

Forbes Billings," Rogget moved from behind the tree. "Forbes Billings," he said louder.

The folk stopped his whirling and cursing and turned to Rogget with red, tear-stained cheeks.

"Rogget." The slender man fell to his knees, covering his face with his hands.

Startled, Rogget turned back to the trees at the children, fear and confusion on his face. Fenn led the others into the clearing and they all stood and stared at the dejected folk.

"What is it?" Grayson asked and moved to put a hand on the man's shoulder.

"I've lost my writ," he cried and sat back onto the ground. He threw up his hands and then let them drop aimlessly. "I've lost my writ."

Grayson looked at Fenn, but Fenn could only grimace. Rogget knew him, so the folk couldn't be completely insane; but he was clearly beside himself. When Grayson sat beside the man, Fenn turned, alarmed, to Rogget, but Rogget simply stared, agog.

"Who is he?" Fenn asked.

"It's Forbes Billings."

"I guessed that much."

"I grew up with him, in Timber. But I haven't seen him in nigh on ten years."

"What happened to your writ?" Grayson asked the man. "Go on, sit down," he told the others.

They dutifully dropped to the ground, Rogget hitting unceremoniously and all his huntsman's gear falling away from him. Forming a semicircle in front of the whimpering man, they waited to understand.

"You remember, Rogget. You remember my writ. Given to me by the prince himself."

"What's a writ?" Sadie said.

"It's a decree issued by the king, or his master of the guard," Grayson said.

"Like a law?"

"Or an order. Yes."

"I think my da has printed some of those."

"I remember the writ," Rogget said. "You've kept it all these years?"

"O' course."

"But Forbes, you can't expect Welk to settle on it. You don't think he actually meant it, do you?"

"O' course I do. He's king now, ain't he? And it decreed, 'Upon ascending to the throne.'"

"But Forbes, he was drunk."

"King Welk was drunk?" Sadie turned to Grayson, astonished.

"Aye, he was," Forbes said. The flow of tears stopped and was dutifully wiped from his face. "He came into our camp, carousing and drunken, with his circle of noble folk. They wanted cards and dice and some of our'n stew and loaves. We obliged, o' course. We hadn't much choice. And I won the writ fair and square in dice. You remember Rogget. I got sixes."

"I remember." Rogget was subdued and Fenn scanned his face for clues as to what it was all about.

Forbes burst into tears once more and fell full-bodied onto the forest floor. "And now it's gone. It's gone."

"What happened?" Grayson asked him again, standing to pull the man back to sitting.

Forbes choked on his tears for several seconds, wiped his face with his sleeve and managed to whine out something of the story.

"Soon as I heard he'd been crowned, I dug up the entire yard looking for it."

"You buried it?" Rogget said.

"Indeed. Such an important doc'ment. I couldn't let it get lost." Here he cried again for a moment before continuing. "I dug ever'where until I finally remembered where I'd hid it. Down in the basement in a jar. I thought, Lil, you'll ne'er forgive me for what I done to your garden, and all the time it was in the basement."

Sadie turned to Fenn wide-eyed and grinning.

"I went all about Woodside, boasting on my writ. Then I walked all the way to Town Village in Aaronland to see my brother. We went all over town, all the pubs and inns showin' off my writ. They all toasted me and wished me luck."

"What does the writ say?" Sadie asked.

"But after dark, when we stumbled out of The Crown, we was beset by thieves. They rifled through all my pockets. All they took was the writ."

"That's a might suspicious," Rogget said.

"Aye." Forbes fell into tears once more.

"Well, what did it say?" Grayson said.

Forbes only shook his head and cried.

"Forbes was married young," Rogget said. "His wife was with their first child when she was banished to the wasteland for shooting a guard."

"She shot a guard?" Fenn said.

"Only in the foot. She mistook him for an intruder. But no

matter. He happened to be one of King Arnot's third cousin's second in-law or some such nonsense. And her firearm was illegal. They hauled her off to the wasteland without much of a trial nor two thinks on it."

"Oh, my Lil," Forbes wailed.

"And the writ freed her?" Grayson said.

"Aye, it done more than that," Rogget said. "The prince was drunker than a brownie on honey mead. He promised to pardon all the wastelanders once he became king."

"What?" Fenn said.

"That's right. Now Forbes, you know as well as I do that there weren't no possibility the king would honor that writ."

"It was signed by him," he said. "And the nobles with him. It's the law. He has to honor it."

Rogget sighed and shook his head sadly. "We all knew what had happened to him. They say he was run off to wed an eisen against the king's wishes. Welk was betrothed to Panter of Damon Wall, but he wanted none of it. Rumor had it, King Evan set the guard after them, had them all killed."

"Killed," Sadie's voice echoed.

"It was that bloody Sorgood." Forbes sniffled. "He was the only one willing to lead the party, so they say. Relished in it, if you ask me. And now he's Master of the Guard. Such wicked injustice."

"When was all of this?" Grayson said.

"Oh, before you were born, likely."

"It were nigh onto twelve years ago," Forbes said. "Twelve years of waiting for my Lil to be freed."

"Forbes, you can't seriously think King Welk would have honored it. He was grief-stricken drunk."

"It's the law," he cried.

"Rogget's right," Grayson said. "Don't fret over losing it. You have to realize the king would never acknowledge it."

"If anything," Rogget said, "you'd be banished yourself and

never heard from again and your property gone to your King Ricker. And who would care for your children then?"

"That's probably true," Grayson said.

Forbes looked to Sadie and Fenn. Fenn turned to Sadie and nodded. Together they nodded their agreement at Forbes.

"Ah, maybe you're right." He sucked in a few ragged breaths. "But I thought I'd finally have my Lil home. I thought..."

"*Don't* think on it," Rogget said.

"Did you get a good look at the thieves?" Fenn said.

"Oh, sure. I seen the like of them before. They got that leader Clutch, the vilest folk in the hill country. They come through Woodside often, and no matter how much we give 'em, they always got to take more. I recognized 'em all right."

"What are you doing in the woods alone?" Sadie asked him.

Forbes threw up his hands and slapped them down on his pants. "I don't know. I left Aaronland after them, without my sack, without supplies. I can't go to Banished now and face Lil. She'll have heard about Welk being crowned. She'll be expecting to be set free. So I thought I'd get on home. And then I decided I'd be better off just sitting here in the woods until death found me."

"Don't be stupid," Rogget said. "You're going home."

"How can I go back to Woodside and face them all?"

"It's easy," Grayson said. "You tell them you were robbed. Regale them with a story. They'll forget it soon enough."

"Oh, sure they will. I'll be the fool who failed to get his loved ones out of the wasteland. That's who I'll be. I can't go back there."

"Where will you go?" Sadie said.

"I can't face Lil. I can't face home. I don't know what to do."

"Come on," Rogget said to them. "Let's set up camp and get him some food. Maybe we can figure this out."

Chapter Eight

A s he emerged from the orchard hiking toward Michelruud Castle to the north, Lucas saw in the distance that the folk had convened at the gathering stage. He walked past the guards' barracks on his left; all was strangely quiet there. He came to the jail, but several of the townsfolk were standing in front of the guard, their arms folded across their chests, so he passed and moved along toward the gathering. The crowd was shouting and raising fists in the air.

Lucas made his way around the outskirts of folk, hoping he wouldn't be recognized too soon. Dunham, privy to King Welk sat in the listening chair while Karner Hardy, owner of the general store in Path, and Lancet Wolf, the leather worker, stood on stage before the throng.

"Their parents should be forced to tell," Hardy shouted. "Dragged out of the jail house and put into the stocks or shown to the noose. They must know where their children have gone with the evil bairn—as surely as they are parents."

The crowd shouted its approval.

"We must give time for King Welk to weigh the evidence and his options," Wolf said.

A folk in the crowd shouted out, "King Evan would have

had this done long before now."

"Evan sent your children to Steingefan. Let them rot in that drafty old prison on the merest chance they might have the mark of prophecy," Wolf said.

"Aye, and it was because he had that great idea that we found the evil one," Hardy shouted. "The bairn led the escape. Why, Evan couldn't have planned it better."

"And walloped your own boy on the head, Wolf," someone in the mass of folk shouted. "Would you not have your retribution?"

"Please, I beg of you all," Wolf said. "The High Priest of Hass is due at any time. We must prepare—"

"The Hass could help us find the evil one," Hardy said and the crowd roared its approval.

"The Hass?" Wolf said. "The very folk who treat us so vilely? They lash our children in the streets for playing, send us to the stocks for the slightest affront. Think of those they've killed. The stationer and the innkeeper make regular visits to the burial grounds and you would ask favor from the folk who put their children under tombstones?"

"We would only ask that they capture the bairn," someone mumbled.

"But you would risk the lives of Sadie and Grayson," Wolf said. "And you would dare ally yourselves with the Hass when instead you should spit before them as they trod our villages."

"They deserve the respect of their station."

"It is not respect you show them, but fear."

"They have soldiers and firearms to outnumber ours by far. They can help us find the boy and kill him."

"Kill him?" Wolf stared at the crowd, stunned. "Folk, listen to yourselves. We don't have all the facts. We don't know the truth. And already you are prepared to ally yourselves with your enemy and murder a child."

"If our enemy will help us in this, why not ally with them?"

Hardy said. "Dunham, what says the king?"

Dunham stood and raised his hands to quiet the crowd. "I will take all of your concerns to his Highness. In the meantime, the stationer and innkeeper are to be left alone in the jailhouse. I assure you King Welk takes the threat of the bairn very seriously."

"Then why does he let the parents of his accomplices sit in jail? Why does he not publicly interrogate them?"

Dunham again raised his hands and shook his head. "I will relay your message." He took the steps off the stage, the crowd mumbling against him.

Lucas made his way back to the jailhouse. He was pleased to see the angry folk were dispersing, apparently realizing there would be no public accusations this day. He stepped up to the guards and threw off his hood, shocked to see his friends. They too were surprised to see him.

"Edgar," he said. "I heard you were injured."

"Aye." Young footman Wolf showed off the now healing bruise on the side of his head. "The evil bairn hit me with a rock during the Steingefan escape."

"He did not hit you with a rock," Tildon Weeks, the other guard, said. "It were one of the other kids. Why do you keep saying—"

"What difference does it make?" Edgar said. And turning to Lucas, continued. "Your Father Treacher being run off to the port, they asked Ma'am Hardy to tend to me, and she told me I ought to be laid off active duty for just a while. So, here I am."

"This ain't *in*active duty," Tildon said. "It's very active."

"Aye." Edgar smirked. "'Tis very active standing at the jailhouse all day making sure no one goes in to bother the prisoners."

"Who do you have in there?"

"The usuals," Tildon said. "The pirate, the madman, and the witch."

"And the stationer," Edgar said. "You're forgetting the most valuable ones."

"Oh, right. The stationer and his wife, and the innkeeper. They got the best stalls, but still sleeping on straw. It ain't right, if you ask me."

"Oh it ain't right, is it? You didn't get hit in the face with a rock, did you? All in the aid of the evil little bairn, did you? No, you didn't."

"That don't make it right none, to lock up the stationer or Ma'am Stationer, of all folk."

"They should tell us all what they know, they should."

"They don't know nothing." Tildon turned to Lucas. "They don't know nothing. No sense keeping them locked away."

"Think what the townsfolk would do to them if they were freed, Til," Lucas said.

Tildon stared at him for several seconds before his face lit up and his mouth fell open. "Oh, aye, that's it. That's what they're in the jailhouse for."

"What are you going on about?" Edgar poked Tildon's shoulder.

"Protection."

"They protect the likes of the folk that brought me this?" He pointed to his face.

"Ah, Wolf," Lucas said. "It's all healed now. And it wasn't the stationer's fault."

Wolf shook his head. "They can stay locked up until the gray is gone around my eye at least."

"Might I see them, do you think?"

Tildon laughed. "Are you out of your mind, there, Lucas? Nobody is allowed in. By the king's orders."

"But, I'm one of the wissenry orphans. And without Father Treacher about, I'm practically next in line."

"Your lesser wissendes over there to the wissenry already tried that one with the madman."

"The madman?"

"Aye, their regular visit to tend him and calm him and feed

him. Same with the witch though she don't want none of it."

"And you didn't let them in?"

"No one goes in. Didn't you hear me? No one."

"Who's feeding the prisoners then?"

"We are, o' course," Edgar said.

"I just want to make sure the stationer and innkeeper are all right."

"They're all right," Tildon said. "There. You made sure."

"Come on, Til. You won't even let *me* in?"

"Are you saying there, Lucas, that I do not take my position in the king's guard seriously?"

Lucas sighed. "No. I'm not saying that. Of course your duties are important."

"Indeed they are. So don't even think about trying to visit with them prisoners. I'm going to be on especial lookout now that I know you want to. I know how sneaky you think you are."

"He is sneaky, Tildon," Edgar said. "He don't just *think* it."

They both stared at Lucas with their eyes closed up into slits of suspicion and nodded slightly. He would have to figure out another way.

Chapter Nine

Leah's mind was numb and her body tingled when she moved to take the steps up to the porch of the inn at Path. The day was done and darkness had fallen. She'd spent the carriage ride forcing herself to think of anything but the brownie's head, bleeding in the sack on the floor near her feet. To be out of the carriage and away from it only brought it back to her thoughts and her stomach turned.

Prenalin held the door to the inn open for Kirche and his guard, the porters, and finally Leah. They stood in the lobby, looking on at the few folk left in the dining area beyond the staircase. A fiddle screeched out a rustic ditty somewhere in the distance and glasses clinked together. Prenalin leaned toward her and whispered, "They have a pub here in Path."

A pub? Leah began to regain her composure and her eyes widened. She'd heard Kirche speak of pubs on the second day of their trip east, aboard the *Treasure of the Seas*. Prenalin explained their purpose and that she would pass several while in Cold Sea Port. It was quite a feat for her to manage to look through the open doors of those they passed without Prenalin or Kirche discovering her curiosity. Pubs and public drunkenness were forbidden in Ruhm.

Kirche led the party up the staircase to the second floor and Leah, tired and weary, wanted only to find her bed and her journal. High-pitched giggling met her ears and she glanced up to see a little girl with red, bouncy curls bounding down the stairs. The child lost her footing and fell into Kirche's leg. Kirche raised an armed and smacked the child off him as if she were a wasp, sending her tumbling down the stairs.

Leah reached out for the girl, but she fell past in blur of ruffles and socks, landing in the lobby with a dull thud. Instinctively, Leah stepped down toward her, and several folk shouted, but Prenalin's hand held tight to her arm. She turned to him, and beyond him, saw Kirche continue up the steps without looking back.

"She will be tended to," Prenalin said sharply, pulling Leah to move along upward.

The child lay still at the bottom of the stairs and Leah forced herself to turn away once more and go to her room. Once inside, she heard the little girl begin to scream. Leah stumbled to a chair at a desk and sat staring into the darkness until a woman knocked and opened the door.

"My apologies, mistress," the woman said and lit the lanterns. "I was delayed."

A porter followed with Leah's bags; he set them with a thud on the floor under the window and hurried out. When the room was lit and the walls flickering with shadow and light, Leah realized there was a looking glass on a stand in the corner. She smiled at the memory of her mother brushing her hair back home in Ruhm.

As the woman pulled back the covers from the bed and fluffed the pillows, Leah turned and watched her. Her dress fell loose over her wiry frame and gray hair dangled about her face, escaped from the severe bun on the nape of her neck.

"Would you like the bed warmed, miss?" the woman said without looking at Leah.

"It's not nearly cold enough for that," Leah said. "But thank you for the offer."

"Yes'm. Can I bring you anything before you turn in for the night? Unpack your bags?"

Leah shook her head. "Is the little girl all right?"

The woman looked hard at her with a frown. "I'm sorry to appear rushed ma'am. I will do for you anything you wish."

"I understand. You need to get back to her. But please...is she going to be all right?"

For several seconds the old woman glared at Leah. Then she said, "Looks to be a broken arm. And she was out dead cold for a few moments. The wissende is gone, lesser wissendes are not well versed, and so she's off to Ma'am Hardy, but—" She stopped with a nod and a quick breath and turned to the door. "My apologies, ma'am. To have bothered you."

Leah wanted to stop her. To learn more. But she felt as if her mind and body were a step behind and the woman was gone before she could raise a hand. Weary, she dug open her bag to find her night clothes. She hid behind the dressing screen and changed. Stepping out, she went to stand before the glass and untied her hair. She ran her fingers through her long locks, pulling them out, away from her head. Then she spun, and caught glimpses of herself with her hair twirling about her in the mirror. She stood admiring its length for some time before taking out her brush from her bag and giving her tresses a long, thorough grooming.

That chore gladly completed, pulling her journal and a lead writer from her knapsack, Leah fell across the bed and lay there with the book open, willing herself to write.

But words would not come to her. Homesick. Confused. Angry. Disappointed. Leah could not bring herself to write the reality that she had been wrong about Kirche. No. Not wrong about him. Wrong about herself. How stupid could she be?

"Oh, Madam Always," she whispered. "You would not be proud of me now."

Chapter Ten

At midnight, Lucas moved silently in the darkness, past the sleeping Tildon Weeks and Edgar Wolf, dutiful soldiers in the king's guard. He lifted the latch and entered the stone jailhouse of Michelruud. The innkeeper's snoring echoed throughout the building and he followed it to its origin, down a long, cold hallway, peering into each barred cell as he passed. The pirate, smelling of whiskey, slept between bouts of unconscious cursing; the madman of Michelruud, frail and harmless, and a relative to the king so not to be sent off to the wasteland, tossed about as if frustrated by fleas; and Ma'am Eer, the sorceress, imprisoned again for setting fire to someone's summer crop was a solid lump of motionless slumber. The wastelanders had once more refused to allow Eer entry and as there was never any evidence against her, she spent much time in the jailhouse.

All slept as he strode past without sound. The innkeeper snored in a cell at the end of the hallway, and across from him, in another cell, lay the stationer and his wife.

"Stationer," Lucas whispered.

Ma'am Stationer sat up. "Who is that?"

"Lucas of the Path wissenry. Wake the stationer."

In the dark, Lucas watched her shake her husband awake.

"Pratt. Pratt, wake up."

The stationer's head popped up, turning this way and that. "What is it?"

"Lucas, of the wissenry. Come to the bars; we must speak."

He sat up, rubbed his face, and crawled forward to the cold, steel bars of his cell.

"It is too dark; I cannot trust it is you."

"Do you not recognize my voice?"

"It's him," Ma'am Stationer said. "I'm sure it's him."

"But you told me the guard took him with the others." Pratt turned back to his wife.

"They did. 'Tis true."

"Aye, the guard took him," Pratt peered through the bars. "So, how might he find himself here?"

"They let him go, husband. I tell you, it's Lucas."

"We have no time for bickering," Lucas said.

"What do you want, then?" Pratt said. "Do you have Sadie and Grayson?"

"The children are in the care of Rogget, a wissenry guide. They are safe as can be expected."

"Does the king believe this bairn nonsense?" Ma'am Stationer whispered.

"He is confused. He does not have access to the histories, as you do."

Pratt's mouth fell agape for a brief second before he spoke. "How do you know about the histories?"

"Never mind that. Understand that war is approaching. Forces from the west and the north are rising. We cannot fight them both."

"What does this have to do with me?" Pratt said, disheartened. "I am jailed as a traitor to the king."

"Yet you remain the stationer of Michelruud. Welk is not so arrogant as his father was. He will find he requires your support. I feel you must trust him."

Stationer Pratt's eyes lowered to the ground. "There are things I should not know," he said. "Things I should not possess."

"I am aware," Lucas said.

"If I trust the king, I give myself up to the law for punishment."

"Perhaps. But you may save the Ruud in so doing."

The stationer's brow creased and he shook his head. "How?"

"Trust me in this. Knowledge is necessary at all times, but especially when one is faced with enemies he does not understand. You have knowledge the king needs."

Pratt nodded. "I see. But I have not heard of any threat, from the west or the north. I only hear the ranting and rumors about a bairn."

"That is the concern," Lucas said. "Our folk are disturbed and afraid. Our enemies will use this to their advantage. You know of whom I speak, Stationer. You know the threat the Great West poses."

"But how do *you* know this?"

"I cannot say. Remain skeptical if you like. But remember what I have said, when you are brought before the king."

"It is so highly unlikely that I should be brought before the king, that if that one small miracle occurs, I will consider you a great sage and follow your advice."

Lucas smiled. "I am no sage," he said. "I just know where to look for information."

Chapter Eleven

They'd spent the late afternoon the day before comforting Forbes Billings. Once Darnit rejoined them, Rogget took a brief hunt while they scoured for wild roots and berries. After they ate what they could, Rogget left Darnit as guard while he went off to scout the location of the thieves.

Fenn's sleep was troubled without dreams and visions. And when he woke, Rogget had bitters warmed over the fire and told him to drink.

"You look like a harpie's ghost."

"Thanks." Fenn was weary and his body felt as if it moved through mud. Something ached inside him for his charm—not thought, not feeling, but the emptiness of longing. The morning was cold and damp and did nothing to raise his spirits. When Forbes woke, he offered a weak smile.

"They've made their way into the port at Cold Sea," Rogget said. "Your writ is long gone."

"All right." Forbes' shoulders sank as all his hope seemed to leave him. "I'll go on home. I'll pack up the children from their grans and we'll have to go meet up with Lil. She has to know the truth." He shook his head. "I am one dumb folk."

"Don't be so hard on yourself," Grayson said wiping the

tired from his face. "You were just hopeful that's all. Nothing wrong with that."

Forbes shrugged.

"I didn't realize," Sadie said, "that you could go and visit the folk in the wasteland."

"Oh, sure," Forbes said. "They rely on family, and the wissenry, to bring them supplies and food. It's a harsh life."

"Why don't their families stay with them?" Grayson said.

"Some have been known to. But they leave behind their property and the king takes possession."

"Aye," Rogget said. "If you want your children to have it, you have to stay in the Ruud and keep claim to it."

"Where are you four headed?" Forbes asked.

"Aaronland," Rogget said.

"Well, then, I'll go with you. I'll get my belongings from my brother and then head home to collect the children. No sense trying to make it all the way through the divide wood with nothing to eat and no knife."

As they hiked through the woods, Fenn lagged behind with Sadie and Grayson while Rogget and Forbes talked of their days of childhood in Timber.

"Are you sure that writ's no good?" Fenn asked Grayson.

"No. But no sense making Forbes feel awful about it."

"I think the king could be forced to acknowledge it," Sadie said. "If I learned anything from my da, it's the importance of the law."

Fenn nodded absentmindedly. The thief had his charms and hemp rope. And he had Forbes Billings' writ. In a way, he thought, Clutch had stolen both their dreams.

Chapter Twelve

Leah was groggy when she opened the door to the old woman again. She nearly shoved Leah aside and hurried to pull open the heavy curtains at the window; morning light streamed in across the floor. Next she busied herself making up the bed.

"Good morning," Leah murmured and went to the window to look out over the small town square.

"Morn. Bitters or tea? In room or down to the dining area?"

"I'll meet my party downstairs."

The woman nodded. "Will that be all, then?"

"How is the little girl this morning?"

"She'll be fine."

"What is her name?"

The woman stared at her, frowning. "Matilda Steppe. Daughter of the innkeeper."

"How old is she?"

"Eight."

"Are you the mistress of the inn?"

"No, miss."

Leah paused, wishing the woman would say more. But she stood stiff and imposing as if awaiting orders.

"And what is your name?"

"Dowling."

"Dowling?"

"Yes, miss."

Leah frowned and let out a short sigh. There would be no friend in Dowling, apparently. She turned to the window once more.

"This village isn't like the others I've seen of the Ruud. It's so small."

"It ain't small." Dowling joined her in looking out at the town square. "This village evolved more than it was built. It were once no more than the path from the original castle, now Steingefan, to the river."

"Path," Leah said and nodded. "So, this isn't all of it?"

"No, miss. Path is spread out into the woods and over through the orchards to the new castle. These here are the main square buildings. But you'll find the wissenry over into the woods and the smithy and chandlery, too. No, there's much more to Path than meets the eye."

"Thank you." Leah curtseyed.

Dowling's eyes closed up and her chin lifted. "Hmph," she said and left the room.

Downstairs, Leah found Kirche in high spirits at a small corner table finishing up his kaff. She picked at a biscuit and ate a bit of sausage until Prenalin arrived and sat with them.

"Today we investigate the woods to the north," Prenalin told her. "And then we meet with the king at his table."

She tried to smile but found herself dazed and saddened. Kirche and Prenalin chatted until Kipling, Alphonse, and Redd, Kirche's bodyguards, arrived to lead them. They left the inn through the back door, Leah absentmindedly following Redd down the steps. When she looked up to find her way, she was staring into the eyes of the brownie Kirche had murdered the day before. She shrieked and fell backward onto the wood stairs.

Prenalin forced Alphonse and Redd away from her and pulled her up by the arms.

"What was that about?" Kirche said, his smooth purr of a voice now more sinister than mysterious to Leah.

"I'm sorry," she managed. "The brownie. I didn't..."

"Oh, yes," he said, smiling at her. "Drying out a bit before the preserving cloths can be placed."

The brownie's small head was mounted on a stick stuck into the ground outside the back door to the inn, his face frozen in a grimace, his eyes wide open; dried blood ran the length of the post to the dirt.

"Do you think it would be better to move it away from the building?" Prenalin said.

"And have some wild animal take it? Or worse, let the felidae claim it? No, no. Dowling said it would be fine here."

"Dowling?" Leah said.

"Yes. She runs the inn. Rumor tells us our innkeeper has found himself in jail. Dowling is his mother-in-law, I believe. Dour isn't she?"

Leah nodded and let Prenalin take her arm as they made their way into the woods. Gretchen and Zelda had come along to carry their baskets for a mid-morning snack and their formal cloaks for the later visit with King Welk. Xavier, the youngest porter, was charged with carrying the small chest in which Kirche's formal head wear, his tall mitre, was nestled. They traveled a series of paths for hours, Gretchen chatting along about this and that and nonsense, with Kirche and Alphonse occasionally veering off to investigate a hole or a cavern. Leah imagined they must be searching for the elusive kell stone and let herself chuckle.

She supposed her suspicions had been right all along. Kirche had no idea where the stone was and no plan for finding it. He seemed to quite enjoy the adventure of his visit to the Ruud, however, and that was no doubt the true point of the trip.

"Are you all right today?" Prenalin asked.

She nodded with a slight smile.

They stopped for a picnic at the edge of the woods looking out over a brief plain and the ruins of a castle.

"Steingefan," Prenalin said as he sat on one of the blankets with her. "A prison now, but once a castle. Beyond that is a path through a field of lilac clover that leads to the wastelands, where they banish their folk."

"Lilac clover. An entire field of it?"

"Yes, I hear tell it spans miles eastward. It helps to keep the banished from returning home. You've heard of it?"

"There is a patch southwest of Ruhm, beyond Madam Sponhide's mine. We were allowed to study there in school—capture fairy bees for..." the thought made her stomach lurch just a bit.

Prenalin nodded knowingly. "Yes, you see? This is how we are raised. They are not sentient beings, but zoo animals."

"The fairy bees are only somewhat sentient. And not fairies at all, in truth," she said. "Not really bees either."

He raised his brows and smiled.

"They are the gemein," she told him. "Angry little creatures. Powerful bite that often scars badly."

Prenalin took a bite of an apple. "So you did not mind so much harming them?"

"I didn't dissect mine."

"No?"

She shook her head. "Madam Always allowed me to defer that assignment."

He smiled at her and wiped apple juice from his chin. Leah turned to gaze at their party, the bodyguards and porters lounged and snacked while Kirche had Alphonse plodding with him about the edges of the wood examining flora.

"Do you remember on the boat over, you told me that Kirche could barely stand these visits?"

He tilted his head and his brow furrowed. "Did I say that?"

"Yes. You told me how base and crude the folk were here, and I asked you if Kirche felt the same."

"And you think I spoke a lie?" A slight smile lit up his face.

"I think Lord Kirche enjoys the visits here, yes."

Prenalin laughed—a loud, stout chortle that surprised her and made the others turn to watch them.

"Nonetheless, Leah Hallowsing," he said, grinning. "The standard answer will always be that the Ruud is a dreadful place and our Lord Kirche cannot wait to wipe its mud from his boots."

Leah couldn't help but giggle and shake her head. She felt the others' eyes on them both but she didn't care. Kirche was too busy walking this way and that, peering into the woods and pointing at birds to notice *her*.

"Pren, is this a test?"

He balked. "What?"

"Am I being tested?"

"Why would you ask such a thing?"

"Because I feel as if I am being tried. And found lacking."

He turned from her and watched the rest of the group eating and chatting. "Not a test. No," he said.

Leah could almost hear the rest of his answer hovering somewhere in his head, not daring to be spoken. When they'd finished their rest, they packed up and headed toward Michelruud castle.

Chapter Thirteen

King Welk gnawed on roast pig and spiced, stewed apples in the great hall. The noble folk, all kin to the founder of the Ruud, Michelruud himself, lounged about the heavy wood tables and benches lining the walls enjoying food, drink, music, and dancing. Welk sat at a table in front of his bed-chamber doors, next to the stairs to the upper floors. He watched the empty throne dais across the room and the young couples resting easily across its steps.

As a child, Welk would sit at his father's feet during meal times watching in amazement as servers, who knelt on either side of the king, held his food tray steady above his lap while he ate. Two others stood at his sides holding his golden chalices ever ready to let them go when the king grabbed at them for a guzzle. Welk shook off his disgust as the chamberlain approached his table.

"Tom Britt, from the wissenry at Cold Sea, Sire," he announced.

Welk waved a hand for the lad to approach and speak. The boy pulled a scroll from under his robes, unrolled it, and read.

"The wissenry of the Ruud wishes to make it known to King Welk of Michelruud that it is sorely grieved to have caused his Highness unpleasantness in the scandal involving the evil bairn of prophecy. None of our wissendes were aware of the origins of said bairn, nor understood the meaning of the mark he bore. He has thus been banished into the hill country, never more to take refuge in the wissenry. Let this be the end of our involvement. By your leave, Father Britt, Head of Affairs, Wissenry of the Ruud, Cold Sea Wissenry."

The lad bowed. "Return message, Sire?"

Welk shook his head and waved him away. The boy handed the scroll to the chamberlain, bowed and left.

"Is Sorgood still about?"

"Yes, Sire, still readying for another journey to the port."

"Summon him."

While he waited, Welk finished his meal and drank his wine, his stomach churning with fury. When Sorgood approached with several of his elite guard, he did not hide his anger.

"Why have you not left for the port?"

Sorgood bowed too slowly. "I have already sent a detachment, Sire. I meet with them shortly."

"Give him the scroll." Welk waved a hand to the chamberlain. He watched Sorgood as he read the declaration from the wissenry.

"But, what does this mean?" he stammered. "Did they have the boy and let him go?"

"It doesn't say...does it?"

"Does this mean he is traveling through the Ruud toward the hill country?"

"Or is this a ruse to keep us away from the port?" Welk added.

"I will call up two hundred men, Sire, and we will accost the wissenry at Cold Sea. They cannot be allowed this treachery."

Welk fumed, not looking at Sorgood, thinking about what that would mean. He could not move against the wissenry without losing the heart of the folk. They were with him, thus far; their fear of the evil bairn and the destruction of the Ruud kept them loyal to Welk. But they were devoted to their wissendes, who counseled them, represented them in the courts, gave them aid and comfort. No, he dare not take the wissenry by force.

It was likely the boy was being hidden under Father Britt's care all this time, even as the guard searched the port more than a week ago. But what else could he do? It was enough, for now, to be seen trying to find the bairn of prophecy. Welk turned to Sorgood, repulsed. Soon enough, he would have to take real action against the boy. This was no time to question his nerve.

He shook his head. "No. We will leave the wissenry alone... for now. You will strengthen your patrols on the borderlands. Build your perimeter. Go to Aaronland first and demand from Arnot all available guards. See to it they cover the border in the divide wood. Then go to Damon Wall and do the same and only after you have secured the northern and eastern boundaries, go to Cold Sea and see what you can learn of ships transporting children away from the Ruud."

Sorgood bowed. "You suspect he remains here still?"

"I do. They are children. They will be loath to leave their homes. And they travel slowly."

"We will find him, Sire."

"Do you have any in your ranks who are familiar with the boy and can recognize him at a distance?"

"Aye, Sire." Sorgood's face lit up. "A volunteer has come to aid us." He reached out his hand and beckoned a young folk forward and Welk sucked in a small breath in astonishment.

"Lucas Foster of the wissenry, Sire." The boy bowed stiffly, as if he was forced into the obeisance.

Welk stared at him, so much like his old friend Belfen his heart leapt. Frieden. Young Frieden would now enlist in finding the bairn of prophecy.

"Lucas was raised with the boy at the Path wissenry." Sogood smiled broadly.

"Of course," Welk managed to say. "Yes. Very good. Thank

you for your help."

The boy nodded and rejoined the other guards. Sorgood turned to leave just as Welk's chamberlain approached flustered, and said, "Sire, the High Priest of Hass has entered the castle grounds."

Welk thought he saw Sorgood flinch before he turned to make his way across the lobby.

"Is it autumn already?" Welk said, watching Frieden, small and frail among the guardsmen. "Allow them entry."

The group, cloaked in soft shades of red, except for the priest, in purple, crossed the room making a great show of their patience and grace. Welk sneered. The priest still wore the same funny hat he remembered as a young lad sitting at his father's side. This priest was much younger than those he recalled visiting his father. The hat seemed larger, too, than Welk remembered.

They approached his table and stood before him. Each of them wore a chain and hanging from it was a large circular charm carved of white marble, etched and painted with a picture of a tree lit in flames.

Looking about haughtily, the priest moved forward but did not bow. The representatives of the Hass of Emorah never bowed before the king. Welk remembered questioning this practice when he was very young. But his father waved him away and learned to send him off on some errand or other whenever the Hass arrived.

"Allow me to express my sadness at the passing of your father, King Evan," the young priest said.

Welk nodded. His eye caught sight of a young girl in the group, her eyes roaming about the hall.

"I look forward to many years of service to you, my lord." The priest smiled. "It is customary," his voice rolled smoothly in the air, filled with disdain and charm, "for the king of Michelruud to stand before the high priest of Hass."

"Is it?" Welk sat back in his jeweled dinner chair and eyed the high priest curiously. He glanced at the girl, her attention suddenly on the conversation, and offered her a smile. Her glance flew to the floor and her cheeks flashed a blush.

"Yes," the priest said.

"My father stood before the Hass?"

"He did."

Welk shrugged. "I find that odd."

"Nonetheless," the man purred with expectation.

"I will not stand before you," Welk said. "But I will invite you to sit."

He raised his hand and called for chairs.

"It is customary for the priest of Hass to sit in the king's chair."

At that Welk laughed aloud and a silence fell over the great hall as folk turned to watch the meeting.

"My father gave you his chair did he? Did he also give you his throne?"

The priest smiled viciously at Welk, but Welk was not intimidated.

"Sit, or don't sit." He motioned to the low wood chair placed before him at the table. "But either way, tell me who you are and what you want."

For a brief second, the priest looked concerned, but his face quickly regained its snobbish glower.

"You are not familiar with the Hass of Emorah?"

"Of course I am."

"I am Kirche, High Priest. I have come to see the King of Michelruud as is customary, every year before winter."

"Aren't you all called Kirche?" Welk said.

The priest barely nodded. "It is customary for the king to receive us in his chambers."

"And why might that be?"

"It is no concern of mine."

"Then what is your concern?"

"Tribute."

"Tribute?"

"Yes." Kirche sighed and appeared angry. "The kings of the Ruud, Michelruud in particular, pay tribute in the form of monetary compensation and statements of fealty, to the Hass of Emorah."

"I believe you are mistaken." Welk frowned. "The kings of the Ruud pay tribute to the Kingdom of Ruhm."

"The Hass of Emorah *is* the Kingdom of Ruhm."

"Again," Welk said, smiling. "You are mistaken."

The young priest stepped closer to Welk and sneered. "I will not tolerate this insolence, young king."

Welk leaned forward with a clever smile and picked up his fork, just as a servant set a plate with a slice of berry pie on it before him.

"Apparently, you will," he said. "I am king in Michelruud. You are my honored guest, a representative of the Kingdom of Ruhm. That is where we are. You may sit, or you may stand, but you do not have my chair, nor my throne."

The priest fumed and glared at Welk as he ate. The young girl's eyes widened and she gawked at him. He chuckled and ate a second bite of pie. After several seconds, the priest took the chair and accepted a plate of food. Chairs were brought for his aide on the left, and the young girl on the right; the others in their party were sat at the far end of the table.

"I am Prenalin, Secretary to the High Priest of Hass," the aide said. "And this is Leah Hallowsing, Aide to the High Priest." They both bowed and sat before Welk.

Welk then turned his attention to Kirche who glared at him, his eyebrows raised.

"You needn't be insulted," Welk said. "I believe you were only given my father's chair near the end, because the king was too weak to sit in it himself."

"Are you accusing the Hass of taking advantage of the sick king?"

"Isn't that your *job*?"

The young priest leered at Welk for a moment, then smiled slightly and nodded. "Perhaps we will get along, after all."

They ate for a few moments in silence. Welk watched as Leah picked, uninterested, at the fowl and potatoes. Her hair was gathered at the nape of her neck and fell down the back of the chair nearly to the floor. Her features were delicate, and while her eyes were filled with curiosity at everything they came upon, Welk could see a strength of will behind them. Hers was very different from the dull, practiced gaze of the priest.

"I have often, as a lad and young prince," he said, raising his mug. "Wondered what tribute does the Kingdom of Ruhm need from our little realm?"

Kirche shrugged. "None, naturally. A token gesture is all that is expected. Your father sent pretty gold chains from the ore mines dug in the northern hill country."

"Very well."

"One day, if you're daring enough, we'd like to see a relic or two from the ice realm. Your father once promised us a rhinobear pelt. Alas, he fell ill shortly after, and was ill every year after that."

"I might visit the ice realm one day for adventure. I'll pick something up for you. Or is that...for the king of Ruhm?"

"Yes, yes of course." Kirche smiled devilishly. "For the king."

Both Leah and Prenalin looked to Kirche when he spoke and nodded in agreement often.

"Who is king of Ruhm these days?"

"Roren."

"I am told the king has always been a child, these past five generations."

Kirche nodded and his aides followed suit.

"Do many children in Ruhm die so young?"

Kirche shrugged but said nothing, while Leah looked squarely at Welk as if she'd never heard such a question.

"Is that an odd thing to ask?"

She seemed to realize she'd been looking at the king, shook her head and looked back to her plate.

"They do not die while king," Kirche said.

"If they do not die, how are they removed from the throne when they reach adulthood?"

Kirche frowned and stared at Welk. "These are questions regarding law and order in Ruhm and are not your business."

"Ah." Welk stuck another fork full of pie into his mouth and chewed with a smile. "But I'm wanting to know. Is it beheading? Banishment?"

Kirche shrugged. "Our kings are granted the privilege of tranquility at the end of their reign. It is a great honor. And none of your concern."

"Well, we'll find something appropriate to send the current boy king, anyway, shall we?"

"You are having troubles with a boy of your own, are you not? An evil little bairn running amok in the Ruud? Your folk are worked up into a frenzy over some ancient prophecy."

Welk nodded and eyed Kirche who seemed to have lost the edge of his sarcasm. They both ate in silence for a moment.

"You could use this situation to your advantage," Kirche said.

"And yours?"

"Perhaps."

"Explain."

"If you kill the boy, you can create a devotion surrounding him. You can make his memory whatever you wish and use it to calm the folk, to direct them."

Welk looked at him skeptically. "If I *kill* him?"

He could almost feel the energy bottling up in both Prenalin and Leah as their bodies tensed and they stared hard at their plates.

"You would not do it yourself, of course," Kirche said smoothly, ignorant of the turmoil he caused his aides. "The folk themselves will ask that it be done."

Welk creased his brow. "They will ask that he be killed, and then accept a devotion surrounding his memory?"

"Yes, it can be done. It was done in the southern lands long ago. Do you not know the story of Rett?"

"Ah." Welk nodded. "But I am of the wissenry line, you recall, and my ancestors did not subscribe to superstition and dogma."

"True, true. But you would be wise to consider them useful. Your position now, as king, cannot rest on truth and realism alone. Folk want to be led and they want to be comforted."

"Comfort is the duty of the wissenry."

"Hah. The wissenry of the Ruud is a mere shadow of its former days in Ruhm." Kirche nearly spat with this statement and Welk flinched, surprised at his passion.

"Perhaps we didn't battle the superstition of the Hass, here in the Ruud," he said, expecting to see Kirche fume.

Instead, a calm apathy fell over his face and Kirche waved his hand. "Enough of our bickering. I assure you, if you have the child killed, and convince the folk it was by their wishes the deed was done, you can then plant seeds of devotion in the land. A great superstition will arise from his death. The folk will worship him."

"And then?"

"And then you appoint a high priest to tell them *how* to worship."

Welk eyed Kirche carefully. He saw Leah, out of the corner of his eye, pull the cloth napkin from her lap and hold it to her lips.

It was all very familiar, what Kirche was saying. He'd been

told the story of Rett when he was a child. His nurse implored him never to repeat it, though he'd asked for it over and over again.

"All right, dear prince," she would say, tucking him into his bed each night. "But remember, you must not share the story."

"But why?"

"It is forbidden."

It was long after Nanta had died that Welk had the epiphany: if it was forbidden, how had his Nanta known it? And why would any story such as that, a silly tale of superstition, be forbidden? Now, twenty years later, here sat the high priest of Hass alluding to the same story as if it were true.

Very odd things were happening of late. The Hass calling for the murder of a child; a child of prophecy with the mark of the faire. Welk frowned as he sat at table listening to the young priest of Hass regale him with stories of the greatness of the kingdom of Ruhm. But he paid little heed. His father told him many a time the Hass was all bluster and exaggeration. "Believe half of what they say, but suspect them double."

"You will find our ways very useful, should you require them," Kirche was saying; and Welk was sure now that he was desperate, deep in some part of him, for Welk to agree to his plans for the young bairn.

"I'll consider your words," he said.

"Good, good. And now, what news of the stone?"

"Stone?"

Kirche tilted his head and raised his brows. "Surely your father told you."

"I know nothing about a stone."

Kirche scowled, even while his secretary and aide relaxed and finished their meals. "The Hass has been assured that the entire realm has been searched for our stone."

"*Your* stone?"

"It belonged to Ruhm and was stolen by your ancestor. We

will have it back."

"Who stole it?"

"Michelruud, who founded your kingdom, but he gave it back, eventually."

Welk laughed softly. "Then what's the problem?"

"One of our wissendes secreted it away and returned it to you."

"How would that then be our concern?"

"Your king received property stolen from us." The priest fumed.

"And you are certain of this?"

Kirche turned to Prenalin. "You have the declaration?"

Prenalin reached under his robes and pulled an envelope from his vest. Opening it, he withdrew a yellowed piece of parchment, unfolded it, and handed it to Kirche.

"When I was in the Ruud last, your father asked to see the proof. And here it is. Wissende Ferdwick Elson, in his own hand, tells of taking the stone from our most sacred museum of artifacts and sailing with it to Michelruud, returning it to its rightful place."

"Well, then," Welk said. "I imagine you will find it there, wherever that rightful place is."

Kirche glared at him. "Do you take us for fools? We know the beast do not have the stone."

"I see." Welk peered at him. "My apologies to the great representative of Hass." He smiled cleverly. "I know nothing of this stone, but I assure you I will look into the matter."

Kirche shrugged. "I am told the stone was a matter of great importance to the folk of the Ruud in the early days. How can you know nothing of it? Is your education system so poor?" He made a face as if he smelled a skunk.

Welk smiled broadly at him. "Indeed, we live rustic lives of farming and brewing. History is for scholars and priests." He turned to Leah. "Our deepest apologies for the debasement you must endure here."

To his surprise and delight, the young woman smiled and nodded; Welk knew that she was in on his joke.

"Do you require lodgings? I do not recall the high priest ever residing in the castle."

"We do not," Kirche said. "We have always stayed at the inn in Path. We still have more touring to do. We sail for home in a few weeks' time."

"Must be a tedious job having to leave the splendor of Ruhm and suffer the hardships of camping in the Ruud. Do you require a guard? I hear tell of a bear loose in our midst."

"Absolutely not. We are heavily armed."

Welk shrugged. "Very well then. Enjoy the hospitality of our folk. We will see you again next year. Chamberlain," he called. "Do we have a tribute to the king of Ruhm?"

He nodded. "Aye, Sire. It was prepared a month ago by your father's steward."

"Then it is goodbye," Welk said. He remained in his seat, smiling at Kirche, knowing that Kirche was waiting for him to stand. But he would not stand in the presence of this high priest of Hass.

After a long pause, Kirche rose and his attendants gathered around him. "I do not think you understand the nature of the relationship between the Hass and the Ruud, young king."

"I believe I understand what it has been, young priest," Welk said. "It is you who do not understand what it is now."

Kirche's jaw set hard and he glared at Welk. "There are ill omens in the air. I am thinking we will see each other again before the year is up."

Welk nodded. "Very well."

As the priest and his folk made their slow walk across the lobby toward the castle door, Leah turned back to give Welk another smile.

Welk looked to Chamberlain. "I could swear his hat is bigger than that of the last."

"They are taller hats every year, Sire." Chamberlain smiled and Welk laughed aloud, his voice ringing through the great lobby behind the Hass of Emorah.

"Dunham," he said, and Dunham appeared at his side. "Prepare lodgings here in the castle for the parents of our fugitives. I will tell you when the time is right to move them from the jail."

Chapter Fourteen

They returned to the inn after their meeting with King Welk and Leah went upstairs to put away her cloak. She was to meet Kirche and Prenalin downstairs for a late afternoon trek into the woods once again, for what purpose they didn't bother to tell her. She should lie down and rest, but her thoughts would not let her alone.

She dared not write in her journal her feelings of late—of Kirche's odd split in personality from a heartless killer to a prideful child; of her feelings of pleasure in being in the Ruud; of her homesickness for her mother even while she didn't want to return to Ruhm. But more and more, the gnawing realization in her mind that her father did indeed know the location of the kell stone wore her down.

After a quick brushing out and retying of her hair, she left her room and plodded down the stairs into the lobby. There was a foyer to the left of the front door and a large window let in light upon a set of chairs and a table. Leah went there, intending to sit in the sun in hopes the warmth would chase away the ache in her forehead, but instead, she found, on a dais, a stand holding a large, open book, covered in a thick layer of dust.

Using the bottom hem of her over tunic, she wiped the dust

away. Closing the book, she read the title: *The History of the Ruud.* After looking back to see if anyone were watching, Leah lifted the tome and brought it to a chair by the window. She opened it on her lap and began reading.

In the year 1043, the great wissende Michelruud traveled to the eastern continents with his family, many wissendes, and others of Ruhm looking for adventure, where they settled into the three realms of the Ruud.

Leah skimmed the pages looking for any mention of their reasons for fleeing Ruhm, or of stealing the kell stone, or sending it back with Dakenruud, but none of that was mentioned. In this history, Ruhm was gracious enough to help rid the Ruud of its beast problem and all now lived in peace.

Pages and pages of genealogy followed and after that, stories of the various kings and queens of the Ruud and their children. Leah closed the book and a poof of dust billowed into her face. She sneezed, got up, and replaced the heavy tome onto its lonely dais; she now understood why no one ever looked at—she'd never seen such a boring history book.

Heavy footsteps thudded down the stairs and Leah saw Prenalin turn into the lobby. She followed and watched as he crossed through the dining area and entered the pub at the back of the kitchen. As she entered behind him, she heard Dowling in the dining room.

"That's no place for a young miss your age," she said.

Leah turned to her, curtseyed, but chose to ignore her warning. Prenalin had taken a seat with his back to her at a table by a window. An ink bottle sat in front of him and he dipped a quill into it and scribbled something. Several folk sat on stools at a long bar and they turned to watch her as she walked through the pub.

"I'm sorry to disturb you," she said as she approached.

Prenalin hurried to pull a blotting sheet into his journal and closed the book, setting down his quill. He smiled up at her.

"Forgive me," she said. "I didn't realize you were journaling."

"It's all right."

"I thought you were working sums for Kirche's inspections."

"No, no. Truly. Sit down. Join me."

She sat opposite him and the barman approached with a bottle and a small glass. He poured an amber liquid for Prenalin and asked, "Would the miss like something from the bar?"

"Tea for the young lady," Prenalin said.

Leah watched as Prenalin put the small glass to his lips and tipped it up, emptying its contents in one sip.

"Don't look surprised." He smiled. "Spirits are quite allowed in moderation—for the inner circle."

"Of course." She hated to behave like a child in front of him. She certainly knew that folk in Ruhm often took spirits. But it was highly regulated and public intoxication severely punished. Few folk bothered with it, so far as she knew. And she'd never actually seen anyone drink them before.

The barman brought tea in a dainty cup and once again, Leah was astonished. Tea in Ruhm was a treasure; the Ruud was seeming more and more like home all the time.

"I wanted to ask you about our meeting with King Welk," she said. "I'm confused about so many things."

"Of course you are. This trip was planned long before you were chosen for your present position. Once we return to Ruhm your duties and schedule will become more...defined. Now you must feel tossed about and unsure of what to make of much."

She smiled. "I feel very much like that at present, yes. But tell me. What was Kirche saying to King Welk about Rett? He made it sound as if Rett was killed on purpose—to be made into a devotion for the folk."

"Did he?" Prenalin shifted in his chair. "I don't think he meant to say that. Only that it worked out that way. The folk did call for his death, when they thought Rett had betrayed them. They only found out later the truth of what he'd done to save them from the manipulative power of the beasts. It's in the *Book of Rett*. You've read it, surely."

"Yes, of course. But what of the southern lands?"

He accepted another glass of amber from the barman and held it, but did not drink. "What do you mean?"

"Kirche said Rett was killed in the southern lands. But it says, in the *Book of Rett* that he was taken to the outer boundary of Ruhm, to Galdred."

He drank, but this time only took a small sip and set the glass back to the table.

"Are you certain you recall the conversation accurately? I can't imagine Kirche would make such a mistake. But then, the tales we've told the folk of the Ruud are vast and varied. It's possible he was simply keeping up a pretense."

"Do we have reason to keep the truth of Rett from the folk of the Ruud?"

At this, Prenalin sat up and leaned against the back of his booth, turning his gaze to the window. "These questions are unbecoming, Leah."

She sipped her tea. "My apologies. But..."

Prenalin chuckled. "Yes, all right. Just one more."

Smiling, she said, "What of the document about the wissende Ferdwick Elson taking the stone from Ruhm and bringing it to the east?"

"What of it?"

Leah shook her head. "Kirche himself told me that Michelruud, who led his folk here, gave the stone to an emissary who brought it home, and was instructed to hide it. No one is sure where. While Kirche believes the stone to be here in the east, we can't be certain. Can we?"

"Well, a little white lie to force the hand of the King of Michelruud does no harm, does it?"

"But why not name the emissary? Why make up the name of Ferdwick Elson?"

Prenalin eyed her, his head atilt. "Why do you say the name is a lie?"

Leah realized then that she'd made a mistake. How could she know that Elson was not the emissary? Kirche had certainly not told her it was Dakenruud who took the stone from his brother Michelruud and hid it somewhere.

"Perhaps..." Her mind raced wildly for some excuse. "I merely expected it was a lie because the document was."

"Of course," he said. But Leah was sure she hadn't fooled him.

It occurred to her that she ought to tell Prenalin that she knew that the emissary was Dakenruud. What harm could it do? But then, he might ask her where she learned the name. And she'd certainly not learned it from school. There were books in the school library, of course, that told small bits about the legend of the stone and the power it gave the beasts whenever they were near it. But she only learned of their quest for the kell stone from Prenalin when she accepted her position as Aide to the High Priest of Hass.

"We're off on our annual trip to the Ruud," he'd said so many weeks ago it felt like years. "We will visit, make notes, observe, and of course, look for the elusive kell stone."

She'd only made a questioning face and he'd continued. "Ah, yes. You'll learn all about that soon enough. Suffice it to say, we've been looking for it for years and haven't come close. But it's there. It must be there."

And that was the extent of her knowledge until her father told her about it being stolen from the beasts and hidden for centuries. Michelruud, brother of her ancestor, Dakenruud, had stolen it back and intended to hand it over to the beasts on the eastern continent. Instead, he'd given it to Daken in exchange for Ruhm's help in ridding the eastern lands of the beasts.

But she couldn't tell Prenalin what she knew. He might suspect that her father knows more than he should. She must find out for herself, first. Only if she could find the location of the kell stone could she explain to them her connection to it. Once Kirche held the stone in his hands, her short term of deception would surely be forgiven.

Chapter Fifteen

Lucas sat on the ground with the riders of the king's guard on the Michelruud side of South Bridge. He leaned against a tree, munching an apple. Across the river lay Aaronland. The guards were suspicious of the delay. Sorgood had run them all over Michelruud and into the port at Cold Sea and now had them pausing when they should be moving into Arnot's kingdom in search of the bairn. Every minute they waited meant further distance between them and the boy.

"Something ain't right, I tell ya," Brinkley whispered for the third time.

"It don't matter," Phil replied again.

"Don't you think something's not right?" Brinkley turned to Lucas and Lucas nodded.

"Look, we stopped 'cause we got to eat, don't we?" Phil said.

"You don't stop to eat when there's an evil bairn running loose in the Ruud."

"Yeah, well, you don't keep changing your mind about where to go, either."

"Sure you do. You got to go where you think the enemy is, don't you? But you don't stop and have a picnic by the river."

Phil shrugged. "You think too much. Just follow orders."

Lucas pondered the situation. The guard had left Michelruud Castle after Sorgood met with King Welk and made straight for South Bridge. That in itself was not surprising, as the news was that their new destination was Aaronland Castle for King Arnot's troops. But they'd stopped at the bridge and settled down for lunch. And while Phil was correct in that they had to eat—they were riders of the king's guard and could very well have eaten apples and hard tack while trotting across Aaronland.

"You really planning to turn the kid in?" Brinkley asked Lucas.

"You've asked me that twice already."

Phil and Brinkley looked at him keenly.

"Why wouldn't I turn him in? Wouldn't you?"

"Well, sure. He's the evil bairn and all. But you *knew* him."

"He came to the Path wissenry before you left for the guard. Don't you know him, too?"

They shook their heads and their eyes widened. "Oh, no. We don't know him. Never heard of him."

Lucas smiled. "Chickens. Squawking chickens."

"Not chickens. We're riders in the guard," Phil said. "What are you? A wissende?"

"You implying the wissendes are weak, Phil?" Brinkley said. "They ain't soldiers."

"It's true, Brink," Lucas said. "There's no offense. Wissendes are thinking folk, not great warriors such as yourselves." He couldn't help giving them a wink.

Brinkley nodded. "So, you really planning on turning him over?"

"Wouldn't you?"

"Course we would," Phil said. "He's dangerous. Even if he don't seem so. I mean, look what he done already with the prison kids."

Brinkley chuckled. "That weren't nothing. We could have done that ourselves."

"But we wouldn't have, would we? It's against the law. Against the king."

Lucas watched Sorgood about twenty yards north; he tossed a knapsack over one shoulder, patted his horse on the back and trudged through the makeshift camp, disappearing into the woods.

"Well, then," he told his friends, not remembering the gist of their conversation. "There you have it."

He stood, stretched a moment to look unconcerned, and excused himself to make a trip into the forest.

Phil muttered behind him. "I don't think he ever did answer your question, Brink."

"Don't be running off now," Brinkley called after him.

Lucas turned back and smiled. "You know I wouldn't get you into trouble."

Brinkley laughed. "You're legend for trouble."

"I'll be back soon, don't worry." And neither Brinkley nor Phil followed.

Lucas made his way silently through the shady wood, winding around wide trees and over roots, sliding furtively through dense shrubs, until he heard horses and Sorgood's voice.

"Yes, Lord Kirche," the master of the guard said. "I am certain we can find him."

Hiding behind a thick pine, Lucas knelt to the ground, and slowly peered around it. There in the wood stood Sorgood, short and bent, looking up as if subordinate to a tall, blond folk—Lord Kirche, the High Priest of Hass. Lucas remembered passing him as he left King Welk's table earlier in the day. With the priest was another folk, darker of hair and eyes, and a girl with a long braid down her back.

"Carry on, then," the priest of Hass said. "You must find the boy and appeal to the folk for his death; but be careful that you do not request it directly. The folk will demand it, if the options are presented to them in the right manner."

"I understand," Sorgood wheezed and though he couldn't see it, Lucas could almost hear the man's slick smile at his lips.

"Welk is not quite as you said," the priest continued. "He is defiant, not at all timid. But he allows circumstances to take him where they lead. He is not a true ruler. He does not shape the world to suit himself, as a king ought to do."

"Aye."

"You should have little trouble using him."

As he was about to turn away, the young girl caught sight of Lucas' face in the woods; her eyes flew open but she stood mute. Standing, expecting her to alert them to his presence at once, Lucas stepped back and made his way quickly and silently back to the guard to pack up his sack to leave. Sorgood approached from the woods several minutes later and gave no hint that the girl had said anything about Lucas' spying.

"We move into Aaronland this evening to camp," the master announced. "Tomorrow we will enter Town Village to enlist the Aaronland guard in setting up a perimeter on the north border. Change out of your uniforms. We will dismount at the outskirts and walk through the village separately, without arousing interest. I will take Welk's orders to the first castle gate on the east side. If you see anything of the boy, contact me immediately."

The soldiers dug out their civvies and began to change as Sorgood approached Lucas, his dark face set hard in a frown. Lucas swallowed heavily, ready with his excuse for listening in on the vile man's private conversation in the woods.

"You'll stick with your guard," Sorgood told him. "And if you see the boy, you will alert them."

"Of course, sir. I serve the king." He bowed with a smirk.

"You ain't gonna turn him in," Brinkley said after Sorgood returned to his horse.

Lucas smiled and waited for them to get dressed.

Chapter Sixteen

They'd spent the day before hiking through the divide wood, with Rogget setting off on brief hunts to increase his load of rabbit and squirrel to share with Forbes for his long trek back home, and to trade for goods in Town Village. "You've never been good with the bow, Forbes," Rogget chided him. "Admit it."

"It's true; I'm a farmer through and through."

They camped at the edge of the wood overlooking the plains of Aaron and woke to cross in the morning light. Dew wet their shoes and the ankles of their trousers as a soft breeze worked to dry the grasses. As they neared the village, Aaronland castle stood tall and imposing in the distance. At the southern outskirts of Town Village, Rogget sent Darnit off to the north.

"How will he find us again?" Sadie asked, watching him lumber off.

"Oh, he'll sniff me out one way or t'other."

They made their way into the village and familiar sounds of the waking town hit their ears. They waved hellos several times to folk off to market with their push carts, or tending to their cottage chores, feeding chickens and ducks, or beating rugs, hung from low tree limbs, with brooms. Rogget told them to act natural, but Fenn felt nothing like it as he pressed a worried smile to his lips. Once they arrived in the bustling town square in front of the castle, they bid their goodbyes to Forbes.

"Everything will work out all right," Fenn told him.

Rogget glared at him.

"It will," Fenn said. "I promise."

Once Forbes disappeared into the crowd, Rogget said, "You ain't got no right to promise such a thing."

"I don't have to mean about the writ."

"But you know that's what he thought you meant."

Fenn shrugged. "Maybe."

In his heart, he did believe it would all work out. There had to be a way to persuade the king to honor his promise to Forbes.

A short distance away, on a small wood stage by the well, a young man called out, "Hear ye! Hear ye! Proclamation from His Highness, King Welk of Michelruud."

Fenn stared at him in a panic and along with Grayson and Sadie inched closer to Rogget, but he continued walking, pushing them away.

"You don't see anyone else gawking, do you?" he said gruffly. "Keep walking, like it's none of your business."

And it was true; the villagers went on with their morning tasks, paying little heed to the town crier. As they passed through the center of town they heard him shout, "Three children, alone. The evil bairn, Fenn Foster of the wissenry at Path with a distinctive mark on his right shoulder."

Rogget put his arm around Fenn. "See there," he said. "They're looking for three runaway children. But you're with me, aren't you? You just tell anyone who asks that you're my kids."

Fenn raised his eyebrows at Grayson. They didn't look at all like siblings; nothing matched, neither hair, nor eyes, nor noses. And none of them looked like a child of Rogget's.

"Adopted," Rogget added.

The huntsman handed money to each of them, instructing them which shops to visit. Sadie was to get fresh and dried fruits from the market. Grayson was sent for flint sticks and candles. And Rogget would trade his rabbits for more wool blankets. Fenn was sent off to the butcher's with five coins for jerky.

"You wait for us out back of the butcher's," Rogget told him. "We'll meet up there and take the wood paths to Waverly wissenry before we try to cross the boundary."

Fenn walked through town keeping his gaze on the ground, but he felt that someone was following him. He wanted to look around, to see if there was a guard watching him, but feared that would give him away. When he reached the butcher shop north of town, he suddenly felt free, as if whoever was watching him had given up and left. He shook his head at his own silliness and entered the shop. At the counter, the butcher was chopping meat for the cure when he looked up and smiled at Fenn.

"I'd like five packets of jerky please." Fenn laid his coins on the counter.

"Well, son," the butcher said. "You either like your jerky quite a bit or you're heading out on a long journey."

Fenn flinched, but the butcher went about the business of wrapping the jerky without another comment. From the corner of his eye, Fenn saw someone approaching and turned. An old man hobbled close, looking at him with a peculiar, pinched face. He came to a stop in front of Fenn and put a long, bony finger out almost touching his nose.

"I know you," the old man said.

"I don't think so."

The butcher behind the counter handed him his packets and said, "Are you not from Town Village?"

Fenn shook his head and stuffed the jerky into his sack. "I live out in the divide wood with my da." The butcher peered at him suspiciously. Fenn moved backward to leave but the old man grabbed his arm.

"I have something of yours," he said.

"No, you're thinking of someone else."

"Ah, leave him be, pa," the butcher said. Chuckling, he went back to his meat chopping.

"It belonged to your mother," the wrinkled man said.

"How do you know my mother?"

The old man tilted his gray-haired head at Fenn. "Come this way," he said and walked to the rear of the shop around the corner of the counter.

The butcher watched, still smiling, as Fenn followed the old man to the back of the store and into the butcher room. Fenn shuddered at the sight of beheaded, skinned, sheep carcasses hanging from large silver hooks along one wall. The crooked, limping old man kept on, waving him through the room and out the back door.

"Where are we going?"

A grizzled smile lit up the man's face; he pointed to a small hut just beyond the yard and hobbled toward it. Struggling to lift his feet up the few stone steps to the door, he pulled it open and disappeared inside. Fenn stood at the bottom step for a second or two, shrugged, and followed him. It took several moments for his eyes to adjust to the dim light of the one-room house. It was crowded with a desk and a bed and along every wall was a collection of oddities. Ticking, moving timepieces; chain mail; wheels of varying sizes connected by rods; metronomes, clicking off time; a firearm that looked like new. And in the corner, hanging from a nail was the most amazing thing of all: a wissenry robe.

The old man was rummaging in papers strewn all over his small wooden desk. He stopped, stood straight, turned and looked at Fenn. "What did I come in here for?"

"You had something for me. Something of my mother's. But I don't think you knew my mother."

"Oh, yes, yes. It was long ago."

Fenn didn't believe him, of course. He was an ancient folk, the oldest man Fenn had ever seen, and obviously, not completely in charge of his mind.

"Where did you get the wissenry robe?"

"Eh? Oh, oh, that. Yes, that's it, you see. I was a wissende many years ago. It was then I met your mother."

"I didn't know you could stop being a wissende...once you were one."

The old man tilted his head at him again and said, "Eh? No? None ever told me I wasn't one anymore...so maybe I still am."

"Then why don't you live at a wissenry?"

"I was banished, you know?"

Fenn shook his head. "No, I didn't know."

"Oh, yes. Banished." And as he talked, he continued to file through the papers on his desk that were covered from top to bottom in very small, but neat and squarish, writing. "I joined the wissenry after my dear wife Iselda died. I had the three boys, of course, and I know it was all selfishness to leave them to my brother. But I had to get far from the memories. And the wissenry took me. Ah, I was so very distraught. I didn't act quite right, for the wissenry, that is. And I was banished."

For a folk who must have been one-hundred years old, as old as the trees, he could say a lot in one breath.

"Well, then," Fenn said. "You aren't a wissende, anymore."

"Oh, no son. A banished wissende is still a wissende. I was sent to the hill country to tend to the rejected. And to the wasteland, to care for the poor castaways."

The hair on the back of Fenn's neck prickled. "You were in the wasteland?"

"Yes, yes. And then I left and came home. So, I'm not really banished anymore, except I don't know if the wissenry knows that. I suppose I'm something of a rogue wissende." He let out an airy laugh. "If you will." He put the papers down suddenly and said, "That's it. That's what I have for you. I couldn't remember.

Merry me, but my mind isn't what it used to be."

The huddled figure stood in front of Fenn but gave him nothing.

"Well, what is it?"

"Ah, yes." He held up a finger. "Information."

"Information?"

"Yes. I have a name for you. Clara. In the wasteland, in one of the middle villages, on the outskirts, in a small cottage by a creek."

"Which village?" Fenn asked, curious, but still believing the man must be addlebrained and wrong.

The old man waved his hand. "I don't rightly recollect the name. And I have to tell you...I'm not sure...but I think...maybe ...I have given this information to others." He put his finger to his lips and stood there thinking, his eyes closed up and his wrinkled face squinched and focused.

"Is Clara my mother?"

"Oh, no, no," he whispered. "That name cannot be said here."

"Do you know her name?"

The old man waved both his hands in front of him.

"How do you know who I am?"

"You look like your parents."

"Who are my parents?"

The elderly folk looked at him sadly and shook his head. "I can't recall..." And he went back to the papers on his desk.

Fenn insides fell with disappointment. He should have known. The man was crazy, poor fool.

"They took my great grandsons," the old man said without turning back to Fenn. "Here, at the butcher shop, weeks ago. They took them because they thought one of them might be you. They thought maybe I took you and raised you. But I didn't. I gave you to the wissenry."

Fenn sucked in a small breath and stood still, a tingling

spreading over his body.

"They told me you let them go. You freed them from Steingefan. I know who you are."

Fenn could see that parts of him were lucid and parts were lost. He knew, somehow, that if he reached out and touched him, he could sort through and find the lost things. He could know what this old wissende knew but couldn't remember. He stepped toward him and held out his hand, reaching for his shoulder.

With a bang, the door behind him flew open, hitting the wall. Arms grabbed Fenn from behind and dragged him out of the tiny cottage. He saw the old man's face lit with horror before the door swung back again and Fenn was dragged down the stone steps into the butchery yard.

Chapter Seventeen

L eah was surprised when Prenalin told her she had the entire day free.

"Walk about Path," he suggested. "Visit the local shops or the orchards. We are allowed to take apples—as many as we wish."

She thanked him and left the inn, knowing exactly where she would like to spend her time—but first, she had a chore to see to. Most of her travels in the Ruud were by carriage, but once, she'd been asked to ride a horse, when Arnot insisted on taking their party along a trail to view the blooming fall flowers in a field west of Aaronland Castle. And Leah had watched, envious, the queen and her ladies straddle their mares easily, wearing pants. She'd not had much practice riding horses in Ruhm, going everywhere on foot or by carriage, and she struggled to keep herself properly covered sidesaddle while never finding a comfortable position in her dress and over tunic.

The tailor's shop was west of town nestled in a woodsy spot, shaded and cozy. Tailor Small welcomed her, though he was clearly nervous to serve her, and let his daughter measure Leah for riding pants. They would be delivered to the inn by day's end.

When she found herself once more in the small village square, she was exhilarated, and frightened, not knowing if she would be able to bring herself to wear pants in front of Prenalin and Kirche.

Two buildings south of the inn was the stationer's office, where Leah was certain to find comfort. The streets of Path were not crowded, but there were folk here and there who nodded and cast their gazes to the ground at her feet as she passed. Several folk gathered on the porch in front of the general store and eyed her suspiciously; she smiled and waved, but they did not respond.

In Path, the stationer lived on the second floor, just as her family did over her father's shop in Ruhm. The Path building had a wide porch with steps all around and on each side of the house were trellises in which it appeared Madam Stationer had attempted climbing roses with little success.

Leah walked up the steps to the front door and pushed it open. The air inside was stifling of books, papers, and ink and all sound was muted, soaked up by the tomes lining the walls.

Leah breathed in the memories of home.

"Hello?" she said, but no one answered.

A ticking clock paced the seconds somewhere nearby, but all else was silent. She walked through the first two rooms, letting her hand slide along shelves and spines and stacks of books.

"Hello," she said again.

There was a door, ajar, at the far end of the second room. She knocked on it lightly and it glided open. Stepping into a tiny office, tears filled her eyes as she thought of her father. How she missed him.

She sat at the desk and looked about at the disarray. Piles of paper sat precariously on the edges among books, inkwells, and a bin of pencils. The room was so much like her father's she smiled, but a tear trickled down her check. Leaning over, she put her elbows on the desk and wiped at her face, knocking several pencils to the floor.

She sat up and pushed herself back, bending down, searching for them. One had rolled far under, toward the wall, so she got onto her knees on the floor and reached for it. She had to laugh as she found more books and papers beneath the desk. Was it a rule that stationers must be untidy?

Grabbing at the writer, she noticed the title on the spine of a large tome. She pulled it from under the desk and sat on the floor with it. *The Book of Katze*. It was leather bound and looked very much like the *History of the Ruud* she'd seen at the inn. But it was much thicker and heavier.

On the first, yellowed, parchment page, in large calligraphy was the introduction: A Telling of the Kell Stone by The Modest Katze, Humble Servant to Our Sire, King of Michelruud. Leah turned the page and began to read.

Within these pages is the proper and unadulterated history of our Ruud, which begins, as all history must, with the beast. It is true that I, Modest Katze, have led a life of debauchery, drunkenness, and revelry. For that I was banished from the wissenry. But I was not the first and will not be the last. One must admit that at least a modest sum of eccentricity is necessary for a full life. I did my best. Perhaps I overly indulged. It will be for the future to decide. But despite this illustrious reputation, I adamantly swear that I have set down the story of the beast of the northern lands as the tale was given me by the beasts themselves. And the history of the Ruud is just as it was written by the sage wissendes of the days of old.

As all stories of the beast must begin with the kell stone, that is where I shall start...

Leah read until the light in the tiny office had shifted and a door opened and closed. She looked up and around the room, remembering where she was, the heavy book now open deep into the first half on her lap. Before she could gather her wits about her, the door hit the wall and a young man wearing round glasses, with a blond mustache at his upper lip, stood staring down at her, shock in his eyes.

"Who are you? What are you doing?"

"My apologies." She struggled to get to her feet with the heavy book in her hands. "My sincerest...I'm so sorry."

"What are you doing with that book? Why are you in here?"

Leah managed to get to standing and put the book, still open, on the desk. She curtseyed. "I'm dreadfully sorry. I wandered in, only looking for a feeling of home." A giggle escaped her and she slapped her hand to her mouth.

The young man glared at her and she feared he would shout some more, but instead, he stood aside and motioned for her to leave the office as if she were an unruly child. She stepped quickly past him into the next room. He closed the door with something of a slam and locked it with a key.

As Leah followed him into the front room, he said, "I'll be sacked for sure if anyone finds out I left that door open. No one's allowed in the stationer's private office. No one. Not you and not me. I'm in big trouble."

"I won't tell anyone. Honest, I won't."

He calmed down a bit, but wrung his hands on his apron. "I should have been here to greet you. It's my fault, really. What did you say your name was?"

"I'm Leah of Ruhm."

"Ruhm? You're not with the Hass?"

"Yes. I'm the aide to Lord Kirche, High Priest. I'm on the annual tour."

The young man's eyes widened and he stammered. "I see. My apologies. I could hardly have refused, had you come in and asked to search the premises. I didn't know, that's all."

"It's quite all right. My fault completely."

Leah curtseyed several times finding her way backwards to the front door. Giggling, she hurried outside, down the steps and back toward the inn.

Chapter Eighteen

Flung from the arms that dragged him from the hut behind the butcher's, Fenn turned to find a young guard standing before him with his firearm raised to Fenn's chest. Beside him stood Sorgood, the king's master of the guard, hunched and grinning like a rat with a slice of cheese. Fenn had seen Sorgood before, riding through Path, and then in the village square on the morning they'd rounded the children up to take them to Steingefan. He was much uglier up close, with black, greasy hair hanging to his shoulders. And beside Sorgood—

"Lucas?" Fenn said without thinking.

"This is him, then?" Sorgood sneered.

The young guard said, "It's him. It's him."

And Lucas nodded. "Yes."

Motioning to Lucas, the master of the guard said, "Tie him."

As Lucas moved forward, the door to the hut behind Fenn burst open and a shot rang out. Before he knew what had happened, Fenn saw the young guard's aim move from his chest to a point behind him and Fenn raised his arms as if to push the guard away and—whoosh! The guard, Sorgood, and Lucas all fell backward to the ground.

Fenn turned to see the old man standing behind him with a

smoking firearm in his hands.

"Run," the old wissende said.

Fenn did as he was told and ran past the three on the ground, now stirring to get up, and toward the butcher shop where he saw Rogget, Grayson, and Sadie, their faces alert with fear.

"What was it? We heard a shot."

Rogget called out, "To the woods, quickly."

They darted into the forest behind the butcher's shop and ran north. Breathless, they stopped after a mile and began to walk.

"What happened?" Rogget asked.

"One of them must have spotted me in the village and gone for the other two when they saw me go into the butcher's." Fenn remembered the feeling he'd had of being watched. He would never again doubt his own senses.

"But what happened?" Grayson said. "They were on the ground. Did you shoot them?"

Fenn shook his head. "The old man did. He took me into his hut and told me about my mother. And then he shot at the guard."

"Mighty good shot to knock 'em all to the ground." Rogget said.

Fenn only nodded. What *had* happened? They fell to the ground after the shot—after he tried to push them away. But he was four or five feet from them. And even if he had physically tried to push them down, he wouldn't have been able to do it. He was a scrawny kid and there were three of them.

And Lucas. With the guard; helping them find him and identify him. Were those the skills Father Treacher had in mind when he told him not to worry about Lucas? Treachery? Betrayal?

"Well, I'd say we need to try to run again," Rogget said. "The guard will be alerted soon enough. We'll need to bypass the wissenry and head straight for the border."

"No," Fenn said. "We need more food. We'll just have to be

106

quick about it."

"But it's a two-hour walk. They'll be alerted."

"They'll be expecting us to go straight for the border. They'd never suspect we'd turn west for Waverly."

Chapter Nineteen

Waverly wissenry was a large, square, two-story building, with a kitchen in the back, like all wissenry buildings. It was set on a large parcel of cleared land in the middle of the forest with easy paths leading out to the villages. Mother Carroll stared at them aghast for too long as they stood at the back door in the late afternoon sunlight.

"What's this?"

"As you see—" Rogget began.

"But why haven't you left? You should have been into the hill country."

At least they didn't have to explain themselves—they simply shrugged and offered her downcast, guilt-ridden faces and she hurried them into the kitchen and filled their knapsacks with biscuits and pieces of roasted fowl, and fresh fruits and vegetables to go along with those Sadie had purchased.

The kitchen was much like the kitchens of all the wissenry buildings—always a pot of stew over the fire. A desk or two in the corners. Oil lanterns hung over the center table. No one else was there and Mother Carroll wasn't at all concerned about keeping her voice down.

"Britt warned me you weren't the sort to go off and do as

you're told. Fenn Foster, as I live and breathe, you'll never make wissende proper this way. A wissende is, above all, dutiful. Don't make that face—it's true. How can you come to be trusted if you don't first practice trust."

Fenn had no answer for that. He should tell her, he reasoned, that trust was meant for weeks ago, before he learned about secrets. He should tell her that Father Treacher and Father Britt couldn't be trusted—how was he to learn to trust from them?

"These are troubling times, Mother," Rogget said. "The boy hasn't even begun his training."

"Aye and it doesn't look like he will."

At that, Sadie grimaced and Grayson looked grief stricken.

"Oh, none of that children. Think of it as a grand adventure. You're off to explore—something few children of Path ever even dream of doing. Well, all right, they dream. But dream is all. You are living it."

"Thank you, Mother," Grayson said taking his now heavy sack and slipping it onto his back.

Mother sighed and put her hands to her hips. "You will take care, now, won't you?" she asked Rogget.

"Aye, Mother. I will let no harm come to my charges."

"And Fenn, when you—if you return to us. You will be oh so much wiser than you are today."

They were hurried out the back door and shooed from the porch. "Go on," Mother said. "And do as you're told, for once."

They jogged across the yard and disappeared into the north woods.

"Well, we can't be seen now," Sadie said. "We'd be caught for sure."

"Why do you say that?" Grayson said.

"Because my pack is so heavy, I'd never outrun a guard."

"Drop the pack then, silly."

"And give up all these supplies?"

"You won't need the supplies if you're caught."

Sadie rolled her eyes and shook her head. "Sometimes, Grayson, you don't make a lick of sense."

"*I* don't make sense?"

"Hush now," Rogget scolded. "Sadie's right. We want to keep our supplies, so we'll be quiet and move as quickly as we can."

Grayson turned an annoyed face to Fenn who could only smile.

They'd hiked east through the north wood for over an hour when Grayson said, "We must have crossed the border by now."

"The border is the end of the wood," Rogget said. "We step out of the wood and into the hills; that's your border."

They trudged on, silent, for another two hours. Fenn was once again troubled by the quiet. Sadie was angry and sad. But certainly she missed her parents and worried about them. Grayson too, though he just seemed sad. He wondered at himself and how he could go on betraying them by withholding secrets, even knowing that it hurt their friendship. But he couldn't seem to tell them the truth. And he still needed to have a private talk with Grayson about the history and the Hass of Emorah; but they never had a moment alone. Every time he tried to bring it up, Grayson insisted he didn't want Sadie to hear them discuss it.

The forest ended abruptly. They stood in a row looking out over a wide, grassy, shallow valley dotted here and there with shrubs and the occasional patch of trees.

"This isn't what I expected at all." Fenn stared at the darkening landscape.

A rising and falling horizon of hills beyond the valley beckoned them, lifted higher and higher until there was only a skyline of worn peaks.

"Me either," Grayson said. "I was thinking it would look like a lot of really big, green, haystacks...of a sort. If you know what I mean. And we'd be hiking up and down...or better, making a path around and through the valleys."

"Me too," Fenn said. "But it's just..."

"Slopey?" Sadie said.

"Aye, it slopes. Beyond are the hills. You can't see 'em now, but when we get closer, you'll find the sort you describe. Gnomes made 'em—all sizes. And look there." He pointed northeast where the setting sun lit up rocky mountain peaks in the far distance. "Beyond those mountains is the ice realm."

"How long will it take to get there?" Grayson asked.

"Oh, I'm thinking a few weeks walking."

"Weeks?"

"Probably more. It ain't so much the distance," Rogget said. "It's only maybe fifty miles through the hills. That'll take a few days for us. But then you've got maybe another hundred through the mountains. Much slower going, I'd think."

"Sadie has a rough map of the hill country," Grayson said. "And I'll see what she's got on the ice realm. We can make a good estimate in the morning."

"How will we find enough food?" Sadie said.

"How will we keep from getting caught?" Fenn asked.

Rogget began trekking down the slope into the valley and they stood watching him until he turned back to wait for them.

"What's your hurry?" He laughed at himself.

Fenn looked to Sadie and Grayson as they stared out into the darkening country in front of them.

"One more step," Grayson said, "and we're out of the Ruud."

"You hadn't been out of Path before a couple of weeks ago," Fenn said. "It's no different now."

Grayson looked at him, his eyes open wide. "No difference? The Ruud is home, just as Path is home."

"He's right," Sadie said. "This is the first real step toward adventure."

"Adventure," Grayson murmured. "I could do with a lot less of it."

"But look." Fenn walked out in front of them. "It's no different. See, I'm in the hill country. And now," he walked back. "I'm back in the Ruud. There's no real difference. There's no line. The Ruud is part of the eastern continent. And that is part of Kell. It's all the same. The border is all in your heads."

"And our hearts." Sadie smiled and moved past Fenn to where Rogget stood waiting for them.

"Sometimes Sadie can be very smart," Grayson said.

"Only sometimes, waiter boy?"

"She's a lot smarter than you give her credit for," Fenn told him.

"Waiter boy thinks anyone who doesn't read two books every week is downright dumb."

"I never said that."

Rogget rocked back onto his heels and fell forward a few times. "Any time you three are ready to move along..."

"You're awfully eager to leave home," Sadie said to Fenn.

"I wouldn't say I was eager. But the sooner we figure out how to get out of this mess, the sooner we can get back home and back to normal."

"You still think we can fix this?" Grayson said. "We're on the run, abandoned to the hills. We're refugees now. Nothing more."

"The guard isn't coming after us out here, are they?" Sadie said.

"Exactly," Fenn said. "We're banishing ourselves. We don't have to run anymore."

"And how is that better?"

"Living out here is better than running and hiding all the time. And without being chased, we can figure out a plan to get back home."

"Now, I wouldn't assume that," Rogget said. "It's true the guard is spread mighty thin. Most were headed toward the port at first because the prison children said you were headed south;

then they turned and started fortifying the borders—until Welk got a message from the wissenry saying you were banished."

"I've been banished?"

"You just said you were," Sadie said.

"It's not the same if you do it yourself."

Rogget chuckled. "Not to worry. Your banishment is a ruse. And a clever one at that, I'd say. They've got the guard turned around so's they don't know what they're doing. First it's to the port, then to the perimeters. Then to the port again. And now they've caught you in Town Village at Aaronland. I don't know how they can rally quickly. And they don't know if you've left east of the castle, or north at Waverly."

"If the wissenry says they've banished him, they'd never expect us to have gone by Waverly to see Mother Carroll," Grayson said. "They don't know where we are at all."

"So, you agree with me. We're out of trouble," Fenn said.

"For now, we can get ourselves well into the hills. And Welk has little choice at this point but to accept you've escaped and spend time bulking up his perimeter to make sure you don't come back."

"That's a relief," Sadie said. "I guess."

"But that doesn't mean there won't be guard sent out into the hills after us. And that's going to be a problem."

"Why, exactly? Is it easier to find folk in the hill country?"

"In a manner of speaking. There's loads of gangs out here. Gangs like we ran into in the divide wood. They'd be only too happy to turn us over for a reward. We got to keep ourselves private and be careful who we trust. Don't start thinking we're out of danger."

Fenn turned to Grayson and nodded toward the hills. Grayson took in a long breath and let it out slowly before adjusting his knapsack on his back and trudging across the border and into adventure. Fenn smiled, following. They could fix this, he thought. They could fix everything. Just as they'd saved the children of Path from Steingefan, they could make folk understand that there was no prophecy and Fenn was not an evil bairn. And if he could find out who his parents were and have King Welk honor Forbes Billings' writ at the same time, more the better.

They walked on through the valley, up slopes, and down again, sometimes along brown dirt trails, other times in ankle deep grasses, until they'd climbed high above the timberline behind them, and down once more into a deep vale. The farther into the hill country they trekked, the more Fenn thought about Father Treacher and his wild grey hair and never seeing him again, never hearing him squeak with anger at Lucas again. Lucas. Fenn's heart sank. All that worrying he'd done about him being eaten by felidae only to find him a rat. Skills. Some skills— traitoring, and lying, and stabbing folk in the back. Now he didn't mind if he never got to go home again...so much.

"Well, I'm glad we're relatively safe," Fenn began, after they'd hiked in silence for some time. "Because I'm planning to head to the wasteland."

"You're what?" Rogget said, as they stopped to gape at him.

Fenn turned back to them. "I saw Sadie's map. Just into the hills there's a stone bridge crossing the river into the wasteland. And beyond it are several villages. I'm going to look for information about my parents."

Grayson's face gathered together into a glare and he opened his mouth to speak, but Rogget stepped forward.

"Do you ever plan to do what you're told?" Rogget asked.

"I can't answer that, really." Fenn smiled. "I might one day, though."

They stared at him in silence for some time, silhouetted against the deep red of the sinking sun behind them.

"You all can go to the ice realm without me, if you want," he said.

"But we made a pact; we stick together," Grayson said.

"What would be the point, anyway?" Sadie said.

"She's right. I think we're stuck going where you go, pact or not."

"So the pact stands," Rogget said.

"Of course it still stands. Pacts are forever," Sadie said.

They walked on, turning slightly north and set up camp against a slope out of the wind and slept on the soft grasses. Fenn bolted awake in the early morning light—he'd had no dreams, no visions. He reached for his hemp rope and charm, but there was no unusual heat on his neck. He was sickened at the thought of his charm against the skin of Clutch, the thief.

Chapter Twenty

The next morning, Leah was to travel with Kirche, Prenalin, and the bodyguards to visit Timber. They woke early, before dawn, for the long carriage ride south. Leah put on her riding pants, tucking one of her nightshirts into the waistband under her tunic. But she couldn't bare it. She liked the feel of the pants, but the look in the mirror was eerie and unfamiliar. She would have to wear the pants under the dress. At least she could hike it up and ride astraddle that way.

Timber was a bustling village without much of a town square. All the buildings and houses were huddled together in chaotic bunches on a plain nestled up against a northern wood.

"To the south," Prenalin told her, "is the beast forest. The villagers are wary of being carried away and eaten."

Leah smiled. "Certainly not."

"It's what we are told."

Leah remembered her chats with Wanda Kay at the Snapping Turtle Inn at Cold Sea. Wanda treated the relationship between the folk and the beast more as a rambunctious rivalry than a vicious battle. Though she did say the folk feared a war with the beast.

After their duties were settled in Timber, they took to horses provided by the villagers. When Leah waved away the side-saddled mare and asked to ride astride, her cheeks burned flush and she caught sight of Kirche's smirk. Neither he nor Prenalin said a word as she hiked up her skirt a bit and straddled the horse, exposing her new pants. She smiled, but Prenalin frowned and turned away.

They rode across the plain to the edges of the beast forest. Kirche told her it was necessary to patrol the area on his visits to be sure the beast were not flouting the laws that kept the most dangerous of them deep within the forest and away from the folk. And while he assured them all of their safety, he insisted they carry their bows for protection and he and the bodyguards had scabbards for their firearms draped over their horses' backs.

"What keeps them in the forest?" Leah asked.

"They were defeated once," Kirche told her. "And they know should they harm a folk here in the Ruud, all the soldiers of Ruhm will not think twice in slaughtering the lot of them."

They rode casually along the southwestern border of the wood and Leah watched as Kirche smiled up at the enormous pines. He was enjoying his tour immensely, she knew. But his smile soon disappeared and his right hand shot up in the air. They halted and Leah peered around Alphonse and Prenalin to see what was the matter.

Rooting around the trunks of the pines along the edge of the forest was a bevy of brownies. Tiny brown creatures wearing pale tunics, they were on their knees digging and sniffing, and moving to dig some more.

Kirche turned back to the party with a finger at his lips. He pulled his firearm from its scabbard and slipped off his mount. Prenalin motioned for Leah to dismount as well and she fell to the ground with a thud. But the noise didn't deter Kirche. He prowled steadily closer and closer to the brownies and raised his firearm. Leah put her hands to her ears and closed her eyes tight just as the shot rang out.

When she opened her eyes, the horses were scurrying, Kirche and the bodyguards were running forward toward the brownies, popping off arrows, and another loud shot echoed through the air.

"Come," Prenalin said, and he took her hand to lead her forward, but she balked.

"We should not be separated." He forced her to jog to where Kirche and the others stood still attacking the brownies as they scurried away and into the trees.

Just as she reached Kipling and Alphonse, a thunderous clatter echoed from within the forest, and through the trees stomped a herd of centaurs. At their feet were enormous wolves and black cats. The ground shook and Alphonse fell in front of her, trampled by an enraged centaur.

"Run, Leah," Prenalin called above the shouts and screams. "Get to a horse."

Tripping, she fell to the ground, rolled several times to avoid a centaur's pounding, then clamored to her feet and ran blindly north. She saw no horses and seeking cover, ran into the trees to her left. Stumbling over roots and shrubs, she ran until her own terrified panting was deafening.

As the forest grew danker and darker, Leah slowed her pace and looked around her. Everywhere, she heard scampering, hooting, squawking. She was being watched and followed. She turned several times, changing direction, but she couldn't tell east from west. A terrified choking sound left her throat and she began to sob and shake. She was lost in the beast forest and, despite Wanda Kay's reassuring words, feared for her life.

When she saw shimmers of light twinkling ahead, Leah made her way toward a glen where streams of yellow sunlight sparkled with dust specks, warming the ground. She stood at the edge, alert to the sounds of creatures all around her. And then she saw it. At the opposite end of the clearing, encircled by a halo of light. Leah shuddered.

"It can't be," she whispered. "It can't be."

Unconsciously, she reached for her necklace and charm, but she wasn't wearing them. The marble amulet, much smaller than the one Kirche wore, etched with the flaming tree of Hass, was only worn for ceremony. But she knew the tree. She could trace its lines in her sleep, and recall the flames licking at its limbs. And there it stood before her in the beast forest. Its wide branches reaching out for her, alight in blazing red and fiery orange leaves glistening in the sun.

It was not possible. According the *Book of Rett*, when the folk of Ruhm learned of his betrayal, his love for the beast, they bound Rett's hands and feet and dragged him behind horses northeast to the flaming tree on the rocky, dry border between Ruhm and Galdred. They wrapped him in chains, hoisted him into the tree, and fastened him to a lower branch. Then they dug a circle pit around the base of the tree and lit it with fire.

When Rett's echoing screams ceased, the tree burned and fell quickly to ash, and the folk knew they had made a terrible mistake. And at that moment, every flaming tree on Kell fell in an instant into a pile of burnt embers. That is why there are no flaming trees left. Anywhere.

Of course it was just a story. Leah had known, deep within her, all along. But standing there in the beast forest looking at the tree, her heart fell. What she had always known was now at the fore; it could no longer be ignored. The *Book of Rett* was a lie.

She made her way, stunned, to the tree, staring up at its enormous limbs. Reaching out, she put a hand to its rough, flaked trunk. Was it called the flaming tree because of its scarlet leaves, she wondered. Or because they'd burnt Rett to death in one? She knew that one day she would have to find the answer—all of the answers.

A twig snapped and she turned, startled.

"H-hello?" she said.

A gray rock sailed across the glen, cutting into the sun's rays, and pelted her on the forehead just above her right eye. Leah fell to the ground against the flaming tree, dazed. She reached up to touch the spot and felt warm sticky blood oozing out of a gash in her skin. Another rock hit her on the arm. And another on the chest. More pummeled her face.

"Stop," she cried out.

"Murderer! Murderer!"

Brownies came out of the trees on the other side of the clearing screeching at her, throwing sharp pellets and branches. Leah curled herself into a ball and screamed.

"I know where the kell stone is!"

It did no good; the brownies moved closer continuing their attack. She raised a hand away from her face as if to block the stones and the ground shook as centaurs entered the glen.

Chapter Twenty-one

It was sudden, Sire. There was no time to gather the rest of the guard."

Sorgood bent low before the king in his chambers by the hearth. Welk sat in his comfortable chair staring at the round bald spot on the top of Sorgood's head. A few of the guard, and young Frieden, stood behind him. Welk was relieved that his shock upon seeing the son of Belfen was wearing off. No doubt he would be seeing more of the lad now that he was nearly grown. He was glad to be comfortable in his presence; it gave him a melancholy hope for the future.

The guards' faces were bowed, but Frieden watched Sorgood with disgust.

"You found him at the butcher's hut?"

"Yes, Sire. I dragged him out but the butcher followed me with a rifle and fired at us."

"It wasn't the butcher," Footman Weeks said. "Begging your pardons." He bowed curtly. "It was old Father Wold. I fired back...or tried to."

"Poor shot."

"But it was old Father Wold. I couldn't..."

"Are you a footman in the king's guard or a wissende in

training?" Sorgood shouted.

"Enough," Welk raised his hand.

"That's when this oaf knocked us all down." Sorgood pointed at young Frieden.

"I was protecting the master of the guard, Sire," he said.

Welk nodded and tried hard not to smile. He could not tell where Frieden's loyalty was—but it was certainly not with Sorgood. And it was now clear that all the digging, and marching, and packing and unpacking, setting up tents and false perimeters—none of the guard's training had prepared them to do anything more than ride about on horses chatting with the guards of Damon Wall and Aaronland. How was he to fight off the eis or Ruhm with these folk?

And what of the bairn? He'd now met with the butcher Wold—the old wissende from the wasteland who told Sorgood weeks ago about the boy's birth and his mark. How did the boy know to go there? He must know more about his origins than the wissenry admits.

"And you let him out of your grasp," Welk mused.

"If I hadn't been knocked down, Sire."

"You'd have been shot," Welk said. "You were unprepared, Sorgood. I am, I have to say, beginning to doubt your worth."

Sorgood bowed lower. "I am sorry to disappoint, Sire."

"Why did you have so few guards in town?"

"There are not enough soldiers to patrol the towns as well as the borders, Sire."

"And no need now, I'm sure. He would have made for the hills by now, certainly."

"Yes, Sire," Sorgood mumbled. "We had yet to put the border in place north of Aaronland."

"As we should have done in the beginning. The boy has outwitted you," Welk sneered.

"He travels with an adult male, Sire. A woodsman."

"No, the boy is the intelligence that betters you, Sorgood.

The sooner you realize that, the sooner you will learn to overcome your weakness."

"Yes, Sire."

"I believe I told you the boy would remain in the Ruud some time before slipping off. You would have done well to patrol the villages. But you chose to ignore my advice."

"Oh, no, Sire. I did not act quickly enough, it is true. But I heeded your words. Indeed, I did."

Welk shrugged. "I trust that at least *now* you will build your perimeter, Sorgood. Now that the boy has escaped us."

Sorgood hesitated before bouncing in a groveling nod. Welk dismissed him and his guards, watching Frieden's back as he left. How tall he stood, despite his frail folk form.

Once alone, Welk relaxed into his chair to ponder the situation as it was. Perhaps it was best that the search for the boy would now end in the hills, and not in the Ruud among the folk. They could be appeased and their lives return to nearly normal. But Welk knew he could not let the boy run amok in the outer lands for long. The folk of the Ruud will be complaining that one day the bairn of prophecy will return to destroy all. No. He must capture Fenn Foster and imprison him, as soon as can be.

The Hass of Emorah would like to see the bairn turned into a local devotion. But what trouble might that bring? And how might the Hass use such a situation to their advantage? And to kill a boy? The folk may be in a frenzy of fear, but to call for the death of a child...not likely.

"Dunham," he called and waited knowing the man was always just outside the door, perched, waiting to be summoned. As expected, a light knock sounded, the door opened.

"Sire."

"Where are the prisoners?"

"Hidden in the bower, Sire."

The bower? Welk looked at Dunham in surprise. The bower had been closed off many years ago after his mother's death.

"I am sorry Sire, if opening the room has offended."

"No, no." He waved his hand in the air. "It is good the room can be used for something."

He caught Dunham's slight smile as he turned toward the large double doors at the far end of the king's chambers.

"Come see what I have done," Dunham said, asking Welk to follow him.

Welk resided now on the first floor, in his father's old rooms. The bower, the queen's suite of rooms, would now await his wife, should he choose to marry. The thought hadn't occurred to him before.

"You see I have sent in the ladies to dust and air out the linens," Dunham said as they walked through the lobby and into the queen's bedchambers. "The prisoners are there," he motioned to a set of doors. "In the closet, where they would not be seen."

"It is a large closet, I presume."

"Indeed, Sire. The queen enjoyed a large closet."

Dunham held Welk in something of a hopeful gaze and Welk couldn't help feeling kindly toward him. He was more a father to him than his own father had been. But the queen's chambers did nothing to elicit in him a desire for marriage. He had little memory of his own mother and none whatsoever of these rooms heavy with tapestry and brocade.

"Very well, bring them to me in my chamber room."

The three folk of Path shuffled into Welk's chamber, wide-eyed and gawking, and bowing again and again as they approached him at his large, comfortable chair. The innkeeper, Steppe, a thick and intimidating figure, sported a shock of deep auburn hair, a face full of freckles, and pale green eyes. The Pratts were round and healthy, both with their pudgy fingers clasped at their bellies.

Welk's room, though once his father's, was simple. The bed had been cleared of its crimson velvet covers and the dark rugs exchanged for lighter, colorful throws. The wall above the fireplace was now freed of the ominous, dull-eyed stares of the eleshag and elk heads—those given to the guards at Steingefan for their cardroom. His father's jeweled throne was taken out and put into the hall and Welk's aged, soft chair from his old quarters brought in. Welk hoped the ease of his chamber would be comforting to the folk.

But once before him, they fell to their knees and cast their faces to the rug on the cold stone floor. Welk first fell forward to lift them to their feet, afraid they'd fallen ill, but remembered himself and sat back again.

"Dunham," he said. "Chairs, please."

Dunham looked surprised and hustled about the room dragging chairs over and doing his best to get the folk off the floor and into them.

"Please," Welk said. "Please sit."

They balanced on the edges of their seats, looking down still.

"Stationer to the King," Welk said and the stationer nodded. "This behavior is unlike you, is it not?"

"I am a prisoner of the king now, Sire. Begging only not to be hanged."

"Hanged? Please, I implore you all. We have much to speak of that concerns the Ruud. Can you please see me as an ordinary folk for a time?"

Ma'am Stationer nearly spit with surprise and looked up at Dunham who shrugged.

"We are not Ruhm," Welk said. "Have we not enjoyed a less formal hierarchy here in the Ruud?"

"Yes, yes." Innkeeper Steppe examined his hands in his lap. "And yet the folk of Path, Sire, as we were in the jail, would scream at us through the windows, telling us we would be hanged or tortured."

Welk shook his head. "My apologies for leaving you in the jailhouse for so long."

They all nodded their bowed heads.

"How can I speak with you if you will not look at me?"

127

The stationer finally raised his head and looked directly into Welk's eyes. "Sire, please tell us the fate of our children."

At that, Ma'am Stationer dared to glance up at his face briefly and the innkeeper nodded and wiped his eyes.

"Last news I have has them safe and off into the hill country with a woodsman."

"Rogget, the wayonder?" the innkeeper said.

"I am not sure who he is. But they are safe. I was hoping they would come to you at the jailhouse and we could capture them and be done with this mess. But they are led by Fenn Foster and he is clever."

"Aye." Ma'am Stationer smiled a bit. "He is a clever boy. He would not want any harm to come to them."

"We have no intention of harming your children," Welk said.

"I fear they are loyal to their friend, Sire," the stationer said. "But I do not think they understand the situation."

"Stationer," Welk said, leaning forward and looking at him closely. "I do not think I understand the situation. I was hoping you all could help me sort it out."

Ma'am Stationer looked directly at him now in surprise.

"It is true. I am confused. Certainly we must capture the boy and punish him for his escapade at the prison."

Ma'am Stationer's mouth hardened and her eyes shut into an angry glare.

Welk said, "All the children would have been returned home soon enough. We were desperate at the time to find this bairn foretold. The folk are concerned."

"Concerned, yes," she said. "But not so much as to see our children in Steingefan."

"Perhaps it was a hasty decision. But as I am at a disadvantage for information, I must stand by it. You see, I have here a history of the Ruud."

Welk put his hand atop the large book sitting on the table

next to his chair.

"But I suspect this book is not the true history."

The stationer blinked rapidly.

The innkeeper spoke up. "We have the same book at the inn. It's available to all."

"Yes, but it isn't correct. You see, there is an error in it. I suspect this history of the Ruud is not accurate. Stationer, what can you tell me about it?"

"I..." The stationer looked to the ground and then back to Welk.

Welk felt for him, sensed his awe, and regretted it. While he'd spoken to a few folk from time to time as prince of the Ruud, and seen his father speak to them occasionally while sitting atop his horse on a tour, he knew that to sit in the presence of the king of Michelruud, especially in his private chambers, was, for the ordinary townsfolk, a miracle to be sure. Welk had long been disgusted with the hierarchy.

The stationer however, cowed as he was, held his own, as if pondering his options on what to say to him. And he finally spoke.

"It is my understanding Sire, that your sixth great grandfather, Roarn of Michelruud, commissioned the rewriting of the history."

The innkeeper looked at the stationer and seemed to chuckle. "What would he do that for?"

"The original history began with the Kingdom of Ruhm," he said. "It told of King Michelruud and his journey here, to establish the Ruud."

"This history begins there, as well," Welk said.

"No, Sire. It's not the same. The new history begins with Michelruud landing with his family and followers in the new land. It speaks of great adventure, freedom, bravado and the like. The original history begins much earlier and tells the story of why he left Ruhm."

Welk nodded. "I see. Why is the story of the prophecy different?"

"There is much that is different, Sire. The new history was commissioned after the Great Beast Revolt of 1070. The prophecy was supposedly made when the beast were defeated and driven off the lands surrounding the old castle. Many things that occurred shortly after were to be kept hidden...but..."

"But what?" Welk said.

"There was a wissende who was banished for a time for carousing. He apparently secreted away a copy of the original history and spent many years with the beast. He grew wise and determined to tell the truth. He added much to the history, about the beast folk, and published copies for all the wissendes under a pseudonym."

"A pseudo-what?" the innkeeper interrupted with another chuckle.

"A false name. He called his history, *The Book of Katze*. He knew to publish copies of the true history was worthy of punishment. But what he wrote about the beast could get him hanged."

"And why would that be?" Welk said. The innkeeper's head bobbed up and down in agreement. "Why was the history rewritten? Why was it forbidden? And why don't I know about it?"

"That, I believe, was the hope of Roarn, and all of the kings of the day. They wanted to erase the old history and hide what they'd done."

"What had they done?"

The stationer began wringing his hands together in his lap and his wife reached over and placed her hand over his.

"You are not supposed to have this information," Welk said.

The stationer shook his head. "No, Sire."

"How is it that you have it?"

"I do not know for certain how it came to be in the possession of the stationer, Sire, but my office has a copy of this *Book of*

Katze." He began to talk quickly now, nervously twitching in his chair. "I have tried to cleverly ask about it at the wissenry, but of course, by law, we cannot speak of such things. So, I do not know if I possess one of the wissende's copies, or another. But my grandmother told me, she had it that a stationer to the king of Ruhm left it at our office in her grandfather's day, though she doubted the story greatly, Sire."

Welk smiled. "Does it not seem odd to you that the kings of the Ruud would not have this history? But the wissenry and the stationer do?"

"Oh, indeed, Sire. Indeed. But we who have dared look inside the book, Sire, we know that it was forbidden and the punishment is death. We dared not bring it to anyone, not even a king."

"Death?" Welk smiled broadly. "What could be in such a book to bring death on any who read it."

"I fear it is not so much what is in the book, Sire, as what is in the hearts of folk."

Welk tilted his head at the stationer and peered curiously at him. "I do not take your meaning."

"The book only tells the truth."

"If you are led home under guard, can you secure the copy for me?"

"Yes, Sire, yes."

"Very well. Dunham," he called, and Dunham appeared from behind a curtain looking curious and excited. "You will gather a small guard to escort the stationer to his office in Path. Before you go, find the lady of the upper rooms and have her prepare quarters for our guests. They will reside here secretly."

"Can we not return home, Sire?" Ma'am Stationer whispered and bowed her head.

"Aye, your lordship," the innkeeper mumbled. "I fear the state of my inn."

"I will send an emissary to the inn immediately to relate

news back to you," Welk said. "Cook often travels there for your beef pies when she is too lazy to make her own. She would be an excellent spy, would she not, Dunham?"

"Must we hide?" Ma'am Stationer said and curtseyed.

"Indeed. The folk are caught up, I'm afraid. We'll let them think you are still held in the jailhouse for a time. And I'm sure you'll find the rooms here more comfortable."

"Thank you, Sire," Ma'am Stationer said. "I didn't mean to shun your kind hospitality. I think I'd rather like to live in the castle for a spell, even hidden away."

"I think you will like it. And you will have all the news of your children as soon as I have."

"Oh, thank you," she said.

Chapter Twenty-two

I know where the kell stone is," Leah cried out once more. But rocks and sticks struck her body and face again and again until she curled as tightly as she could into a ball, covering her head with her arms, waiting to be stoned to death. "That's enough," one of the centaurs roared and pounded the ground near her head with his hooves; the attack ceased. The brownies nearly shrieked with each heavy, irate breath they let out and Leah lay still, huddled against the flaming tree of Rett, bruised and bleeding on her head and arms. Her body trembled violently. She was sure she would die. The centaur kicked at her.

"Get up."

"She is one of them," one of the brownies shouted. "Kill her!"

"Get up," the centaur roared and Leah forced herself to move.

First she lifted her head and squinted up at the silhouette of a centaur blocking out the bright rays of sun. Shading her eyes with a hand, she struggled to sit up.

"I know where the kell stone is." She was hoarse and her voice trembled as she spoke.

"Liar," the centaur said.

More centaurs and several wolves surrounded her. A deep growling hum rattled her through to her bones.

"What is this?"

The centaurs moved aside for one of their own to approach Leah.

"Red Lichen, she is one of them," a brownie said. "You must let us have our vengeance."

"She mentioned the kell stone," another centaur said.

Red Lichen looked down at Leah and she gave a slight nod.

"What do you know of the kell stone?" he asked.

"I am descended of Dakenruud." Blood trickled down her upper lip and she took hold of her tunic, wiping it away, wincing at the pain.

"What is that to us?"

"I know you know of Dakenruud. I read about it in *The Book of Katze*."

"She lies," a brownie said, glaring at her.

Red Lichen shifted his hooves on the grass. "If the Hass knows where the stone is, why are they still here looking for it?"

"They don't know. I haven't told them."

"We should kill her," a brownie shouted.

"Wait," Red Lichen said. "We will take her to Dag Voorspeld for his counsel. If he decides that she is lying, you may have her."

"And if she is not lying," a brownie said, "we will torture her until she gives up the location of the stone. And *then* kill her."

Chapter Twenty-three

A cool, damp mist hovered among the slopes and valleys of the hill country. Back home in the Ruud, Fenn would be listening now to sparrows, cardinals, and chittenbirds chattering and peeping. Here in the hills, the stillness of the late morning was broken only by the occasional crow cawing far in the distance.

Rogget had a fire going and was warming kaff in a pot over the flames.

"Would you like some bitters?" he asked. "It's strong."

Fenn shook his head and packed his new blanket into his sack. Groggy with sleep, they sat around the fire while Grayson looked at Sadie's map of the hill country.

"It looks like the bridge is just before the larger hills begin. So if we keep heading northeast, we ought to find it."

"What makes you think you'll find out anything about your parents?" Sadie asked him.

"I was born in the wasteland, according to Father Britt."

"Just like the bairn of prophecy," Grayson said. He glared at Fenn, but his face softened quickly.

"I'm not the bairn," Fenn said. "There's no such thing as prophecy. The future isn't written yet; how could anyone predict it?"

"But you have the mark. And now we find out you were born in the wasteland. Even you must think there's something strange in all that."

"It's just coincidence. And anyway, Dag Anfang didn't say born in the wasteland; he said cast into it. There's a difference. And he didn't say anything about a mark. See? You're looking for reasons to think the prophecy is true and I'm the one. But I'm not."

They frowned at each other for several seconds until Rogget coughed.

"It was years ago," Sadie said, and Fenn was grateful for the interruption. "How's anybody going to remember anything about it now?"

"But, before you were saying that it ought to be easy to find my parents."

"That was when I thought you were born in the Ruud."

"She's right," Grayson said. "Finding your parents in the wasteland would be harder than in the Ruud. I doubt they keep track of births there."

"Well..." He hesitated. "The old man behind the butcher's told me my mother's nurse was named Clara and I could find her in a village in the wasteland."

They all raised their brows at him.

"How could he have possibly known that? He doesn't even know you. Nobody knows you, Fenn. You're an orphan."

Fenn shook his head. "I know it sounds strange, but I believe him. He had a wissende's robe in his hut. I think he did know me."

Grayson nodded. "If he was a wissende, I guess it's possible he knew you as a child."

"And..." He hesitated again and took in a large breath. He'd have to get it all out at once and act like he wasn't crazy for saying it. "And-the-fairies-told-me-to-go-and-find-the-truth-about-my-mother-in-the-wasteland-so-I-can-prove-there-is-no-prophecy."

"What?" Rogget said. "Huh? The fairies did what, you say?"

Grayson leered at him. "You heard fairies again?"

"I did. In the glade. Saw them, too."

"And they told you to go to the wasteland?"

"They did. Yes."

"Maybe you imagined it," Sadie said.

"I didn't imagine it any more than I imagined them in the beast forest making fun of Grayson's big feet."

Grayson laughed. "Well," he said. "He does have the faire mark. So..."

Sadie shrugged. "I suppose."

Fenn could tell they didn't believe him. Nobody, Grayson had told him, could understand fairy talk. Nobody. He wanted to tell them that his hemp rope and charm burned his skin, that he had visions of his past that were real, and that he thought he became the thief when he touched him, and he was sure he knocked Lucas and the guards over without touching them at all. Then maybe they would see that there was something odd happening and understanding fairies was the least of it. Then again, maybe that would convince them that he was crazy.

"Doesn't matter, either way," Sadie said. "If Fenn wants to go to the wasteland, we go to the wasteland."

"I thought you liked an adventure," Grayson said.

Sadie smirked. "You're right. Like Mother Carroll told us. It's a grand adventure. I'm just tired."

They were silent for a long time, enjoying the warmth of the fire in the chilly morning, waiting for the sun to dispel the mist and warm the air. Rogget put out the flame and drenched it with his leftover bitters and they all got up to leave.

"We'll get your parents out of jail," Fenn said. "We'll save them. We'll figure this out and end it, somehow. I promise."

Sadie tried to smile; she nodded bravely.

"I'm sorry," Fenn said.

"Don't keep apologizing," Grayson said. "It gets annoying.

There's nothing we can do about it now and it wasn't your fault, anyway."

"He's right," Rogget said. "Let's just work from where we're at and not concern ourselves with how we got here."

Fenn looked at them all, standing there staring at him with half-smiles on their faces.

"All right then," Rogget said. "Let's get moving."

"Didn't you ever have folk at the inn come in from the hill country?" Fenn asked.

"If they did, they didn't brag on it. We got a lot from the port, heading out to the hills, so they said. And we got them from all over the Ruud. But I didn't ever hear any tell of being here."

"Then you'll have stories of your own to tell when you get back," Fenn said.

"If I ever get back."

"Haven't you ever been to the hills, Rogget?"

"I stick to the Ruud. But there are plenty who come and go. Most of the encampments will be nearby, close enough to sneak in and out of the Ruud."

"They get them mostly in Aaronland and Damonwall," Sadie said, and they all looked at her in surprise. "My da told me. He travels through the Ruud a lot. Folk from the hills don't come through Michelruud, mostly because it borders Steingefan and the wasteland."

"And why are the wasteland villages so far north?" Fenn asked. "Wouldn't they want to be nearer to the Ruud?"

"Well, now, they're banished out there. They're not allowed to be too near the Ruud." Rogget said.

"Aren't the folk in the hills banished?"

"Not exactly. But they would be, if anyone got the chance to banish 'em." He laughed. "In the hill country, the land is green and pleasant, so I was told, and so I see is true. The criminals and loners took control here. The banished stick to the wasteland and out of their way."

"Aren't the banished criminals?"

"Not always. Sometimes they're just folks who found them-selves in a bad place and maybe made a mistake. Some of 'em, I hear tell, aren't quite right and leave the Ruud on their own."

"Yeah, that's what we hear," Grayson said.

"So, keep your ears and eyes wide open," Rogget said.

"How does a folk close his ears?" Sadie laughed.

"I think it's a metaphor," Grayson said.

"A metaphor," she murmured as if she liked the sound.

"What's it like in the wasteland?" Fenn asked.

"I hear tell the ground is rocky, bad for planting, bad for grazing. The folk there are very poor. Look there." Rogget pointed to an archway dug into the side of a slope and covered with rocks. "Gnomes. Watch for the holes; you don't want to fall in."

They laughed, but stepped carefully.

Sadie recited, "Stick a gnome, stick a gnome. Far from home you'll have to roam. Fall into the deepest hole. Never will you come back home." And she giggled, a sound that echoed off the slopes and hills and made Fenn feel lighter.

"I can't believe you remembered that," Grayson said. "I barely remember Bob Biddle."

Sadie began, "Kit kiddle, bob biddle."

Grayson joined in, "Tell us Brownie Tom's riddle."

Fenn and Rogget exchanged looks while Sadie and Grayson laughed together.

"Maybe there's something in the air," Rogget said.

Suddenly Grayson and Sadie stopped. Fenn followed their gaze to see two eleshags several yards in front of them stomping at the grass, wary of their presence. They were wide as small cabins and nearly as tall. Shaggy, brown coats of matted hair fell all over them and they shook it out, glaring at them impatiently.

"It's all right," Grayson whispered. "They're supposed to be very gentle."

When they all began to breathe regularly again, the eleshags went back to grazing. From around the hill three horses loped over to join them.

They heard a cry from the sky and looked up to see roster fiends and falcons circling in the east.

"Hunting for ground squirrels and hundrats, I imagine," Rogget said.

The autumn day wore on, the sun just barely warming their heads. They wandered the small valleys between the slopes keeping on a general northeastern path toward the bridge until they came to a row of curled, yellowed parchment signs on sticks stuck in the ground, about ten feet apart, leading around one of the large hills.

Rogget looked puzzled. "Now, I don't read well, mind you," he said. "But it looks to me like that says Scray Buts."

"It does," Grayson said. "What could it mean?"'

"It's an encampment perimeter. That much I know. I hear tell they put out signs to warn you so you don't bother 'em. Usually a mean-looking picture of something. But...Scray Buts. I'm not sure what to make of that."

"Hey, oi!"

A barefoot man approached them from around the hill, rags draped over his shoulders, his britches ripped to shreds at the knees. His face was black with dirt and mud, and his hair matted against his head.

"Toggle off with you," he yelled. "Didn't you read the sign? Go on...off!"

"But..." Grayson pointed to one of the parchments.

"Get out," the man yelled and two others joined him from behind the hill. They wore dirty, hole-filled tunics, their eyes were dull, and they had rags tied around their heads.

"We did read the sign," Grayson said.

"What are you still doing here, then?" The man picked up a

rock.

"All right, all right." Rogget ushered the kids away. "We're leaving."

"What was that all about?" Sadie asked.

"Like I said. They're camped there, probably in the little valley between the slopes. Don't want us around."

"Well, they need a better sign," Grayson said.

"Let's get away from them and stop for some lunch," Fenn said. "I'm tired."

After lunch they hiked another two hours and came across another row of posted signs. These were sturdier, the parchment nailed to thin wood boards, and each had a picture of a bloodied gnome with Gnome Eaters written on the top and bottom in red.

"That's more like what I expected." Rogget smiled.

Sadie looked at him, disgusted. "They eat gnomes?"

"Well, now, for some, a gnome is not much different from a ground squirrel."

"Rogget," Sadie cried. "That's horrible."

"But you nab them," Fenn said.

"Just because we pick on them and carry them around as a lark doesn't mean we'd eat one."

"Do folk eat brownies?" Grayson asked.

"Grayson!"

"I'm only asking."

"I don't rightly know," Rogget said. "I've never heard of it. But the brownies are forest creatures. You won't find them out here."

"But they can talk," Sadie said. "How can you eat something that talks?"

"Just because you don't understand what ground squirrels are saying when they bark doesn't mean they aren't talking," Fenn said.

"It's not the same thing at all."

Grayson laughed. "She's right. The gnomes are beast folk—sentient. There's a difference."

"We'll see. Maybe we'll meet one," Rogget said.

"Well there you go," Sadie said. "You never talk about *meeting* a squirrel, do you? Anyway, I've met plenty of gnomes in the Ruud. They don't like being picked up. And they tell you about it."

"A ground squirrel will tell you about it, too," Grayson said. "And you'd understand his language perfectly well, then."

"I don't think squawking is language, Grayson. Honestly, you think you're so smart."

"Hey there," a strange voice bounced off the slopes and they looked up to see a gruff and dirty man standing next to one of the signs.

"What's all the noise?"

"Sorry," Rogget said. "We'll be moving on."

"Best be. You're all too fat to eat. What kind of spits you think we got over here? Battering ram spits? They don't' make 'em that big. So go on; off with you."

"We're not that fat," Sadie protested.

Rogget put a hand over her mouth. "No, no, you're right. Much too fat for the spits. We'll be moving on now."

But the man walked toward them, his eyes squinting and his head atilt.

"Is that Roggester? Roggester Reynold?"

Rogget peered closely at the man and Fenn saw his face brighten. "Wiley Arbus, is that you?"

"Tis! And you, what in the Ruud are you doing traipsing about the hills...and with children."

"They're my charges." Rogget beamed with pride. "Fenn Foster, Sadie Pratt, Grayson Steppe, this here's Wiley Arbus. We was stationed in the guard together years ago."

"You were in the guard?" Fenn said.

"His name is Roggester?" Grayson said.

"How do you do?" Sadie bent into a slight curtsey, holding out her hand.

Wiley gave her hand a gentle bobble. He took Grayson's with an enthusiastic pump and Fenn's with a jerky shake.

"Good to meet you as well, kidlings. Come along to camp; we won't eat you, really. I'll get a replacement guard so's I can hear all the news of the Ruud."

He led them around the slopes into a deep valley and Fenn was surprised to find a settlement with tents, even a few wood buildings, lines of rope hung with clothes drying in the dim morning sunlight, fire pits, pots and pans hanging at a mess tent, and dozens of grimy men lying about, smoking pipes, and playing cards.

"Hey, oi, Tanner. Go to the post. I found an old mate."

Tanner sneered. "It ain't my time yet."

"I says it's your time, now get."

Very slowly, Tanner rose and made his way out of the camp, huffing and grumbling as he went.

"Come on, sit here by my fire pit. This here's my tent."

They sat while Wiley built up a small fire and hung a pot on a spit over it. "I got a big treat for you kids. Some sweet honey brew. I wouldn't normally share, but I ain't seen a child in nigh on five years."

"You been out five years now?" Rogget said.

"I have. Left right after you. The guard just weren't no fun without you."

"You were in the guard?" Fenn said again, looking at Sadie and Grayson in amazement.

"He was," Wiley said.

Another man joined them around the fire saying, "Roggester Reynold, I never thought..."

"This here's Bruck Lerned, kids," Wiley said. "Aw, what d'you look all scared for? We ain't criminals. Well...well, yeah we are. But we ain't going to harm you none."

"No, they won't do us any harm," Rogget said.

"What sorts of criminals are you?" Grayson asked in awe.

Wiley shrugged but Bruck said, "Thieves mostly. We try to steal seeds and farm and such. But we ain't much for it. So we tend to steal food from town."

"We don't steal it from town," Wiley said. "In Aaronland, they got a mound near the border where they leave things for us. Kind folk. We have to steal from the Brutes and the Wretched. The Brutes mostly, cause they's the stupidest folk you'd ever meet. We try to keep away from the Wretched; ain't none meaner in these parts."

"Brutes!" Grayson said. "Scary Brutes! Is that what their sign's supposed to say?"

Wiley nodded. "Aye, it is." And they all laughed.

Wiley's honey tea was delicious and Fenn drank his fill, apologizing for taking so much. But Wiley seemed pleased to see them enjoy it. Grayson opened the map and showed them the stone bridge they were looking for.

"Passing Bridge. Over to the wasters. Just up north a bit. You're close now. But what do you want in the wasteland?"

"We're explorers," Fenn blurted out.

"Explorers, now?"

"That's right," Rogget told him.

"And Rogget here's your guide...your protection, I'm supposing?"

They all nodded.

"Well, that's a fine story. As fine a story as I've heard tell in these parts." He laughed. "Tell me the news, then."

They listened to Wiley and Rogget talk of the guard and the new King Welk of Michelruud and Rogget told him about Steingefan and the children of Path."

"Aye, we heard of that. The rumor of the evil bairn's been all over the hills for years. Came right out of the wasteland, he did."

"That's all the guard's about these days," Rogget said frowning. "Chasing after children, looking for this bairn."

"Well, they'd lost the adventure well before we left." Wiley said.

After their conversation began to lull, Sadie asked, "Do you eat gnomes, then?"

"Ard, no," Bruck said. "We call ourselves that to make 'em leave us alone."

"Are they bothersome?" Grayson asked.

The two men laughed. "We settled our camp here over a gnome city," Wiley said. "They didn't care much for us. They'd come out their little holes at night and tie our laces together, or pour honey in our pipes. Devilish little critters."

"So we changed our name to Gnome Eaters and that about did it."

"Just that?" Sadie said.

"Well, there was the unfortunate accident with the little gnome in the fire."

Sadie gasped.

"It was purely accident, I swear. But when he went off screaming like that, telling 'em all we was trying to roast him. Well, I guess they figured we were serious and they packed off right quickly."

"Well, Roggester," Bruck said. "I always thought you'd go back to the guard after your troubles were settled."

Rogget shot a glance at Fenn and shook his head. "Nope, nope."

"It weren't your fault. You know that by now, I figure."

"I don't rightly want to talk about it; and no I don't figure that. It was my fault. I didn't have to do it and I done it."

"You did have to do it," Wiley said. "It was a direct order from your superior. You kill the dang thing or you get hanged or something."

"I told you I don't want to talk about it. But I could have

run right then. I don't think they'd a shot me in the back. Heck, they only had one firearm at the time and I was the one holding it."

"No, you did what you had to do."

"I said I don't want to talk about it."

"Fine then. But I can't believe you've been carrying it around for five years still thinking it was your fault."

"It *was* my fault. I don't care who told me to do it. It was wrong. And you know, sometimes I think he only told me to do it 'cause he knew it was wrong."

"Aye, I'll grant that," Bruck said. "I heard other stories about what they made guards do. But with most they start out when they're little ones, like these fine children here. And by the time they're old, like you was, they'll shoot a centaur with no more'n a blink of the eye."

"I told you I don't want to talk about it."

"You shot a centaur?" Sadie mumbled.

Rogget got up and took off his sack, bow, and quiver. "I'll be off for a stroll round about your lodgings, now, if you don't mind." He stomped heavily across the camp.

Wiley nodded and called out, "Rogget here's my friend. Give him leave." Several men looked up, a few waved and they went about their business of lounging and cards.

"Did Rogget kill a centaur?" Grayson asked.

Wiley nodded. "He was ordered to. He hesitated long time, hoping the darn beast would leave. But it didn't. Just dared 'em to shoot."

"But why?"

"The centaur was out of the forest, on the king's land, and we had orders to kill any beast we found without a pass. Lieutenant gave the firearm to Rogget, as he was new and all."

"So, he didn't join as a kid, like most?" Grayson said.

"No, he signed on older. His family needed the money and Rogget weren't no good at tailoring."

"Rogget's dad is Tailor Small?" Sadie said.

"In Timber," Wiley said.

"Oh, I don't know the tailor there."

Wiley nodded. "I joined up with him. Thought it'd be fun. And you make some good gold for your family. But neither of us took to it. And Rogget left after the centaur. Said he was going into the forest of the beast lord to ask forgiveness, but I don't think he ever went."

"And now he probably thinks it's too late for apologies." Fenn said remembering Rogget's refusal to enter the forest.

"True, true," Wiley said. "And he figures the beast folk have some sort of recip...recip ...uh, equal? What's the word, Bruck?"

"Give and take? Tit for tat?"

"The reciprocal law," Grayson said.

"What's that?" Sadie asked.

"It means Rogget thinks he'll have to give his life for the one he took."

"That won't bring the centaur back, will it? And anyway, it does sound like it wasn't entirely his fault."

"It's going to get a might cold here soon," Wiley said. "You kids have some warmer clothes with you...I hope."

They shook their heads.

"I don't think we thought we'd be running—"

"Exploring," Fenn interrupted Sadie. "We didn't expect to be exploring this long."

Wiley smiled and nodded. "Well, you head back through after you explore the wasteland and maybe we'll have found something for you. You know, something just lying around."

"Maybe you could find stuff lying around at my house," Grayson said. "I wouldn't feel so guilty about wearing it."

Wiley winked at him. "That's a possibility. But if not, you might can barter some stuff in the encampments on your adventures. I don't think they'll have anything in your sizes, though."

"Where you planning to explore after the wasteland?" Bruck said. "I don't think the hill country is someplace kids ought to be wandering about."

"We were headed to the ice realm," Fenn said. "They say it's beautiful."

"Aye, and filled with eis and angels. Beautiful and dangerous."

"No," Wiley said. "No. You can't be heading out to the ice realm. There's war coming up that way."

"War?"

"Aye, I'll be telling Rogget about it. Keep you out of trouble."

"Why war?" Grayson said.

"Ard, it's a mess. And the angels aren't helping matters any. They're the ones you got to look out for. I don't think you'd even make it to the ice realm without them taking you."

"Taking us?" Sadie said.

"Aye," Bruck said. "They come swoopin' in, a dozen or so, and they carry you off. They drop you in the ice mountains and leave you there."

"Dangerous and just plain mean," Wiley said.

"Then you got to walk all the way back, half-starved and weak—"

"If you make it back at all."

"True. Too true. Some of us didn't make it back. And up there in the ice, there's no burying the dead. The gargantuan crows and eagles will feast on your frozen, rotting body."

"Gargantuan crows," Sadie whispered.

"Well, technically," Grayson said. "If you're frozen..."

"Then," Wiley said, "a day or so after the poor souls are taken up by the angels, the eis come round with their poison arrows and demand that we take our kind elsewheres."

"And we always tells 'em, we stay here in the hills; we ain't none of your concern."

"But your kind are up there in our mountains, they say. And we say, 'your friends the angels took 'em up there.' But they don't believe us. They killed lots of us until we got the shields."

"What shields?" Grayson said.

"I'll show you one." Wiley stood and disappeared into his tent, emerging with a large silver plate of glistening metal. "They're heavy. But they're the only thing we've found to withstand the eis arrows. They shoot so much faster and stronger than folk."

"Ard, Wiley, they're eis; their arrows are imbued with the beast magic."

"Maybe so."

"Do our guards have those shields?" Grayson asked.

"No, no. They're stolen. Well, the Wretched stole 'em. Off ships that pass through Ice Port over there cross the Plains of Glisch."

"So you stole them from the Wretched?" Fenn said.

"No, they traded 'em."

"But aren't you enemies?"

"Enemies be a harsh and variable word round these parts." Bruck said.

"We're a brotherhood," Wiley said.

"Aye. A brotherhood of enemies."

"We'd run 'em off without a thought, mind you. But when it comes to fighting off the angels and eis, we're all of one mind."

"Not of one mind, Wiley," Bruck said. "There's those what want to fight and those what want to make a peace with the angels. There's no defeating them, some say. They got a knife even more powerful than the eis arrows." Bruck lashed the air with his hand as if slashing Fenn with his angel knife. "You stay away from them."

"Well, who wouldn't stay away from a knife?" Fenn said.

"Aye, but a knife with angel magic. One deep wound from it and you die a slow, slow death. Years! It can take years. Wasting away."

"Yes." Wiley stole a brief annoyed glance at Bruck. "What with the war coming from up to the north and the Wretched around here, I'd say you'd best be back in the Ruud."

"Where do the Wretched hide out?" Grayson asked.

"All over the hills. Land pirates. Steal anything they can find from anybody. No souls."

Bruck picked up a stick and poked the fire, fuming. "One o' these days we're gonna have to do something about 'em."

Wiley nodded. "One 'o these days. None of the gangs out here care for 'em much. If we could get together we could run 'em off. But nobody'll help us."

"Well, I don't see how we would know them...to avoid them," Grayson said.

"True," Wiley said. "By the time you knew who they were, it'd be too late. But they don't head north so much this time o' year. They do most of their foraging into Damon Wall and at the port."

"Is one of them named Clutch?" Fenn asked.

"You've met them already?" Bruck said.

"They robbed us in the faire glade on their way to the port."

"I'm surprised they didn't kill you, even though you are kids. Stay away from 'em if you can."

"We thought they might kill us. But Rogget and Darnit showed up."

"Darnit?"

"Rogget's bear."

"Rogget's got a bear, does he?"

"Sure, hasn't he always had a bear?"

"No, I don't rightly recollect a bear. Can't say as it's odd, though. He seems the type to be traipsing about the Ruud with a bear. Where'd he get it, anyway?"

Fenn shrugged. "Don't know."

"Is it an invisible bear, then?" Bruck looked all around.

"No, he sent it off without us when we went to town for new supplies. It should show up sooner or later. I hope."

"I don't know. Seems to me a bear might cause a disturbance

out this way. Folk are more likely to shoot straight off."

"Are there a lot of firearms out here?"

"More so than in the Ruud."

"But aren't they hard to come by?" Grayson asked.

Bruck nodded and smiled. "They are."

"Do the Wretched steal firearms, too?"

"Indeed they do. They traded a whole lot of 'em to the Breathless to fight off raids from the Brutes."

"The Breathless?" Fenn said.

"Philosophers," Wiley said. "Never shut up."

"Can't understand a word out their mouths," Bruck said.

"But the Breathless turned right round and traded 'em to us and the Brutes as a sign of peace."

"We think that was their goal," Bruck said. "Like I told you—can't understand anything they say."

Wiley spit into the fire and the men chuckled to themselves for a few moments.

"Do you hear much about any of the orphans of the wasteland?" Fenn said.

Wiley shook his head. "There are some, I hear. But I don't know about 'em. Why?"

Fenn shrugged. "No reason."

"Mostly I think they aren't so orphaned as you might think," Bruck said.

"What do you mean?"

"A mother don't want her little one brought up in the wasteland, nor the hills. So she sends her wee one off with a traveling wissende or she sneaks it over to Waverly wissenry."

Fenn perked up at that.

From behind the tent they heard a roar and a scream.

"That'll be your bear, I guess," Bruck said and stoked the fire with a stick. "Don't shoot it!" he called out to no one in particular. "It's Rogget's darn bear!"

Chapter Twenty-four

The stationer sat in the second chair by the fire in Welk's chambers, a chair meant for a friend, an equal. But in the early days of the Ruud, the stationer to the King *was* nearly equal—a trusted confidante. He flipped through the gold-lined book on his lap; it looked nearly identical to the history of the Ruud Welk owned, but this one was larger and its early pages delicate with age.

"Here it is, Sire—the part that I have read. The Beast Uprising of 1070 has occurred and many of the beast were driven into the forest. But the beast lord returned to old Michelruud Castle, Steingefan now."

"I know as much as that, at least, good stationer."

"My apologies, Sire."

"Continue..."

"The beast lord returned with the felidae and created chaos and havoc outside the gate. It was as if he called up a storm overhead and his voice thundered until finally King Michelruud appeared outside to hear him speak. Do you care to read it? Or shall I?"

"You may read it," Welk said.

"Dag Anfang thundered, 'Michelruud, thief of lands, butcher

of beast, heartless intruder, dead you are. Dead you will be. A new bairn, born of a king, cast into the wastelands, will rise against you, and destroy all that you hold dear. The kell stone he will wield and all folk will harken to his command. The dragon flies above him! All laid waste below!' But Michelruud only smiled and turned his back on the felidae, leaving the king's guard to escort them to the edge of the Ruud and into the ancient forest, never to be heard from again."

Welk sat in silence for a moment pondering what he'd heard and then said, "Well, then, there certainly was a prophecy. Of that much we can be sure."

"Perhaps, Sire. However, there is one small item after this entry. I never paid much attention before. But now it seems a bit relevant."

"What is it?"

"Here, in a report given by one of the king's guard. He states that he overheard Dag Anfang say to another felid, 'these folk don't cower and whimper as the others do.'"

"Others?"

"Yes. It is a puzzle, Sire. Though, we know that other folk from the Great West and parts beyond often landed north of Cold Sea Port, at Ice Port, before Damonruud built the harbor piers."

"And you think they are the others Anfang spoke of?"

The stationer shook his head. "I could not say, Sire. But it appears he thought he could frighten Michelruud."

"So, you think it was not a prophecy?"

"As a descendent of wissendes, Sire, no. I do not."

"I cannot believe that this is what Roarn and the other kings wished to hide from the folk."

"No, Sire. It was much more than that and it's all here in this book. Originally, Michelruud speaks of wishing to create a world in which the threat of Emorah was unheard of. He wished to erase the fears of the Hass from the hearts of the folk. They were not to be spoken of."

"But it wasn't he who changed the history."

"No, he did not go that far. Damonruud, his son, had to deal with Emorah for trade at the port. And according to the history, he and the other kings accepted help from them to drive the beast folk out of the Ruud. They led raids and brutally tortured and murdered many of the beast, in the name of the Ruud."

"Ah," Welk said, nodding. "That is something they would wish to hide."

"Indeed Sire. We pay tribute to the Hass of Emorah annually for the deed, but none in the Ruud are aware of the savagery that was leveled against the beast. Even now, after some two hundred years, the main folk of the Ruud have no memory of their ancestors' past in the Kingdom of Ruhm. They believe that Ruhm helped Michelruud out of the west and we pay tribute only because they are our forefathers."

"Do folk forget so quickly, stationer?"

"That is what I meant, Sire, about the hearts of men. They will easily forget what they do not wish to remember. And they will do evil all too quickly in error."

Welk nodded and sighed. "Why did not the Hass of Emorah regain control of the Ruud when they were asked for help?"

"I cannot say, Sire. I confess, I have not read all the history. I haven't much time for doing secret things. Maybe the answer can be found within it. Especially in the history of the beasts that Katze put at the beginning."

"And you never read that?"

"I never found myself much interested before now."

"You are certainly not alone in that."

"I will leave the book with you, that you may read it all." The stationer stood and bowed, prepared to leave but stopped at the door. "One more thing, Sire, of grave import. When I went to retrieve the book from my office, it was not where it was supposed to be. And it was lying open."

"Someone has read it? Your apprentice, perhaps."

Stationer Pratt shook his head. "Jeopard has already read the book—and he didn't know of its last hiding place. Not only that, he is an honest young man and would never stoop to snooping."

Welk nodded. "So, others know what I will soon know. Can that be a bad thing?"

The stationer gave him a helpless shrug and left his quarters. Dunham approached and occupied the empty chair.

"What do you make of it all, Sire?"

"I believe the Hass of Emorah had something to do with the rewriting of the history. Folk who do not know the mistakes of the past are fated to the same errors again and again."

"Yes, Sire. Wisdom."

"I think they are looking for what they see as another beginning—here in the Ruud."

"Sire?"

"I will read the history first. But if my Nanta knew anything, I think she knew how this whole sordid mess began."

Dunham put a question on his face, but rose to prepare the king's plate.

"Will you dine in the hall, Sire?"

Welk nodded. Yes. The noise and gaiety of the great hall would help him think.

Chapter Twenty-five

Rogget returned to the fire when he heard Darnit had arrived and Fenn thought he had become his old self again.

"The thieves that stole my charm," Fenn said. "They're called the Wretched."

"That so?" Rogget said.

"And they have Forbes' writ."

"Aye, I reckon they do."

"What's this?" Wiley said.

"Forbes' writ. You remember."

"He still has that?"

"Not anymore," Fenn said. "The Wretched stole it from him outside a pub in Aaronland."

"Why would he take it to a pub where it could get stolen? Not that it's really worth anything."

"According to him," Grayson said. "That's all they took."

"That's a might suspicious."

"Exactly what I told him," Rogget said. "But like you say, it's worthless."

"Well, you never can tell with the Wretched. They'll steal anything. And they didn't know it was worthless, now did they?"

"I guess not. But why would they want it?"

"Maybe they'll take it to Welk," Sadie said.

"Hah," Bruck laughed and spit bitters into the fire. "I don't think a king of the Ruud is going to take a meeting with the likes of the Wretched."

They spent the rest of the day and night with the Gnome Eaters, sleeping by the fire as the gang sang and played cards into the night. The next day, they woke early, were treated to a hot breakfast and began saying their goodbyes.

"You were going to tell Rogget about the war," Fenn reminded Wiley, anxious to hear the news himself.

"Aye, the war."

"War?" Rogget's eyes lit up in alarm.

"It's the encampments in the northeast," Wiley said. "They're spreading out all over the hills and the eis of the realm don't want 'em any closer. They've sent messengers over to the kings of the Ruud telling 'em to get rid of the folk, but the kings think it's none of their concern."

"Are all these folk from the Ruud?" Fenn asked.

Wiley pointed at him with surprise. "Bright boy, there. No. No, most of the folk up farther north come from the Great West, from the Kingdom of Ruhm."

"Then it isn't the business of the Ruud," Rogget said.

"Tell that to the eis. Anyway, it's heating up near to boiling up that way. We hear rumors of civil unrest in the realm as well."

"In the ice realm? Aren't they peaceful among themselves?" Grayson said.

"Aye, that's what you hear in the stories, ain't it?" Wiley winked. "But they're just as cunning and crafty as folk, as it turns out. I hear tell of the maiden being ousted and planning a revolt to regain her throne."

"Then maybe they'll forget the settlers for a while."

"Rogget, I'm surprised at you. If anything, it only riles them against the settlers more. They got to put the blame on somebody, after all. Anyway, we told the kids last night they'd be better off in the Ruud."

Rogget shook his head. "I'm thinking...not so much. But thanks for the warning."

"Take care on your exploring expedition," Wiley told them with another wink.

They made their way north to Passing Bridge, a wide stone arc over the rapids of the river. The day was cool and the sky clear blue; light breezes whipped at their faces. The water rushed loudly below them as they crossed into the wasteland. Just on the other side of the river the land was changed. Mostly flat with sparse clumps of trees, the ground was rocky and much harder to trek. By noon, they'd headed northwest, upward across a long rise to look down into a shallow valley covered in a blanket of pale purple.

"It's beautiful," Sadie said.

"And dangerous," Grayson said.

"But they're just flowers."

"Grayson's right," Rogget said. "That there's a field of lilac clover—thirty yards wide. I plumb forgot about it." He scanned the horizon. "Blooms its sweetest in spring and autumn. We're smack dab in autumn. And it goes on for miles."

"But there's a wasteland village in the distance." Fenn pointed. "Let's cross."

"We'll have to head north or south to find a way around it," Grayson said.

"What are you talking about?" Sadie said.

"Bees."

"Ard no," Rogget said. "It ain't the bees you got to worry about. Fat, lazy things'll just hover out of your way. It's the fairy bees."

"That's what I meant," Grayson said.

"Fairy bees?" Fenn looked out across the peaceful, beckoning field of violet.

"They're not technically fairies," Grayson said.

"But they're sentient," Rogget said.

"The encyclopedia on the beast of the eastern realm says they're semi-sentient. They're self-aware; but prone to viciousness. They don't appear capable of, or even interested in, learning other languages and they can't be reasoned with."

"And they're dangerous?" Sadie said.

"Very," Grayson said.

"I guess reading my da's books does come in handy."

"You should try it sometime."

Fenn slugged him in the arm and gave him a stern look when Grayson turned to him.

"Sorry," Grayson said. "I guess I'm just out of sorts lately."

"Yeah, well, we all are, waiter boy. So, what do we do?"

Rogget looked at Fenn. "We could hike for miles trying to find a way around. The main entrance into the wasteland villages is north of Steingefan. There's a path through the clover there."

"All the way back to the Ruud?"

"Aye."

Grayson sat on the ground with Sadie's map of the hills and wasteland. "That must be what this hazy marking is. It's the clover. Sure enough," he said, putting his finger on the map. "Right there it says so. The patch runs from just west of Steingefan all the way up to a plain nearer to the ice realm."

"And no other way over or around?" Rogget said.

"There are bridges. The first looks to be about five miles north."

"Five miles?" Sadie said.

"It's not all that wide," Fenn said. "We should try to cross here."

Darnit shook his head slowly back and forth, arcing it down and up like a swing, and let out a deep growl.

"I'll set Darnit off again." Rogget slapped the bear on the backside. Darnit lumbered off northward. "He can meet up with us later."

"How does he understand you?" Sadie said.

Rogget shrugged. "I think he can smell the village. He don't like folk much. Can't say as I blame him. It's not like I trained him or anything. And I reckon he smells me out after a while. I like to think he wants my company. But I reckon it's the jerky."

"Would the fairy bees sting him, too?"

"Nah, they're not likely to sting an animal. They're just vicious. If you upset them, they'll sting you for spite. And they take great pleasure in it. But an animal? Nah. They know the animal didn't mean any harm."

"Well, what if we don't mean any harm?"

"They're fairy bees," Grayson said. "They think all folk mean them harm. We have to hike to the bridge."

"I've heard tell of folks crossing without harm," Rogget said. "But it's a risk is all."

They stood on the rise for some time, watching the field of clover and the village beyond. There was no indication of danger—all was peaceful and quiet.

"Well, what's it going to be?" Rogget eyed Fenn.

"I think we should try to cross."

"That's a really bad idea," Grayson said.

"We can't go back toward the Ruud. Do we really want to walk another five miles up and back for a bridge? Let's just be careful and cross here."

Rogget stared at Fenn longer than usual, making him restless. "Okay then," he said finally. "Let's be quick about it."

They walked downward toward the village and into the clover. Careful at first, stepping around as many plants as possible. Fenn's feet sunk deep between them, flowers grazing his boots at his ankles.

"I don't see any bees," Sadie said.

"Shh," Grayson warned. "Just keep moving quickly and don't talk."

As they trod, fat bees, rose from the ground around them, hovering, landing, buzzing.

"Which ones are fairy bees?" Sadie asked.

"They looked like wasps in the picture I saw."

"Wasps? Ouch!" Sadie slapped at her arm. "I got stung."

She turned this way and that, her arms flinging about her body and swiping at her hair. "They're all over me." She screamed and started to run.

Fenn watched as dozens of tiny bees swirled around her face and hands.

"Sadie, stop!" Grayson yelled. He ran forward and dove for her, tackling her to the ground. She screamed again batting furiously in the air. Rogget roared forward, grabbed Sadie up into his arms and ran through the clover heaving and wheezing.

Fenn ran ahead of him, slapping at the bees crying out, "Hurry, hurry."

Sadie screamed again. Grayson tumbled forward out of the field rolling to the ground knocking Fenn over. Rogget plodded out behind them and fell, dropping Sadie out of his grasp.

"Are they coming after us?" Fenn stood and gathered up his knapsack.

They looked back at the field; it was calm again.

"Sadie," Grayson said. "Are you okay?"

Rogget pulled at the neck of her tunic. She moaned and her head rolled to the side. Large, round red spots erupted all over her neck and face. Rogget looked up toward the village.

"We've got to get her to help fast."

He scooped Sadie up in his arms, gave Fenn a stern look, and headed off toward the village.

"I'm sorry," Fenn said.

"I'm not mad at you," Rogget said. Fenn heard him mumble under his breath, "Only myself to blame."

"Did you get stung?" Grayson asked.

"No. You?"

Grayson nodded. "Just twice. What do you suppose they have against Sadie?"

162

Chapter Twenty-six

Facing the beast lord in his den—a sunlit glade amid the dense, dark forest—her hands bound tightly behind her back, Leah wobbled and weaved, forcing herself to maintain balance. Her right eye was swollen, though she could still open it a sliver to see, and her body ached. Her damp hair was draped over her face and tickled her skin, but she could not shake it away.

Beasts of all sorts prowled about her as if she were prey—pacing wolves glaring at her with yellow eyes; brownies hissing; a fat, frowning troll snorting at her; large black cats padding in circles at the outer edges of the den, their loud purring echoing all about. Tinkling water drew Leah's attention to an enormous boulder with water running down its front and pouring into a basin of rock below.

She'd been marched through the forest by brownies, wolves, and centaurs—the brownies demanding she be killed without delay. When night fell, her hands were bound behind her around a small pine and she was allowed to sleep for a short time, though the fitful squirming on the root-covered forest floor could hardly have rested her. She woke once in the cold dampness of midnight and was glad for the extra protection of her new riding pants; at that thought, she let out a laugh, which only angered her captors.

She'd lost the ribbon for her hair at some point in the attack and sat on her locks—with each shift of her sore, aching body, she felt ripping and tearing.

As they marched her to the den of the beast lord the next morning, she understood how she'd come to be in her present circumstance. The brownies were only too happy to make her aware of her crimes. News that Kirche had murdered a brownie in Aaronland had spread quickly through the beast communities. The brownie's head, drying out on a stick behind the inn in Path, was an added insult.

When they were stupid enough to attack the group of brownies just at the edge of the forest, the centaurs, wolverines, and felidae were already on guard. And there Leah was, enemy to the brownies, running into the forbidden forest of her own volition, and the brownies demanded their right to vengeance.

Once in the lair, the coolness of the day fell in a mist, and introductions of a sort were made to Dag Voorspeld, one of the huge black cats, who nodded his large head and growled something like words that she couldn't understand. He lounged atop a gray boulder overlooking the crowd of beasts, and stared at Leah as if bored.

"Ho-an uchen hin," he grumbled.

Leah watched as the cat trembled, as if shaking off the morning chill, but instead of settling down again, he shimmered and broke into a million tiny shards of shiny black glass, and twirled around in whirlwinds of bits and pieces until coming back to himself as a folk, wrapped in an ebony velvet cloak.

"You claim to know of the kell stone," he said, and every word vibrated across the glade and through her body.

She nodded.

"You will explain," Voorspeld commanded.

Leah fought to stay awake, wishing desperately to wipe the dried blood from her face. Her forehead throbbed and her wrists chafed against the ropes binding them; she could feel warm blood oozing onto her palms.

"My name is Leah Hallowsing." A sharp, slicing burn spread out on her upper lip as she spoke. "I am daughter of Edwin, Stationer to the King of Ruhm. I am kin to Dakenruud who took the kell stone from Michelruud and was commissioned to hide it somewhere on Kell."

She paused and wavered, fearing she would fall. She needed water desperately.

"And how does being kin to Daken save you?" the felid said.

Leah shuddered, realizing that her fate was Voorspeld's to decide. And what if he turned her over to the brownies?

"Before he was taken and killed by the Hass," she continued, trembling, "Daken gave his brother Abueruud a journal in which he told of his adventures across Kell. And in which he related where he hid the stone."

Snickers rippled through the group of brownies and centaurs pawed at the ground.

"She lies," one of the wolves growled.

"I must return to Ruhm and find the journal."

"You don't know where it is?" Voorspeld said.

"You see. She lies to save her life. Do not be fooled."

"Woolrich," Red Lichen said. "Do not insult the lord."

The brownie slunk back into the crowd and another stepped forward.

"She is not the one who killed our Zeelif."

"Do not listen to this one," Woolrich said. "He continues to use name given him by folk; he is traitor to his kin."

"Kwitcher is not traitor," the brownie said. "Like name. Keep it. That is all."

"Stop this bickering." Red Lichen stomped the ground for silence.

Dag Voorspeld gazed at Leah and she begged him with her eyes to believe her, even as she knew she was lying. The journal was only legend. She would have no idea where to find it. And even if she did, there was no certainty that it contained any information about the kell stone. But she surprised herself by how little she cared; she wanted to live. She wanted to get out of the forest alive and go home. And she would tell any lie that might make that happen.

"What would you do with the stone if you found it?" Voorspeld asked.

Trying to sound truthful, she said, "I would consult with my father for advice, of course. But I am sure that he would agree with me that the stone should be returned to the beasts."

"You are a member of the Hass," Red Lichen said. "Why should we believe you?"

"It's true." She lifted her chin in defiance. "I came here as one of them. But I have seen Kirche's careless, even murderous, behavior toward the folk of the Ruud, both beast and mortal. I do not leave as one of them."

Voorspeld purred loudly for some time while Leah tried to stay focused on his green eyes. Somehow, she must convince him that she wanted only to help them. She could hear her father's voice in her head from long ago, after she'd been caught lying at the Hass school.

"A lie will always reveal itself in your eyes," he'd said. "It's there, an imprint on your heart, and your eyes betray you."

"Drop your beloved into the pool," the folk cat said.

Chapter Twenty-seven

As they approached the outer huts of the wasteland village, they found a sign posted on a stump. It read: Banished. They walked quietly along the main road lined with huts—some crafted of clumps of sod, others of branches, and a few of hewn logs. Fenn saw that each had a small fire pit dug just outside its entrance. Thin, sallow folk crouched outside their homes, or gathered in circles on the ground on mats, or in the dirt. Most paid them no attention, despite Sadie, pale and motionless, draped across Rogget's arms.

Banished was rocky and dry, warmed by a constant sun—no trees dotted the landscape, only huts. As they neared the center of the little make-shift town, folk turned to frown at them.

"Newcomers," someone said. But they did not approach to greet them.

As they stood at the well, a short, wrinkled woman with a long mane of gray hair dancing about her shoulders walked defiantly toward them.

"What is wrong with the child?" She reached out to pull the hair from Sadie's face and Sadie flinched. "It's the fairy bees."

"Aye. Have you anything for it?" Rogget said.

"Bring her to my hut, quickly."

They followed the old woman into a dark, suffocating room built of logs with mud, now dried, slathered between them. In the center, the woman pulled at a stick and a flap opened in the roof and sunlight streamed in, brightening up the little space. There were beds along the walls, no more than rags laid neatly on the ground.

"Put her there." She pointed and Rogget fell gently to his knees and laid Sadie on one of the beds. She moaned.

"Welcome to Banished." The woman dug through a chest, pulling out bowls and containers of herbs. "I'm Pinta. Never mind the others. They're leery of strangers. They'll warm up. But you aren't banished, are you?"

Grayson shook his head. "We're adventurers."

Sadie chuckled and coughed.

"She hasn't lost her mind," Pinta said. "So there is hope."

"Lost her mind?" Fenn said.

"The stings. They'll drive you mad from pain. Once that happens, death isn't far behind."

"Death?" Grayson said.

"Oh, don't worry, son." Pinta ground herbs, oil, and water in a stone mortar. "It's only the very weak, or the allergic, who succumb. I'm sure the girl will be well in no time. Now, sit. This will take a while."

They watched as Pinta sopped up her muddy mixture with bits of muslin and covered Sadie's red patches with it, pressing them gently onto the swollen sores. Smiling up at Rogget, she said, "Adventurers, now. Fancy that. You should know how to cross the clover properly."

An elderly man, bent over at the waist, supporting himself on a stick, shuffled into Pinta's hut. He pointed at Grayson and said, "Did you come from Ousted? Did you bring any writs or decrees from the board?"

"They're not banished, Havert. And from the looks of this one, they came straight over through the clover without any foreknowledge." Pinta looked at Rogget. "But...you didn't happen to go through Ousted, did you?"

"No ma'am," Rogget said.

"Where is that?" Fenn said.

"Ousted's the little patch just north of Steingefan. Where there's the path through the lilac clover I told you about," Rogget said.

"It's the first place you go when you're banished from the Ruud," Pinta said.

"There's a board there where the kings have their decrees posted," Havert said.

"Yes, yes." Pinta rolled her eyes. "We haven't had a traveler through in months. But we rarely get a writ freeing anyone, anyway."

"It's good to have hope," Havert said. "At least."

"Ard," Pinta said. "Hope is nothing more than the disappointment that follows. Hollow. And unnecessary."

This reminded Fenn of Forbes. "Is there a Lil Billings living here?"

"Ah, Lil and her writ. Talk about hope." Pinta laughed. She finished pressing her bits of poultice onto Sadie's spots and ladled water out of a barrel. Rogget helped Sadie to sit up and she drank a few sips before smiling weakly and lying back down.

"Lil Billings lives over in a little plot yonder south a bit. She's got too many of us believing her husband's got a writ to set us all free. Any day now, she tells us."

"Do you read? Either of you?" Havert said.

Grayson nodded.

"Are you feeling better, Sadie?" Fenn asked when she rolled over onto her side to listen to their conversation.

"A little."

"She could use some meat." Pinta looked at Rogget. "But that's a rare treat around here."

"Aye," he said. "Meat. If you're of a mind to stay with these kind folk for a time," he said to Fenn, "I'll take the evening and try some hunting."

"They're fine. No harm will come to them in our little village. You'll have to travel far into the hills yonder for anything much."

"I'll bring us all back some juicy rabbit." Rogget adjusted his sack and patted the sheath at his hip. "Sadie will be back to strength in no time."

"Yes, go hunting. But you boys, come out and read for us," Havert said.

Fenn and Grayson followed Rogget out of the hut with Havert and bade him a good hunt.

"What is it you want us to read?" Grayson asked.

"This way, this way." The old man hobbled slowly across the dirt road through the town to another hut. "We keep them in my house, in a box."

"What do you keep?" Fenn said.

"Writs. The last we got we haven't read yet."

"No one here can read?" Grayson said.

"No, not a one. Well, there's a woman over to the river in the mountains, but it's a long trek to see her."

They entered Havert's tiny hut, made of logs without any material packed between; sunlight streamed in lines across the floor.

He pointed to a wooden chest. "There she is. Filled with writs." He lifted the lid and pulled several decrees from kings written on fine parchment. "These we got more than a month ago and we've had no one visit yet who could read them."

Grayson took the papers and looked at them with a frown. "From the stationers in the realms of the Ruud." He looked up to Havert. "Most of these are notices of property being seized."

Harvert frowned and nodded. "Aye. We get a lot of that. If you're not there to fight for it, they take it from you. You don't have to read those. No sense spreading bad news."

"But this one is for a Kindred Aldrick. It's a pass."

"A what?" Fenn said.

"He's allowed to go home for a short time."

"Oh, wonderful, wonderful." Havert clapped his hands together. "You see? We sometimes get good news. Let's go, let's go." He danced out of the hut and back into the dusty little village square. The boys followed, Grayson still holding the writ.

"Kindred, where's Kindred? He's got a pass."

Pinta came out of her hut. "Quiet down, Havert. The girl is resting. What's this all about?"

"Kindred has a pass."

"Is that so?"

"You called me?" A scrawny, bearded man hobbled toward them.

"Yes, Kindred. A writ for you. A pass. Read it to him, read it!" Havert slapped Grayson on the shoulder and shoved him gently toward Kindred.

Grayson nodded, nervous, and read, "Proclamation from Evan, King of Michelruud, attested by Ricker, King of Damon Wall. Kindred Aldrick, thief and liar, banished to the wasteland from his home in Damon Wall for a term of forty years, is hereby granted pass to return to the aid of his ailing parents."

The man shuffled his feet to and fro and cleared his throat with a rough cough.

"Aye," Kindred said. "Thank ye." He turned to leave.

"Don't you want it?" Fenn asked him.

"Nah," he said. "My daughter Lisha came here nigh on a month ago on her way north to join her sister. She told me my parents had passed into the ether."

"But, it's a pass," Fenn said. "Can't you use it to go home."

"It only says I'm granted a pass to see to my folks. They're gone. If I'd use it to get back home now—well, I'm not going to chance that."

"He's right," Grayson said. "It's not a pardon."

Aldrick nodded and left.

"But—" Fenn started after him and Pinta put a hand on his arm.

"There's nothing you can do to help us, boy. Come sit with your friend a while."

Sadie slept on the floor, her body occasionally jerking as if she were being stung again. Grayson and Fenn sat with Pinta as she cleaned out her bowls and mortar and packed away her goods.

"What did you do to be banished, Ma'am Pinta," Fenn asked quietly.

Grayson glared at him.

"If you don't mind my asking, I mean."

"Oh, no. Mine's a funny story. You'll enjoy it." She chuckled and shook her head as if lost in memory for a time.

"My family had all gone. My two sons were lost at sea— hadn't heard from them in nigh onto fifteen years. Their pa drowned when he fell from a fishing boat many, many years ago. And my daughter, poor darling, succumbed to the gasping fever shortly after she was born. So, I had no one and I thought to myself one day—I thought I'd come out to the wastelands with Father Britt and see to the sick in Banished. Father Britt introduced me to Father Wold, he was a banished wissende. He and I tended to the folk here."

"So you aren't banished?"

"No, it's not so boring a story as that. No, you see. We were plagued by a bit of the gasping fever and there were a few women who had babes. I knew I needed more orange root and spirim, and the only place I knew to find it growing free was in Timber at the outskirts of the western wood. So, I went to get some. But it had already been foraged. So I asked the apothecary in Timber if he could spare some. I had no money, so he chased me off. I managed to get some from the kind apothecary in Path on my way back. I came home, treated the sick and thought no more of it. Until some time later, a traveler from Ousted brought a writ declaring me banished."

She paused and Fenn said, "But why?"

Sighing, Pinta shrugged. She reached behind the chest of herbs and remedies and pulled a bag onto her lap. From inside, she found a yellowed, folded writ from the king.

"I'm told it says here, for willfully and recklessly spreading the gasping fever to the family of the apothecary in Timber, resulting in the death of his young son."

She handed the writ to Grayson and he nodded as he read it. "But, did you have the fever?"

"I never got sick."

"Father Treacher could have defended you at a court, at the meeting place," Fenn said.

Pinta laughed. "Maybe so. But as I'd already been banished, I couldn't go back home to try. And no court would have been allowed after the fact, anyway. They accused me and held that I was absent and so found me guilty without representation and no need of court."

"Can they do that?" Fenn said.

"Apparently."

Chapter Twenty-eight

L eah had been given a few sips of water and a biscuit, her hands unbound, and was now being escorted out of the forest. Only the brownie Kwitcher had been allowed to accompany the centaur Red Lichen, as the others could not stop arguing for her death. Her throat remained parched and her stomach growled occasionally, tightening itself into empty knots; her knees wobbled and threatened to give out several times. She struggled to make it out of the forest, fearing if she fell, her captors would leave her where she lay—and at the mercy of the brownies. She had never realized before how vicious brownies could be.

Red Lichen halted in front of her and held up his hand to have her stop. Kwitcher walked into the back of her knees.

"Apologies," he said.

"Shh." Red Lichen put a finger to his lips.

Ahead, Leah heard the crunching of needles on the forest floor and the brushing of shrub branches. A young, frail folk emerged from the wood. It was the boy she'd caught spying on Lord Kirche's meeting with Sorgood in the woods just outside Aaronland some days ago. His face, upon seeing her, told Leah she must look dreadful.

"Lucas," Red Lichen said. "You tramp through the woods like a boar. Have you no sense of stealth?"

"This is my forest, is it not?" he said, his concerned eyes still on Leah. "I have nothing to fear here."

They all stood silent for a moment staring at one another.

"What's this?" Lucas pointed at Leah.

"We are escorting her from the forest. It's a long story."

"I've heard some of it," he said. "I will join you. I am Lucas of the wissenry at Path."

"Leah." Her parched voice was barely a whisper.

"You are with the Hass."

Leah nodded. As they hiked through the wood toward the border at Timber where Kirche had attacked the brownies, Lucas told them that he'd heard there was trouble in the forest.

"The brownies are tightly knit," he said to Leah. "Among their various communities—except, of course, there is animosity between the displaced and woodland."

"Dirty, backward sorts," Kwitcher grumbled.

Leah nodded, not really understanding or caring what Lucas was saying.

"A few in Aaronland told me I was needed—that one of the Hass had been captured and their representatives were calling for her death."

"Dag Voorspeld has granted her reprieve," Red Lichen said.

"On what condition?"

"She claims to know of the kell stone."

"Is this true?" he asked her.

Leah nodded. Lucas looked at her carefully as they walked and she felt as if he knew she had lied. She was unsure why the beast lord had not known it. In his lair, Voorspeld had commanded that her hands be unbound. She was led to the boulder and stood staring at it, trembling with fear. She could hear Voorspeld purring, even in his folk form—an echoing, resonating hum—as he approached her.

"Drop your beloved into the pool," he'd said.

Leah shook her head and tears formed in her eyes. "I don't know what you mean."

"What is it that you cherish?"

She thought about it for a few seconds. "My mother. My father."

"What is your beloved?"

He was insistent, angry, and yet, a weariness tinged his words. Even in folk form, his smooth voice shuddered through her chest. It reminded her of Kirche's soothing speech and yet, she found herself trusting in Voorspeld—his was real and not rehearsed.

What did she cherish? Leah's chin fell to her chest and she closed her eyes; her cheeks burned hot with shame. "My hair," she said.

"Drop your beloved into the pool."

She slid her trembling hands along her head, gathering her locks at the nape of her neck and pulled them over her left shoulder. Kneeling on the ground, she let her hair fall into the water in the basin. While she knelt there, shadows emerged and mingled with the water falling over the face of the rock and Voorspeld stared down at her, then at the shadows, and back, as if reading her thoughts.

"She promised Voorspeld she would return with the stone," Red Lichen said.

"There is more," Kwitcher said. "She is to return the head of Zeelif to his tribe."

"And how will you do that?" Lucas asked her.

"They are to wait in the woods behind the inn tonight." She coughed.

Lucas pulled a canteen from under his tunic, popped out the cork and handed it to her.

"Drink," he said.

"Much obliged." She tried not to appear greedy as she

swallowed several times. "Thank you."

"You may keep it, while we walk," he told her. "You are in more need of it than I."

Leah wished she could stop herself from finishing off Lucas' water, but was unable. She wanted to ask him who he was and what link he had with the beasts and their forest—she suspected he was one of the felidae, like she'd read about in the *Book of Katze*—but as captive, she felt it better to keep quiet. If she could only make it out of the forest and away from them, she would finally feel that her life was no longer in danger.

"The Hass has often had deadly run-ins with our kind," Lucas told her as they hiked. "They've killed felidae, centaurs, wolves. But never the little ones. We heard that your Kirche has been seen trying to hunt the brownies in years past, but he was unsuccessful. They aren't difficult to sneak up on, as they become engrossed in their digging for morels."

"We do concentrate," Kwitcher said.

"His efficiency at the hunt as apparently increased," Red Lichen said.

"He had help," Leah said. "From a folk called Sorgood. It was Sorgood who led him to the brownie."

Lucas nodded as if he knew of Sorgood already. "Here we are."

They pushed through the trees to the edge of the beast forest to look upon the plain of Timber. Leah found herself confronted by two folk on horseback surrounded by a dozen archers.

"There she is," Prenalin called out and the archers raised their bows.

"Frieden?" The king of Michelruud, sitting atop a horse beside Prenalin, gazed in shock at their party.

As the archers drew back their bows, Leah stepped in front of the group and put her arms wide.

"Please don't hurt them," she said. "They have escorted me

out of the forest."

Prenalin dismounted his steed and ran toward her as Lucas, Red Lichen, and Kwitcher fled back into the forest. She fell as he met her and he lifted her into his arms, carrying her to his horse.

"Are you all right?" he said, clearly shaken.

"What have they done to you?" King Welk said when she found her seat on Prenalin's horse.

"Nothing more than I deserved." Tears fell down her cheeks, stinging her wounds. "It was revenge for the murder of one of their brownies. They did not hurt me without reason."

"You give them too much credit." Prenalin gazed up at her. "They should be punished."

"No, please. It would only lead to more fighting and more death."

King Welk nodded at Prenalin. "And what of the guard who was trampled? Does Kirche have plans to retaliate?"

"He has not confided any to me."

"Well, then, I am happy to have helped you, if only by lending you my horse. Let the girl ride back to the inn with you. I'll send someone for the horse later."

"Thank you, kindly, your Highness."

Prenalin climbed onto the horse behind her and spurred it toward Path at a lope.

"Are you sure you're all right?"

"I'm bruised."

"And bloodied."

"It probably looks much worse than it feels."

"Let us hope so."

"Will Alphonse be all right? Was he badly hurt?"

"Alphonse died of his wounds this morning. Kirche has already sent his body off to the port to be shipped home."

"I'm sorry." Leah thought back to the brief attack, and watching Alphonse trampled under the hooves of the centaur.

She could not say if it had been purposeful or malicious. But it seemed at the time that the beasts intended only to protect the brownies. Though their response to her in the forest brought her many doubts.

"Will the soldiers of Ruhm come to the Ruud and kill all the beasts?" she asked.

"What on earth for?"

"But Kirche said, if they dared to harm a folk..."

Prenalin chuckled. "You put too much stock in Kirche's declarations. But he will remember what has taken place here, and use it when he will."

"You engaged the king of Michelruud in my rescue?"

"Indeed. Though he was against it when we first approached him. He believed that you were likely lost forever, led over the falls to the mermaids or worse."

"But you persuaded him?"

"I did." His voice behind her sounded grave with concern. Leah breathed finally—a deep sigh of relief.

"And Lord Kirche, he stayed behind at the inn?"

"A rescue was much too dangerous for the Lord. But he was certainly for it. It was his idea, actually. At least...he didn't need to be convinced."

Once they reached the inn at Path, the others rejoiced in her return. Gretchen babbled continuously as she put an arm around Leah and led her to a chair in the front room where the thick *History of the Ruud* sat on its dusty perch. Zelda produced a ribbon and handed it to Leah, knowing she could not touch her hair.

"Prenalin, go and ask for Leah's room once again," Kirche said and then smiled down at Leah as she worked her hair smooth and tied it. "You look like death has tortured you. I hope you aren't permanently disfigured. We thought you gone forever, I'm afraid—knowing the murderous nature of the beast. We emptied your room and Zelda took possession of all your

180

things. We'll have them back to you immediately."

"Yes, of course," Zelda bowed. "I'll run gather them now."

"Thank you," she said. "For coming for me."

Kirche laughed. "Prenalin would hear of nothing else. Insisted you still lived as if he was connected to you by telepathy. I told him we had no army with which to fight and he was bold enough to suggest asking the king, of all things. But it worked after all, didn't it?"

"I'm so sorry to hear about Alphonse."

"Ah, well." Kirche pulled his mouth into a deep frown. "Such are the dangers of the hunt."

Prenalin returned with her room assignment. "We weren't needed after all," he told Kirche. "She was emerging from the wood when we approached."

"See then?" Kirche said. "Much ado for nothing, as I said. But no matter. Our main business has done and we are off for adventures now. So, you didn't cause us any great delay."

"For that I am grateful, Lord Kirche." Leah smiled as best she could.

Chapter Twenty-nine

Welk returned to the castle at Michelruud and was forced to regale his cousins with the story of his brave rescue of the fair damsel in distress. He embellished as much as he dared, to make the story more interesting than it had turned out to be, but only a little. He was anxious to get back to his chambers and finish his reading of the history.

When he finally closed the heavy tome and lifted it with a heave back onto the table by the fire, he rubbed his eyes and let his hands remain against his face for some time. Finally, he pulled them away and blinked into the flames. The warmth of his chambers had left him; he was cold. He ground his teeth together unconsciously, seething with anger at his ancestors. Fools!

How could wissendes of science and logic have been so overcome with fear and suspicion that they would act with such vile against the beast? He could accept the behavior of the Hass for stealing the stone in the first place and casting the beast folk into confusion and despair. The Hass, after all, were always leading with their fears and insecurities and forever, it seems, hated the beast.

How Welk had applauded the story of the great wissende

Michelruud, discovering the kell stone in the mines of Galdred in the west, risking his own life and those of his followers to steal it, escaping the Hass and sailing off to return the stone to the beast Rad. How his chest had filled with pride in reading that part—only to deflate into shame.

Thousands of years of cooperation among the various beast folk, cast away—their traditions thrown asunder and all because of mortal folk. It was no wonder to Welk, now, why the beast despised them so. His disgust at Michelruud, so easily persuaded by a crown and a castle, was strongest in his heart. The folk quest for power was only won by demeaning and dismantling that of the beast.

Anfang's words now made sense to Welk. He longed for a redeemer, to find the stone and return the Rad to power for the beast. But it was clear that the folk of the Ruud were justified in their fears. If the history was correct, once the kell stone is returned to the beast Rad, the folk are likely to be overcome and their lands retaken, cast off the continent with nowhere to go but back to their motherland and the Hass of Emorah.

Welk remembered Kirche and his desperation for the stone. Kirche and the Hass would not want the beast returned to power, even here in the east. No, the Hass want the stone to remain with the folk. And now it was clear why Ruhm had let the Ruud survive on its own for so many hundreds of years. They wanted, above all, to keep the beast inferior.

Welk sighed. He must find Fenn Foster of the wissenry. The mark! How could he have been so wrong about it? Why did Rue-Anna not tell him what it meant? They were too busy with forbidden love and defying their parents' kingdoms to bother themselves with matters of history. But now he understood. He alone, it seemed, knew who Fenn Foster truly was.

He needed advice. Welk needed to find the only person left in the world whom he could trust. And that task would not be an easy one. Luckily, the emissaries of the usurper queen of the ice realm had given him a reason to take control of the hill country without raising suspicion.

Chapter Thirty

Leah allowed Gretchen to help her up the stairs while Kirche and Prenalin remained in the dining area. Dowling was called to assist her in a bath in the bathing chamber. Leah knew the instant she saw Dowling's face that she must, indeed, look of death. The crotchety old woman nearly cried.

"Is it all that terrible?"

"Oh, miss," Dowling said. "Let's clean you up."

The bath chamber was on the second floor with a flume to the outside in which the used bath water was poured. But each bucket of fresh water had to be pumped from the well behind the inn, warmed over the fire, and carried up the stairs. While the tub was being filled, Dowling sat her in a chair, left and returned with a tray full of towels, soaps, and ointments.

"First, we must clean your wounds. Try not to flinch too much."

Dowling soaked a cloth in warm soapy water and gently dabbed at Leah's face. She winced at the stinging. The wound on her forehead thudded a dull ache through her head.

"We'll put the ointments on after your bath."

Leah stripped to her under slip and with Dowling's help, climbed into the tub of warm water. Her aching body tingled and relaxed.

"Miss, I'm afraid your hair will need washing. There is blood. I know I am not allowed to touch it."

"It's all right; I'll do it."

It took much of Leah's strength to lift her arms to scrub her scalp. She ducked under the water for a quick rinse, then stood and let Dowling climb on a stool to pour buckets of clean, warm water over her. She pulled the water out of her hair, wrung out her under slip, and climbed gingerly out of the tub.

Once in her room, she noticed immediately that Dowling had covered the looking glass with a bed sheet.

"No sense having a look until you heal up a bit, miss."

Behind the dressing screen, she pulled off her wet slip and put on her night shirt. Every muscle in her body demanded she stay still as she let Dowling help her into the soft bed.

"I'll be back shortly to dress your wounds."

After Dowling left, Leah turned to look at the mirror in the corner. How bad could it be? She crawled out of the bed and carried a candle to the looking glass. Lifting the sheet, Leah gasped at her reflection. Eerie shadows cast by the candle highlighted her swollen right cheek and brow. A red gash on her right forehead ran ragged to her hairline; both cheeks were lined with cuts and her right upper lip was fat and grotesque. She let the sheet drop and made her way back to the comfort of the pillow and blankets.

Dowling returned with another tray and set it on the table by the bed. On it was a teacup, on a saucer, with a string hanging over the rim, and a small brown packet of paper.

Seeing the packet, Leah said, "I do not wish to be anesthetized."

"No worry, miss, this is only willow bark, for the tea. It will help ease your pain."

She watched as Dowling pulled open the packet and poured pale, ground willow bark into the tea and stirred. Holding the teacup out to her, the woman said, "Drink it, you'll see."

Leah sipped the warm tea and grimaced. Dowling laughed. "Ah, well, it's an acquired taste."

After forcing her into several more sips of tea, Dowling had her rest her head on the fluffed up pillows while she dabbed ointments on her forehead, cheeks, and upper lip. She gently pressed gauzy fabric over each wound and told Leah to finish the tea before she came back with her dinner.

"You must eat, miss," Dowling said when she returned with food. "And then you must sleep."

After eating, Leah requested more candles and promised she would sleep.

"The dark," she lied, lying coming easier and easier. "I'll sleep better with some light."

But instead, she sat at her desk, despite her aches, writing in her journal, waiting until the wee hours when she must fulfil her promise to Voorspeld and the brownies. Certainly, it was the only promise she could keep.

How would she ever find Dakenruud's journal? And even if it did reveal the location of the kell stone, how could she possibly get to it? It was most likely hidden deep in the kell somewhere, perhaps in the Ruud, but no doubt in a spot inaccessible to adventure seekers, much less a young girl of Ruhm. Even if she could get to it, she would certainly be found out by someone— Lord Kirche, probably, as he was looking for it as well.

No. Leah had told a terrible lie and she knew she'd have to get back home and hide forever from the beasts of the eastern continent. One thing she couldn't fathom, however, was why Voorspeld had believed her.

She shook her head at the thought and nearly dozed off writing mid-sentence. She darted awake when the picture of the flaming tree of Rett came back to her; she could still feel its rough trunk at her back as she lay huddled against it, believing she would die there at its base. Suddenly she realized all was quiet in the inn.

She extinguished the desk candle, stood, wrapped her robe and tied it tightly at the waist, slid her feet into her slippers, and snuck downstairs.

The inn was dark as pitch. She was lucky to know that at the foot of the stairs there would be a clear path to the left, straight to the back door. She'd seen the latch lifted before and found it easily, sliding it up slowly and quietly. Pushing open the door, she let the latch drop so that it would hold the door open for her.

Leah was glad for the moonlight as she left the steps for the ground, grabbed at the stick that held Zeelif's now dried, dismembered head, and carried it into the woods behind the inn, forcing herself not to look at it. She was met by four brownies, glaring at her, tapping their tiny feet on the ground.

"Took long enough," one said.

The others hissed, "Murderer."

The largest of them took Zeelif's head and cradled it in his arms, then turned to her and spat. "Get back to the safety of your inn, mortal, before we stone you to death right here."

"Murderer," they called after her as she stumbled back to the door and ran into Dowling, knocking them both to the ground.

Chapter Thirty-one

Fenn woke once, in darkness, grasping for his lost charm, and realized he was in Pinta's hut in Banished; he let himself drift into sleep again. Rousing himself in the dim morning light, he heard Sadie and Grayson outside the hut talking in low voices. He pushed aside the fabric covering the doorway to join them.

They sat at Pinta's fire pit eating apples and hard biscuits. Sadie's marks were barely pink now and no longer swollen. Pinta was cooking in a pot over the fire and the smell of warm bread and gravy wafted to his nose.

Taking a seat next to Grayson, he said, "All better?"

"Oh, she'll be fine. Weak for a while," Pinta said. "She's lucky. She told me that she smacked a fairy bee and started dancing around. It's no wonder she was stung so many times."

"Pinta says that the fairy bees aren't really vicious," Grayson said.

"But you read about them," Sadie said.

"All I know is what it says in the encyclopedia."

"So," Sadie scooted herself around to face Grayson. "You're telling me that not everything in the encyclopedia is true?"

"Not vicious at all," Pinta interrupted. "Just frightened. Any time you cross the clover, except at night, you'll get stung once or twice. It's a warning is all. Learn to be calm, like an eis, and they'll let you cross."

"Like an eis?" Fenn said.

"Aye, the eis are very calm folk."

"What good are books if you can't trust them?" Sadie said.

"Just because you hear one little thing in the encyclopedia might be wrong, you're ready to toss all the books in the trash?" Grayson said.

"I didn't say that. I'm just learning to be skeptical is all."

"Nothing wrong with that," Fenn said.

"Take a plate." Pinta handed Fenn a few cracked pieces of ceramic. "And a slice of bread. We've got gravy for sopping."

"Where do you all find food?" Fenn asked, taking the bread from Pinta.

"We have little plots. Some of us are strong enough to hunt and share our take. But only once in a great while. We get rabbit, squirrel, and sometimes a boar. We have vegetables and some corn and wheat. We make our own flour."

Fenn raised his eyebrows at her.

"It's true. We don't starve. But we have to cooperate. And of course, we get folk from home on visit sometimes and they bring what they can—and folk travel through willing to trade."

"What do you have to trade?" Sadie asked and Grayson nudged her with a stern look. "What? I'm just asking."

"It's rude."

"Aw, that's all right," Pinta said. "We have our small crops, of course, and we make things. Jonesy has actually managed some fine mud pottery and every so often we get emissaries from the royals out to trade for 'em."

Fenn glanced quickly at the others, hoping they caught that as well. They would not be able to stay here long if any of the Ruud folk might happen along.

"It's a hard life, 'tis true," she said. "But we do what we can."

Fenn thought of Forbes Billings and his writ. If only it were real, all these folk could be freed. What could have been the harm in at least trying?

"What about Lil Billings and the writ?" he asked.

Pinta laughed and shook her head. "Waiting Lil, we call her. She thinks one day we'll all be going home—free as roster fiends in the sky."

"So, you don't believe there is a writ?"

"Writ, schmidt. No king would ever honor such a flimsy thing, if she had one. Don't worry about Waiting Lil. She'll come to terms soon enough. But if that husband o' hers dares to come back stirring us all up again, there'll be some sparring, no doubt."

"I was born in the wasteland," Fenn said, without thinking.

"Were you now?"

He nodded. "I was hoping I could find my nurse. Her name was Clara."

Pinta closed up her eyes and twisted her lips in thought. "There was a Clara out in Chosen, I think. Yes. She was a nurse. Worked with Father Wold for a time."

"That would be her." He jolted with excitement. "I need to get to Chosen."

"Leaving already?" Pinta said. "You should stay. It's dangerous for children wandering about the wasteland."

Fenn nodded politely. "I'm sorry, but I have a lot of exploring to do."

"Sadie at least should stay and rest."

"I'll stay behind," Sadie said. "I feel better, but I don't think I can walk very far yet. You and Grayson go off to Chosen."

"We can't leave you here alone," Grayson said.

"Maybe Rogget will stay with Sadie."

"Ard, what's that?" Rogget came around from behind Pinta's tent carrying three dead rabbits and two squirrels from his rope. "You want me to do what?"

Pinta smiled. "Come on over and join us."

"I've got some bitters if you've got water and a pot." Rogget smiled setting aside his game, shrugging off his pack and rubbing his hands together over the small flame.

"Bitters, now! I haven't had the bitters in forever, not since that fancy man in purple rode through about this time last year."

Rogget prepared a pot to boil their bitters and gratefully took a biscuit.

"Sadie needs to stay and rest while Grayson and I find Chosen," Fenn said. "You can stay with her."

"Hold on, there. I can't let you two go off alone in the wasteland."

"We can protect Sadie," Pinta said. "You boys go off and find Chosen. I can tell you where it is. It won't take but a half day to hike over."

Sadie looked stricken. "I'm not sure I want to stay here by myself."

Grayson sighed. "I'll stay with Sadie, then."

Pinta clapped her hands together. "It will be wonderful to have children about for a while."

"I'll try to teach you some reading," Grayson said to Pinta. "I'll try to teach everyone. To read their names, at least."

"And the words on a pardon," Fenn said.

He nodded. "Exactly."

"You can't teach folk to read in just a few days," Sadie said.

Grayson looked at the ground. "Maybe I should stay longer, then. Maybe I'm needed here."

"I didn't mean that," Sadie said. "I don't want you to stay here alone. And I don't want to stay. I want to go with Fenn to the ice realm."

They each looked quickly at Fenn, then Rogget, then Pinta. All their eyes were round except hers. She looked at them curiously.

"The ice realm? What sort of adventure are you on, anyway?"

"It's a dangerous one, Ma'am," Rogget said. "But very important."

She nodded. "I suppose that's why you're traveling about with three reading children. It must be a great mission for the kings."

"Aye," Rogget said. "But it's a very secret one as well. The children aren't so practiced at keeping secrets as at their other skills. We'd be pleased if you wouldn't spread the word to none of the guard."

She raised her head and looked down her nose at the three of them and then smiled and nodded at Rogget. "Aye, I'll be keeping my mouth shut. Of that you can be certain."

"But what about the situation here?" Grayson's voice held a hint of desperation. "We can't just leave this the way it is."

"Help me to write a proposal to the kings," Pinta said. "We can ask for a reader and a writer to visit on occasion."

"Would the kings offer help to you?" Grayson asked.

She shrugged.

"King Welk might be of a mind to be kind," Rogget said. "Being new and all."

"King Welk?" Pinta said.

"Aye, Evan the Fearsome is dead. His son Welk has the throne."

"Evan dead?" Pinta said. "I thought I heard long peeling of bells some time ago, come right over the wind, ever so faint. That must be why Lil Billings has been smiling so much more of late."

"Ah, about that writ," Rogget said. "Don't let her be getting your hopes up. I have it on good gossip that the writ's been—"

"Rogget," Sadie said.

"Oh, aye. It's all for Forbes Billings to explain."

"Any news of Elrundt?" Pinta broke in as if she hadn't been listening to them. "Now that his father's passed into the ether?"

"Elrundt?" Fenn said.

"Aye, Welk's younger brother, disappeared many a year ago

195

after a row with his father. Any news?"

Rogget shook his head with a sly smile. "None ma'am. No news to be told there."

Fenn caught Rogget's brief glance and crinkled his brow. What was this about? Maybe Ma'am Stationer was right after all and there was a Prince Elrundt. But what would Rogget know about it? So many curiosities and questions to keep track of these days; he couldn't keep them all in his head.

"Yes, as you were saying," Pinta said. "Now would be the time for Forbes Billings to show up and get us all afluster again. I told the children I'd do him harm if he did."

"Ard, no worries there, ma'am. We put him to rights," Rogget said.

"You know him?"

"Long time friend."

"Maybe we'll meet Waiting Lil on our way to Chosen," Fenn said, hoping to end the talking and move on. He felt as if Clara was calling him to hurry.

"No, no," Pinta said. "It's the other direction."

Rogget left his rabbits and squirrels with Pinta for Sadie and to share with the village and in exchange, she'd given them dried apple slices and flat bread for their journey. They headed northeast just as Pinta had told them and hiked the flat rocky plains of the wasteland until, well after noon, they came upon a tiny village nestled up against a wood.

A few huts were neighbored by brick and wood buildings. Smoke poofed out of chimneys. A well sat in the center of the hut circle and folk went about their business, staring at them.

"New?" A man approached them, carrying a small wood pail.

"We're looking for Clara," Fenn said.

The man tilted his head at them then turned and spit into the bucket. "Seems quite a few folk are looking for Clara these days."

"Who else?" Rogget said.

"Soldiers."

"What would soldiers be wanting with an old lady?"

The old man smiled slyly. "It was the stories," he said. "Of the bairn. She lives out by the creek in the woods."

They hiked through the tiny village and over a slight ridge into the brief wood. They could hear the creek tinkling its way around them when they came to a clearing where a little cabin sat on the edge of the water. Fenn's heart pounded and he began to tremble.

"Well, come on," Rogget said. "We didn't come all this way to stand and gawk."

For a few moments, he couldn't move and stood trying to concentrate on the breeze rushing through the pines overhead. Finally, he managed to breathe, and walked to the door and knocked.

A woman, wearing an apron, and holding a damp towel, opened the door. She smiled at them and nodded.

"Clara?" Fenn said, his voice cracking.

She shook her head and motioned for them to enter the hut.

"I'll stay outside, if you don't mind," Rogget said.

"Are you sure?"

He nodded.

Fenn entered the dark hut and stood for a second letting his eyes adjust. The lady who answered the door took his arm and led him over to a bed in the corner. Lying there, propped up on two pillows, was a tiny, frail, old woman. She lay with her eyes closed and her mouth open and Fenn thought at first she was dead and took a step backward. But the lady patted the old woman on the arm and sat Fenn down beside her on a tall stool.

Clara opened her eyes and looked at Fenn. She closed her mouth and swallowed.

"Well, what is it? What do you want?" she said. Her voice was dry and scratchy.

"I..." Fenn couldn't remember what he'd come for at first and stared at her. Finally, he said, "I'm looking for my mother."

"Eh? What's that? Are you speaking?"

Fenn raised his voice. "I'm looking for my mother."

"Well, it ain't me." Clara closed her eyes again.

"But you knew my mother," he said. "You were my nurse."

She opened her eyes and looking up to the ceiling, shook her head. "I was only nurse to one child," she said. "It was long ago after my man and child died here in the wasteland. Father Wold came to me with a young woman." She stopped talking and peered at the ceiling for a long moment. "She was dressed all in white, like an angel," she said. "I was to tend to her. But she faded away so quickly after her bairn came into the world."

"Was that my mother?"

Clara turned her head to him, but instead of looking at his face, looked at his chest. "Do you have the charm?"

"Yes," he said, excited. "I have the charm." He reached for his neck and grappled for it until he realized it was gone. "But it was stolen," he said.

Clara turned away. "The child I nursed would have his charm."

"I did have it. It had a dragonfly on it. And the letters A, o, and E on the back. Can you tell me about it? Would you tell me who my mother was?"

She wouldn't look at him. "I can't tell you anything until I can feel the charm."

Fenn felt tears burning at his eyes and forced them away.

"Fine then," he said. "I'll go get it back and I'll bring it to you."

Clara closed her eyes, a frown at her lips. "You do that."

"But," he stammered. "But you don't know how hard it was just to get here. My friend even got stung all over by fairy bees—"

"Fairy bees? If you are the bairn I nursed, you'd have no trouble with fairy bees."

"Fine, fine," he said. "I'll go all the way back to the hill country and steal it back from the gang of thieves who took it from me."

"I'll be here. I'm not going anywhere."

Fenn sat staring at her, his mind searching for a better way. How could he get his charm back from Clutch? It was impossible. Suddenly, he thought, if he touched her, like he touched Clutch, maybe he would become her and know what she knew. He reached out his hand and put it gently on her arm. It was bony and thin and cold under her night shirt and he pulled his hand away. She did know something, but he felt as if he'd have to squeeze her to find out and she was too frail; he felt he'd break her if he tried.

He came out of the dark hut, squinting into the afternoon light, to find Rogget in the back yard tossing stones into the creek.

"Well?" he said.

"I have to find my charm," Fenn said sadly. "She won't tell me anything until she sees it."

Rogget nodded and paused for a moment before mumbling, "So, I'm thinking you're getting ready to take me into more trouble."

Fenn nodded and Rogget let out a chuckle.

Chapter Thirty-two

Lucas sat at a table in a dark corner of Dylan's Tavern at Cold Sea Port, keeping his hood pulled well over the top of his face. The bar was crowded as patrons drank and yelled and sloshed ale over the tops of their pitchers. Frantic waiters fought through the maze of folk with trays held high above their heads, serving those at table in the bustling lamplit pub.

"They've chased him out of the Ruud, at least," one gruff, unshaven folk called out.

"They should have caught him and hanged him," another countered. "What good is the king's guard if they can't get their hands on a child?"

"He ain't just any child; he's the bairn. Folk say he's got beast blood in him. He's dangerous."

"Aye, they shouldn't have let him escape in the first place." The crowd roared approval.

"We should build up our own posse and head out to the hill country and drag him back for a hanging," one man said, standing up to raise his pitcher and staggering back against his stool. He was applauded.

"Hey, you! Wissende," someone called out. "You kept him

safe all these years."

Lucas looked up and saw Father Britt's terrified face as he battled through the crowd. He rose quickly and made his way across the room, took Britt by the sleeve and pulled him back toward the door.

"That is not a good spot to meet this night," Lucas said.

"The panic has made its way clear to the port. I never expected..."

"Did you not?"

"No."

Lucas glanced at him as they made their way through the streets and to the wharf. There was a quiet alehouse there, more private, with booths and curtains. Madam Henry welcomed them in and showed them to a back booth and left to get them some refreshment.

"Father Britt, why does the wissenry appear unable to come to terms with reality? Is that not the purpose of the organization?"

"Reality has, for some time, been something to be avoided."

"By the folk, perhaps, but not the wissenry."

"What would you have us do?"

"Quell the fear. Speak some reason to the folk. Tell them there is no prophecy. The future is not something that can be foretold. End this madness."

Britt wrung his hands and looked up gratefully to Madam Henry when she appeared with pitchers of ale. How old he looked, how tired and red of face. The wissendes had, over two hundred years, degenerated from men of knowledge, to men of philosophy and comfort.

"We are not equipped to deal with this. We are not the wissenry of yore. We are the wissenry of the Ruud."

Lucas took his pitcher and drank long sips and put it down again.

"I did not know you drank ale," Britt said to him.

"I thought it was about time."

"You are hardly of age."

"I am older than you think," Lucas said, surprised that they had not figured that out by then. Did they not realize that felidae mature sooner than folk? Did they not have books on studies of the beast locked away in their old cabinets below ground? What did these wissendes spend their time on these days?

Britt smiled and shook his head. "You can't be more than fourteen."

Lucas waved a hand to quiet the old man. "Take the news. I must return to the guard. The folk all over the Ruud call for Fenn's death. He traipses about the wasteland with Rogget."

"The wasteland? But he was to—"

"He knows very well what he was told to do but he does not trust the wissenry any longer. He trusts only himself and I can't say I blame him."

"We had to keep these secrets."

"That is a lie."

"He is only a boy."

"He is more than just a boy, Britt. Or did the wissenry not know?"

Britt stared blankly at him.

"It's true then. The wissenry does not know who Fenn is."

"I only know that he has a mark that says he's part beast."

"That is not what the mark means."

Britt grimaced. "Then I know nothing."

"You must know something more. Tell me."

"Well, I hardly think I ought to be sharing our knowledge with—"

"Tell me what you know."

Britt looked at him now, with a hint of fear behind his eyes. "Only that the rumors spoke of a child with a mark. We assumed it was Fenn they feared. We kept him hidden as long as we could and planned to send him far away to the south lands as soon as he was of age to travel."

Lucas sipped his ale. "All right. Listen to me. Spread the word through the wissenry. Go to your cellars and get your books and read. Read them all. If they're under lock and key, they must be read."

"You want us to read?"

"Yes. Read. If you do not understand why we are in this mess, you will be of little help when it explodes."

"You think there will be an explosion?"

"I think so, yes."

"Of what sort?"

"Of the war sort, Father. You must decide on which side you will fight. And you must be available to the folk for information. That is your role. That is the duty of the wissenry. Why have you forgotten?"

"Why do you speak this way, young Lucas? You act as if you know much more than your few years of training would grant you."

Lucas smiled at Father Britt. "That's because I stole Father Treacher's cabinet keys and read all of his books. Now, tell me about my parents."

Britt sputtered. "What?"

"That is the reason I have summoned you. Tell me what you know. Why does King Welk know my felid name?"

Britt nodded and drank more ale. "Yes, he knows you. He was a good friend to your father. Belfen wanted peace with the mortal folk and he and your mother wanted to live the old ways."

"But what happened to my parents and what does Welk have to do with it? Quarn said that my father saved Welk's life."

"Welk was to marry his eisen, Rue. His father and her mother were against it. King Evan was not a folk to be trifled with—he'd already lost one son to the eis, and he would not lose Welk, his only heir, as well. But truth be told, his man Sorgood was all too eager to teach the eis a lesson. Evan sent Sorgood and some of the guard to stop the nuptials—to separate Welk and Rue. But they went too far. They killed everyone—everyone except Welk and Elrundt."

"My parents were there?"

"Indeed. Your father was to stand up with Welk and his brother."

"Murdered on Evan's orders?"

"It is unclear what he ordered. But that was the result. I came upon the massacre the same day. Welk held you in his arms. He...he fought against allowing Quarn to take you. The beast lord was there and he gave his consent to have you raised in the old ways as your parents wanted."

"Did my father give his life for Welk's?"

"Welk tells the story that Quarn and Yew, your other uncle, fled the scene leaving your father and mother to die."

Lucas stared at Father Britt, his jaw set so tight he felt pain and slackened.

"Thank you, Father, for being truthful."

"Have you seen Fenn, then?"

"Yes. And he saw me, I'm afraid. Fenn may end this journey believing he can trust no one."

Lucas stood, tossed a few doars on the table, and left Father Britt in the small alehouse at the wharf to make his way back to Sorgood and the guard.

Chapter Thirty-three

Fenn and Rogget returned to Banished after dark to find Sadie and Grayson sitting at the fire pit in the middle of the village, surrounded by the pale, gaunt folk on mats—the fire blazing, lighting up their faces with a yellow glow.

"They've taught us all our names," Pinta said. "And the word pardon. It's a start, but we sure could use them here all the time. Still, I guess I wouldn't wish such a thing on a free young."

"But, you can leave, can't you?" Fenn asked. "There are lots of places you could go besides the Ruud."

Pinta frowned. "Perhaps. But then they'd never know if they could go home. Here, there's always hope."

"But you don't like hope," Grayson said.

"No. I've never found much to appreciate in it. But they seem to require it." She looked at Havert with a smile.

Fenn turned to Rogget and whispered, "What about Forbes writ? Maybe there's a chance."

"Don't be settin' these folks' hopes on it, Fenn. I warn you. It's a fool's desire. Aren't no king who'd honor such a promise, made in a drunken fury."

Fenn frowned. "You're right, I guess." But he felt a tugging in his heart. There ought to be a way to make a king honor his word.

Rogget preferred to sleep outside on a small patch of smooth grass just behind Pinta's hut, and they decided to join him, curled up on Pinta's rag mats lying in the dark talking long into the night. Fenn told them his plan.

"I have to get my charm back."

"From the Wretched?" Sadie said.

"I've been thinking on it," Rogget said. "The Gnome Eaters know how to find them. We could try to sneak into their camp, but we couldn't let 'em see us. It's not likely at all we'll even get into their camp. And even if we could, how could you find such a small thing. And that's assuming they haven't melted it down already. I don't think you should get your hopes up much."

Fenn shuddered at the thought of the dragonfly melting into a small pool of gold. He fell into a deep sleep and woke in the morning feeling refreshed, but lost and alone. No visions haunted him. He remembered the slender hand, and the wissende's robe. But he'd forgotten his mother's voice in his dreams. He'd spent so much time before wishing the images would stop tormenting him, but now, without them, he felt empty and incomplete. A constant tugging tore at his insides and he felt the urge always to wrap his arms about his middle and weep.

"So you are to leave us now?" Pinta said as they bid their goodbyes.

"We'll be back soon," Sadie said.

"You're sure that the fairy bees won't hurt us if we stay calm?" Fenn asked her.

"I'm sure. But here." She handed Sadie a leather pouch. "It's more poultice, already soaking and ready if you need it."

"Thank you."

Fenn could hear fear in Sadie's voice, and as they left the village behind, she asked what he knew she would.

"Are you sure we have to go through the lilac clover?"

"I need my charm. You can stay in Banished until we come

back."

"No," Grayson said. "We stick together, remember?"

"We'd be together again after I get my charm."

"Grayson's right," Rogget said. "There's still a guard out after us. We got to stay together."

"But can't we go around the clover?"

"Sadie, the bridge up north is miles out of the way." Fenn said. "And Pinta told us the bees are just scared. They don't really mean any harm."

"Tell that to my scars."

"They didn't leave scars," Grayson said. "Don't be so vain."

"I'm not being vain. It hurt. It hurt a lot. And Pinta said if they bite deep enough, they *will* leave scars."

"Well, if you hadn't flapped around like a madman, they wouldn't have stung you at all."

"I didn't know. Did you know?"

"Cut it out," Fenn said. "Anyway, even Clara told me that we should be able to calm the bees."

When they approached the stretch of clover, a sweet, heady aroma floated in the air and this time, they could see the bees hovering inches above the flowers.

"You should go back," Fenn said. "You don't have to come with me."

Sadie sucked in a loud breath. "No. We stick together. I'll stay calm."

They walked on, slowly, stepping gingerly, doing their best not to upset the bees.

"Calm, calm, calm," Sadie chanted. "I'm staying calm."

"Ouch," Grayson yelped.

"Don't slap at them," Rogget said.

"I'm not. Ouch."

"How can you not slap at it if it stings you?" Sadie said. "Calm. Calm."

"Just don't, that's all."

"Ow," Sadie stopped. "Ow. It stung me." She held up her arm and looked at the bee. About an inch long, it had a furry, golden abdomen that it wiggled back and forth teasingly, threatening another poke.

"No," Sadie scolded.

Its antennae were long and curled at the ends into spirals. The bee grabbed one in its front legs and pulled at it, letting it pop back into place before spreading its wings and flying off.

"See?" Fenn said.

"Why don't they sting you?"

"Maybe they sense that I'm a nice folk."

"Very funny. Ouch." Grayson slapped at the back of his neck. "Ouch, make them stop."

"You're egging them on, Grayson."

Sadie screamed and danced around.

"Calm down," Rogget swatted at the air. "Ouch. Darn bees."

"Stop it, you have to stay calm," Fenn shouted, as they dodged bees and slapped at themselves.

Fenn knew he had to do something. He sucked in a long deep breath and closed his eyes, letting serenity fall over him. He imagined his body as a soft yellow light; it filled his chest and his head and shot out from his outstretched hands. Joy spilled out from him and he smiled. When he finally opened his eyes, Grayson, Sadie, and Rogget were standing, staring at him, still ankle deep in the lilac clover.

"What are you doing?" Sadie asked, a smirk on her face. "Why were you walking like a grub zombie?"

"How do you know what a grub zombie walks like?" Grayson said.

"I've seen plenty of kids pretend."

"He was communing with the fairy bees."

"Ard, he's calming them down," Rogget said. "Do it some more."

"That's right," Fenn said. "They stopped stinging you didn't they? You should try some communing yourselves."

Fenn kept his hands held out in front of him, trying to recapture the feeling of light emitting from his fingertips as he plodded across the clover patch.

"Well," Sadie said. "They did stop stinging us. That much is true."

"I am *not* communing," Grayson said. "You can't make me."

They exited the other side of the clover with only a few stings for Rogget, Sadie, and Grayson.

"I guess that wasn't too awful," Sadie said. "I'm going to want that poultice later. And I don't look forward to doing it again on the way back."

"Fenn will just have to commune the bees from the start." Rogget smiled.

They crossed the bridge into the hill country where Darnit roared and charged them, nearly knocking Rogget to the ground for jerky. The hike through the hills was a pleasant one and Fenn felt almost at home. Now all he needed was his mother's charm. It pulled at him from somewhere near.

At the outskirts of the Gnome Eater's camp, Rogget called out, "Oi, there." A young guard came around a hill and waved them over.

"Back so soon, Mr. Rogget?"

"Aye, and looking for trouble."

Wiley was glad to see them and they all relaxed around his fire pit while he and Rogget drank warm bitters and they all noshed on a batch of carrot root that Bruck had just dug up.

"We'll be looking for those Wretcheds you told us about," Rogget said.

Wiley looked around at them all in disbelief, shaking his head.

"I need to get my charm back."

"Consider it gone, lad," Wiley said. "Even if they did still have the thing, you'd never be able to get it back from 'em."

"I have to try."

Wiley sighed. "It just don't seem right. I'd like to help you. But if I tell you where they are, and you should get killed, it'd be my fault."

"I'll take responsibility," Rogget said. "They're in my charge."

"Aye, you're always taking on the responsibility, even when it ain't rightly yours."

"If you don't tell us where they are, we'll just wander all over and run into them by accident. But if we know where to find them, we can sneak up on them."

Wiley nodded. "All right. I'm seeing your persuasion there." He paused. "They have a main encampment some twenty miles from here, in Arrow Valley, nestled up close to the big hills. They're surrounded by wood on three sides and they post their guards well hidden in the trees. You can't come up at 'em from the north and through the valley or they'll see you right off across the brief plain."

They were silent for a moment before Wiley went on. "There's one way, I think. If you come straight at 'em from the Ruud, 'stead of from the north or south, they don't watch as much. They're not expecting regular folk. They watch for us and hungry banished from the north; and the Breathless, and the Hunters, and sailors come from the south. But the west. No, they don't usually get anyone that way."

Rogget nodded and looked at Fenn. "Sadie and Grayson will stay here, with you," he said. "I'll go in and get your charm."

Fenn shook his head. "No. You'll never find it alone."

"I have to say," Wiley said. "The kids are smaller and lighter. If we draw the Wretched away from camp, the children could sneak in and have a look."

Rogget looked to the ground. "Aye. You're not thinking of a battle, are you?"

"No, no. More like a chase. If we go at it right, they'll chase us all the way to Cold Sea Port." Wiley smiled and chuckled.

"They'll leave a few guard behind," Rogget said. "I'll handle them while the kids find the charm." He looked back to Fenn. "You're sure this is important?"

Fenn nodded. "Very important." And for a moment he didn't feel as if he were lying. He needed the visions, for one thing. Maybe they could help him. And the fairies seemed to think if he found out who his parents were he could stop the bairn of prophecy nonsense. So, it seemed true that finding his charm was very important. But what if someone got hurt or killed? He pushed that thought away, and tried to bury it deep inside him.

That evening, the plan was set. Under cover of darkness the next night, they'd approach the Wretched from the west. The Gnome Eaters would shoot fire arrows into their encampment where they were expected to be playing cards, drinking, and carousing. The Gnome Eaters would attack until all the Wretched were joined in and then run south toward the Plains of Glisch and Cold Sea. Rogget and Darnit would tend to the guard left behind while Sadie, Grayson, and Fenn found the charm.

It could actually work, Fenn thought as they crouched behind trees in the wood outside the Wretched encampment the next night. They were staring at a sign posted at the edge of the wood—a wooden plank, stuck in the ground, painted with a red skeleton, black wavy lines rising from it, to denote a rotten, stinky corpse. Very scary, Fenn thought; very much what he'd expect from Clutch and his dirty friends. And just beyond the sign, the land sloped downward into Arrow Valley. They could see the pale glow of firelight in the dark and hear voices of men yelling and laughing. They waited.

Suddenly there was a shout of pain and anger; Fenn imagined one of the fiery arrows must have hit its target. Then screaming rang out, high-pitched and frantic. The Gnome Eaters had attacked. Fenn looked, wide-eyed and afraid, to Rogget but Rogget put a finger to his lips. Darnit sniffed and rocked his head left to right until Rogget turned to the bear with a hard stare.

Grayson and Sadie looked on, edgy and excited, but the battle raged, noisily. Finally the sounds drifted off to the south as the Gnome Eaters led the Wretched out of their camp. Rogget gave the signal and they got up and made their way quickly into the valley.

Right away, Rogget and Darnit charged into the center of the village where Rogget jumped on a guard. Fenn, Sadie, and Grayson split up and began their search. Fenn was to look for a sign of Clutch's tent. He knew it right away. It was the largest, as Wiley had said it would be, and the only one with a chair and its own fire pit out front. Stuck on a stick outside the tent entrance was a sign that read: go away. Fenn darted for it and went into the tent. He stood there in the dark before remembering the lantern. Wiley told him there would be one and had given him a pack of flint sticks. He lit the candle and replaced the glass lid, returning the lantern to its hook. Rifling through the chest in the corner, he found jewels of all sorts, but not his charm. He tore apart the bed, but nothing. He looked all over but found only other folks' lost valuables.

Outside the tent, he came across Sadie and Grayson. "Anything?" he asked. They shook their heads and they all moved on to other tents and searched some more.

Too soon, they heard voices and Rogget whistled the signal for retreat. Fenn panicked. They couldn't return yet; he hadn't found it. But Sadie grabbed at his tunic and pulled him to come along. Reluctantly, he followed. They began to run as the voices drew nearer. As Fenn passed Clutch's tent again, he caught sight of a glint of gold and turned to look. There, hanging from the arm of the wooden chair out front was his hemp braid and his gold charm, with the stone charm the children of Path had given him dangling beside it. He pulled from Sadie and ran over to grab it.

"Come on," Sadie whispered. "Come on."

"I got it," he said, smiling broadly. As he turned to flee, he tripped over a duffle and landed on the edge of Clutch's wooden chair. As he struggled to work his foot out of the duffle's straps, he saw Forbes Billings' writ in the bag. Not believing his luck, Fenn grabbed it and kicked the duffle off.

"Hurry," Grayson called.

They ran toward the wood.

"Stop!" someone shouted from behind them.

Fenn turned to see Clutch and some of the Wretched running into the encampment. They were seen. "Get 'em," Clutch yelled.

They darted into the wood and saw Rogget turning into the trees behind them with Darnit at his side. A gunshot rang out; Darnit let out a painful roar.

Chapter Thirty-four

Leah had spent the last two days resting at the inn, sometimes in her room and often downstairs in the front lobby watching the town square through the large window. This evening she curled up on her bed and gently touched her face. Her wounds were healing, soon there would be little or no sign of the attack; but her soul was forever scarred.

Opening her journal, she wrote, as writing was the only thing that brought her relief from her anguish. There was no one here in the Ruud in whom she could confide. She'd begun her journey wanting nothing more than a coveted post within the inner circle of Hass. Neither Prenalin, nor Kirche seemed unhappy with her; she had no reason to think she could not still become historian if she worked at it. But she was no longer sure she wanted it. Kirche as always, from the time Leah was a young teenager pining after him from afar, was a beacon of all that was kind and beautiful. But up close, his goodness was turning out to be questionable—on the improper side of questionable, truth be told. His practiced smoothness was more facade than real; and his disregard for the beasts cruel, more than ignorant. Whenever she was in his presence of late, she struggled not to look upon him as if he were a murderer.

And now that she had seen the flaming tree of Rett in the beast forest, and knew the *Book of Rett* to be incorrect, at least on that point, she imagined Kirche and the devotion taught to her by the Hass of Emorah to be parallel—both well-crafted, partly good, but also false and cruel.

It was long past time for sleep when she heard a light rap on the door.

"Are you awake, miss?" Dowling whispered.

"Yes, I'm awake."

Dowling pushed open the door and peered in. "I saw the candle light under the door and hoped you were awake. May we come in?"

The door opened wider and young Matilda Steppe wandered into the room looking around, her dark red curls bouncing about her shoulders. Her left arm was in a sling and she wore her nightgown. When she caught sight of Leah sitting up against the pillows on her bed, her eyes opened wide.

"Did you fall down the stairs, too?"

Leah chuckled. "No, I fell on some rocks."

"The child couldn't sleep," Dowling said. "I thought you two might like to meet."

She made the introductions and Leah said, "It's a pleasure. Would you like to sit on the bed."

"Careful," Dowling warned as Matilda climbed onto the bed and bounced.

"Does Dowling make you drink the willow bark tea?" Matilda said.

"Yes, she does."

"She says we'll get used to it." The child rolled her eyes, opened her mouth wide and stuck her finger in, pretending to gag. "It tastes terrible."

"How is your arm feeling?"

"It's sore sometimes. But I'll be fine."

Leah looked to Dowling who sat at the writing desk and

smiled.

"Dowling says you're very brave," Matilda said.

"Really? I don't think so."

"But you are. She said you were in the beast forest, so you must be."

"Well that's true enough, I guess."

"Was it scary?"

"Yes. But only because I didn't know what to expect. And because I didn't know the beasts and they didn't know me."

"But you're all friends now?"

Leah nodded. "All friends."

"Do you read? Would you read me a story? My brother is the best reader, but he's gone away."

"I'd be happy to."

Matilda bounced, excited, and reluctantly, Dowling left to find a book.

"What's this? Your diary?"

Matilda pulled Leah's journal from underneath her and held it open.

"Yes. Do you have one?"

"I did. My da wanted me to learn to write. So I wrote some things. But then my brothers found it and read my secrets."

"Oh, that's very rude," Leah said and her body shook slightly with the realization.

"It's too much trouble to write all the time, anyway."

"It takes practice."

Dowling returned with *Ginger Brown Bunny* and Leah read the story of Ginger Brown and her adventures in the wood, with Matilda resting next to her on the bed. Soon Matilda's eyes were closed and her breathing steady and Leah closed the book and smiled up at Dowling.

"Thank you."

"My pleasure, miss."

"You didn't like me very much when I first arrived," Leah

said.

Dowling looked surprised.

"You didn't hide it well at all, Dowling."

She laughed. "Perhaps not. But you were of the Hass."

"Was? Am I not now?"

Dowling thought for a moment, her brow creased, biting her lower lip.

"When you first returned from your ordeal in the forest, I suspected. You took punishment for what your Lord Kirche did, but you never said anything about it. We all knew what had happened."

"What could I have said?"

She shrugged. "I'm not sure. Maybe nothing. But you took the incident with such grace, I was instantly softened. And then, that night, when you returned the brownie's head to his kin. Then I knew..."

"What?"

"That you aren't really one of them."

After Dowling carried Matilda back to her room, Leah opened her journal and flipped through the pages, tears forming in her eyes. She was a liar. Either she would never find the kell stone and so had lied to Dag Voorspeld and Lucas. Or, she would, and would thus lie to Lord Kirche and Prenalin. Either path she chose, she thought, right now she was lying to them all. She could not be trusted. And it hadn't occurred to her until moments ago, that perhaps, she couldn't trust others, either.

Unwillingly, Leah gathered the pages she'd written since returning from the beast forest—in which she'd confided to her journal her lies, her suspicions, sighting the flaming tree, and her feelings about Lord Kirche—and ripped them out. She carried them to the fireplace and tossed them into the embers watching them burn.

Lord Kirche must never know about the kell stone—until Leah herself did.

Chapter Thirty-five

Run!" Rogget yelled. "Don't stop."

They sprinted without thinking about direction until they were out of the wood. Then they darted up the slopes and down, heading north toward the Gnome Eaters' encampment. Finally, Rogget slowed, and they slowed with him.

"I don't think they're following anymore," he said, gasping. "You kids sure can run." He bent over and put his hands to his knees. "Darnit," he said and stumbled over to the bear who limped forward toward him. "Ah, Darnit. He's been shot."

Sadie gasped. "Is he all right?" She approached Darnit and, for the first time, dared to touch him. Darnit nuzzled her arm with his nose.

"I think it just grazed his back side," Rogget said. "I need to get him into some light."

They hiked on as fast as they could get Darnit to move and finally made their way into the Gnome Eaters' camp.

"It's you." Tanner guided them around the hill. "The others aren't back yet."

"They'll be here soon," Rogget said. "It went well, but I'm afraid we were seen. We'll have to leave right away."

"No worries," Tanner said. "It ain't like we never squawked

at 'em and run before. They won't be back over any time soon.'"

"Is that what you do, then?" Sadie asked. "You fight back and forth."

Tanner nodded. "But usually we gots some reason for it." He smiled. "I like thinking of them darn Wretched ponderin' and ponderin' over what mischief they done to cause us to attack like that."

"I think they'll figure it out," Fenn said. "They're not stupid. They'll know you helped us."

Tanner smiled. "All the better."

"Just a grazing." Rogget relaxed after examining Darnit by the fire. He rubbed the bear behind the ears. "You'll be fine soon enough. But no more scuffles, you hear? Next time, you stay home."

"Won't he follow you?" Grayson asked. "He seems to."

Rogget nodded. "I reckon it'll be hard to keep him out o' things."

"Can you send him home?" Sadie said. "Back to the Ruud?"

"I don't think that's home for Darnit."

"Where'd you get him, anyway?"

"Out to the port. I won him in a game of cards. I think he came over on a boat from the Great West. I hear tell they got a lot of bears over that way."

"Well," Fenn said. "Let's just try to stay out of the way of the Wretched."

"You don't have to tell me twice," Grayson said. "They could have hit any one of us with that shot."

"I think you're right," Rogget said. "Be thankful for their poor marksmanship."

Wiley and the Gnome Eaters returned, whooping and triumphant.

"That was great fun," Wiley said. He saw Rogget patting Darnit nervously. "I see blood. Is the bear all right?"

"He was grazed."

"We heard the shot," Bruck approached. "I'm glad to see they didn't get one of the children."

"Is everyone else all right?" Sadie asked.

Wiley smiled. "Sure we are. We got pelted with some rocks, but they weren't prepared for much more. We need to start making plans for a dummy camp for when they come back at us."

Sadie shook her head. "I think they think they're playing a game."

"They don't have much else to do out here," Grayson said.

She rolled her eyes. "Maybe they could play cards together instead of trying to kill each other."

"Oh, we tried that." Wiley settled himself by his fire. "We ended up killing each other anyway. Might just as well skip the cards, eh?"

Fenn packed up his knapsack, preparing for their trek to the wasteland again.

"We're leaving already?" Grayson said.

"We have to move. The Wretched saw us and might come after us to get the charm back."

"How valuable could it be?" Wiley asked.

"It's very valuable to me," Fenn said. "And I don't want to risk losing it again."

"There's more reason to get moving," Rogget said, looking at Sadie and Grayson.

Fenn remembered Clutch's idea to ransom them to King Welk and he nodded in agreement.

"But it's dinner time," Sadie said. "It'll be dark soon."

"Darker is better." Rogget began packing up his gear.

"You and Darnit can stay," Fenn said. "Darnit needs to recover."

"He's fine now."

But Fenn was thinking more of Rogget recovering from the scare.

Rogget said, "The farther we get from the Wretched, the better I'll feel about it."

That much was true. They needed to get Darnit far from there quickly.

"Can I set you up with any provisions?" Wiley asked and he gave them some extra fruit and jerky. "Stop back and see us if you come back through."

"Aren't you all moving?" Grayson asked Wiley.

"Ah, maybe. But maybe they're expecting us to move and we'll fool them by staying."

The four traveled much of night through the hills and crossed the lilac clover without incident.

"They're asleep," Fenn whispered in the darkness.

"Well, step carefully," Grayson said. "I've seen Sadie when she wakes up. I don't want any grouchy fairy bees stinging me."

Once in Banished, they slept through to noon inside Pinta's hut while she tried to keep the villagers quiet for the adventurers' rest. Fenn tossed and turned fitfully; visions of his mother, his father, the old wissende's robe, and all their voices echoed in his head without ceasing. It was a nightmarish jumble of dreams that made no sense, but reached out for him and would not let him loose. He woke feverish and groggy, the hemp rope damp around his neck.

That afternoon, they were off to Chosen with the charm. When Fenn approached Clara's cabin for the second time, he was overwhelmed with fear that she was dead. But the same old woman opened the door to him, smiled, and waved him into the dimly lit hut and to Clara's bedside where she still lay, gaunt and shriveled.

"Miss Clara," he said. "It's me, Fenn. I brought the charm."

She opened her eyes and turned her head toward him. "Where is it?" She held out her hand; he took the rope from his neck and laid the gold charm in her palm. She looked up to the ceiling and felt the charm with her fingers, turning it over and over in her hands. Fenn suddenly realized that she was blind.

She held the charm out to him. "That's it," she said as he took it from her. "That's the charm."

Fenn's heart pounded in his chest. "What was her name?"

Clara shook her head, still staring at the ceiling. "She never said her name; she rarely spoke. But I called her Eseld. She was the most beautiful woman I'd ever seen. She was eisen."

"Eisen? Are you sure?"

"She didn't have to tell me. I'd never seen a folk look like that."

"What happened to her? Why was she here?"

Clara's face came together as if she were in pain. "It was so long ago and so frightening and the Father—he would not tell me much. I'm not sure."

"Please tell me all you know."

"He told me there had been an attack on an encampment in the wastelands. North, where sometimes the eis hunt. All were dead, but her." She smiled. "What do you look like?"

He grimaced. He didn't look at himself much. He couldn't remember the last time he'd seen a looking glass. "I have dark hair."

"And your eyes?"

"Dark also."

"You must have your father's features then. Your mother was pale, with hair like gold. Her eyes were blue as sapphires. Her face round and soft."

"I think mine's more pointy than round," Fenn said, beginning to doubt that this eisen was really his mother.

Clara nodded.

"Was my father killed in the attack?"

She shrugged slightly. "Father Wold didn't say. And I didn't ask. It was really none of my business. But she mourned as if he were dead, lost forever. So I reckon he was. She was in much pain. Her face and hair shone like the rising sun in the east. But her body was burned and mangled. She'd been felled by arrows. It took all of her strength to carry you those last days."

"Is she dead?" He knew the answer. But he hoped so badly he was wrong that he couldn't breathe.

Clara nodded, and swallowed hard. "She died just a few days after you were born. She was so frail and light, like air. It was too much for her. She tried to hang on for you. She did."

Fenn looked down and they were both silent for a long moment.

"You are the bairn of prophecy. Sent to us to destroy the monarchy and let the banished return to the Ruud." Her face glowed with adoration.

Fenn shook his head, but did not respond.

"I'm glad you haven't been captured," she said.

"Why do you think I'm the bairn?"

She frowned and closed her eyes. Her forehead creased as she thought hard. "I don't recollect. It was something the Father said. You were...to be neither prince of the Ruud, nor of the eis, but..."

"That doesn't mean anything."

"But cast out into the wastelands."

"What?"

"Cast into the wasteland. Orphaned. And you have the funny mark on your arm." She opened her eyes and turned her face toward him. Fenn trembled. She seemed to be looking directly at him.

"How long have you been blind?"

"It started several years ago," she said. "I see shadow."

He nodded and put his hand on her arm. He felt devotion and love travel through him like a wave of warm water and suddenly, he could see her. His mother. Lying before him, pale and drifting out of life. Her golden hair spread across the white pillow cover. She turned her face to him and opened her eyes, stunning him. He was sinking into the blue depths until Clara's nurse pulled him away.

Fenn left Clara's hut and was surrounded by Grayson, Sadie, and Rogget.

"Well?" Sadie said.

Fenn shrugged and began to hike back to Chosen.

"Come on, what did she say?" Grayson said. "You're not going to keep it secret are you?"

"She told me my mother was one of the eis."

Sadie gasped. "An eisen?"

"And my charm has RoE on it. It could be her name began with an R, like Rose. Rose of the Eis."

"Would not," Sadie said. "If it was for Rose of the Eis it'd be RotE."

"Not necessarily," Grayson said. "You don't have to have a letter for a little word like 'the.'"

"Oh, but you have one for a little word like 'of.'"

Fenn nodded. "She's right. It might all be a big mistake."

Suddenly, Rogget, who'd been silent for some time, coughed. "No," he muttered. "No I'm thinking this Clara is, or rather was, your nurse and she's telling the truth."

"I did get the sense she was being truthful."

"So, maybe she's insane," Sadie said. "Insane folk think they're being truthful so it might seem to us that they're telling the truth, but for the fact that, you know, they're crazy..."

Fenn smiled. But no, it was deeper than that. When he touched Clara, he felt deeply that she was telling him the reality of his mother, at least as far as Clara remembered it. But supposing Sadie was right. If a person was out of his mind and believed he was possessed by a doppelganger, for instance, if Fenn touched him, would he see that as the truth, even if it wasn't? What if it was all in his mind? What if he was insane and just thought he could be other folk and see into other folks' minds? That was the most likely explanation, after all. Unless... unless the eis could do it.

Once in the middle of Chosen, they paused.

"So, where to?" Rogget looked at Fenn.

"Well, I guess it's off to the ice realm then. Father Britt wanted me to go there to see the maiden. Maybe, if my mother was one of the eis, that's a good idea."

"Maybe that's why he wanted you to go there."

"I wouldn't be surprised," Fenn said. "He kept a lot of secrets from me. They all did. And I'm willing to bet there are more secrets they never told me."

Rogget coughed again. "All right then, this way." And he led them out of the village, across a broad, rocky plain, and then east along the lilac clover field.

"How about we take our time getting there?" Grayson said.

"Why?" Sadie said. "Are you scared, waiter boy?"

"Well, sure, there's the eis and the feeorin, and angels to be scared of and Wiley told us there was war going on and you should be scared, too. But it's not that; I'm just tired. I feel like I've been walking my whole life. I miss home. I miss doing nothing, you know? Oh, I had plenty of work. But I didn't have to go far to do it. And then when I didn't have work, I could sit at the lake up north for hours, or hang around town. I miss that."

"Or read in my da's shop." Sadie laughed. "I'm used to traveling more; but I'm tired, too."

"We can take it slow," Fenn said. "I'm in no hurry. Unless the guard decides to come after us. But, you all don't really have to come. You could stay in Banished. They could use you to read."

"Are you trying to get rid of us?" Sadie said.

"No."

"Then why do we have to keep saying it?" Grayson said. "We stick together. We made a pact."

"How binding are pacts, anyway?" Sadie said.

"What do you mean? It's a pact. Your honor and reputation are at stake."

"So nobody's going to jail if we break it?"

"Of course not."

"Why would you think that?" Fenn said. "You were the one to suggest the pact anyway."

She laughed. "I did. We stick together, through danger and calm, in peril and peace."

"And we're a team now," Grayson said. "No secrets among us."

"All right then." Fenn knew there were still secrets he hadn't shared. "Pact it is."

Chapter Thirty-six

In the days that followed, Leah found Dowling's mood much improved. She sang while making up the beds and working in the dining room and she smiled much more often, even around Kirche. She'd told Kirche that hundrats had made off with the brownie's head because he'd left it out too long.

"You told me I couldn't bring it into the inn," he'd protested. "So the fault is yours."

"I didn't prevent you from burying it, or storing it in the smokehouse."

This outraged Kirche and he ranted for some time in the lobby that it would have been absurd to bury it and have it overcome by worms or to have it smoked. But in the end there was nothing he could do to recover his trophy.

Once Leah was strong enough, and willing to cover much of her face with a scarf loaned to her by Dowling, she accompanied Kirche, Prenalin, Kipling, and Redd to tour the old prison Steingefan where they heard stories of the bairn who rescued the children of Path.

"It's a sad story that a king couldn't keep hold of a few children," Kirche purred as he grimaced, disgusted by the damp and barren rooms of the old castle.

The next day, they were off to train recruits from Path and Timber. It had been done once already on the day Leah had to herself, but this time she was invited along to see the young men's marching and shooting abilities. There were thirteen boys, small and large, various ages, barefoot and dirty.

"They're not much to look at," Kirche said as Leah stepped out of the carriage onto the field just outside the wood between Path and Timber. "But they're eager to learn."

The boys marched and turned, and played at running and shooting, using sticks carved into the shape of long arms. Kirche enamored them with stories of the military in Ruhm and any time they wished to join, they could travel to the port and ask for passage on any ship of the Hass.

"How many have joined?" Leah asked Prenalin, as Kirche handed out hard candies to all the boys.

He smiled. "Over the years, a fair few have left home for the military. They had little to keep them here. And are you feeling much better?"

"I am."

"You'll have had quite a bit to write about in your journal," Kirche said, after dismissing his charges.

Leah eyed Kirche, but chided herself for her suspicions. Kirche had often mentioned her journal, and she'd never thought much of it before. Knowing what she'd written in recent days, and what she'd torn out and thrown away, on the off chance the book might come into possession of the wrong sort, had made her paranoid.

"I'd rather focus on positive thoughts," she said.

"But your time in the forest," he persisted, as they walked to the carriage. "You should perhaps write it all down in detail. It might later have some meaning."

"For finding the kell stone, you mean."

"Yes, of course. Did you see or hear anything that might lead you to some information about its location?"

Leah couldn't imagine what she might have found fighting for her life in the forest.

"Did any of the beast who harmed you say anything about the stone?"

"Why would they?"

Kirche looked at her as if she were speaking a foreign language. "Because you are a foreign folk, of course. Wouldn't they question you about it? Did they not ask you if you knew where it was?"

"My apologies, Lord Kirche. I don't understand why they would ask me that."

"Folk stole their stone. Wouldn't they question any they come across?"

"The stone was stolen generations ago. It would be highly unlikely that a folk such as I would know anything of its whereabouts."

Kirche smirked and climbed into the carriage. "Seems one would not want to leave any stone unturned." And at his own wit, he laughed loud and raucously, shaking the cart as Leah followed Prenalin to her seat.

Leah did her best to laugh with him. "No, I'm afraid there was no mention of the stone while I was there. They were more concerned about punishing me." She amazed herself at how easily she lied and continued to do so. She didn't flinch at all this time. Clearly, lies came more natural the more a folk told them.

"Punishment, yes. What cruel creatures, to punish you for something I did. Is that the sort of justice system they live by?"

"I couldn't say."

"Well, never mind that. It's over and done with now. Journal it. You may never know what ideas it might spark."

"If I may be so bold, Lord, what are we doing...to find the stone, I mean?"

Prenalin turned his face to the carriage window as the driver beckoned the horses and Leah thought he must wish she would not bother Kirche with her questions.

"We haven't done anything, yet. Not really. Certainly, we take a look when we come across some new cavern or hole we haven't seen before. And on this trip we will take a tour out to the caverns in the north. But in the past we have done little. The folk of the Ruud were charged with finding the stone for us.

Leah nodded. "I see."

"But this new bairn." Kirche beamed with a wide smile. "That's a boon, is it not? If we catch him, we can use him to our advantage in taking the Ruud. And if we do not succeed in that, we need only wait for him to find the stone for us."

"Do you suppose that is his goal, at present?" Prenalin said.

"Of course. That is what the prophecy told, did it not?"

"Do we know the words of the prophecy?"

Kirche let his head rattle back and forth on his neck and rolled his eyes. "We know what the folk tell us it said. Isn't that enough? The boy is meant to find the stone."

Leah shook her head. "Lord, begging your pardon. But I have found no folk here who know what the kell stone is."

Prenalin turned to her. "It's true," he said. "They don't know of it."

Kirche laughed. "The folk of the Ruud know nothing. Haven't I told you they are ignorant? Why, they don't even read. No, no. I understand we first heard the story from an angel eisen in Ruhm. We tried to find her after the story was revealed, but we were unsuccessful. Of all the creatures on Kell to be wary of, the angel eis are the most cunning and vile."

"An angel eis in Ruhm? But I thought they were—"

"Banished. Murdered. Yes. But angel eis have many powers and this one has apparently managed to live among us."

Leah shook her head.

"You are not convinced," Kirche said.

"Forgive me. But, how did you hear the angel eisen's story?"

"One of our community spies overheard her telling the story

to charm folk at a fire gathering. The gathering itself was illegal and that is why he was there—to take names. After he reported, we searched for the eisen and found no trace of the woman."

"Of course. And the spy told the truth. Naturally."

"Naturally," Kirche said, failing to note the skepticism in Leah's voice.

But then, she thought, why would the spy lie? They are trained only to make note of blasphemies and incidents against the moral law. Where might a spy of Ruhm come up with such an idea if it were not true? But an angel eisen in the city? Why would she *be* there? What sort of life could an angel eis have living among the folk of Ruhm?

"Lord Kirche," she said. "Could this angel eisen, then, be a spy as well—for the ice realm, perhaps?"

Kirche's brows rose and his head fell back slightly before he let out another loud laugh. "For what purpose would the angels or the eis spy on the folk of Ruhm?"

The carriage slowed to a stop at the inn at Timber where they would have their dinner and Kirche continued his chuckling as he disembarked.

"It is a thought," Prenalin whispered to her as he scooted past her to leave the carriage.

He handed Leah down the steps to the ground and as they followed Kirche into the inn, Prenalin said quietly, "Kirche and the inner circle of Hass are of the mind that no other folk come near to Ruhm in power, among other things."

"Perhaps the eisen isn't a spy," Leah said. "But such arrogance for Ruhm doesn't bode well if she is ever faced with a real threat."

Prenalin smiled down at her and spoke unusually loudly. "Don't fear, Leah. Our circle is proud, yes, for our love of Ruhm. But is pride misplaced when its focus is valid? Ruhm is the greatest and most powerful city on Kell. Of that, you can be certain."

Leah turned to see Kirche watching them with a self-assured smile.

Chapter Thirty-seven

Darnit came bounding toward them two miles north of Banished and Rogget knelt to give him a rub about the ears.

"Ach. I've been so worried for you, darn bear. I wish you'd just take off. He's such a mind of his own." Rogget turned to the kids, smiling.

"I think you'd be lost without him," Sadie said.

"Maybe. But I don't like these parts, with the criminals and the firearms. I'm thinking the ice realm, even with a war, will be safer for a bear."

Grayson shook his head. "It's rumored that even the criminals won't venture all the way into the ice realm, so I'm not sure safer is what we'll be."

"Oh, they're harsh there, on the criminal folk," Rogget said. "But I didn't ever hear tell of any of the faire eis being unkind to strangers...leastwise until they discovered their intent."

"Intent?"

"Well, sure. You know, there's some go off to the ice realm looking for gold and silver. Or the eisen women. I hear tell they're downright hard to resist...eh?" He looked at them and turned red in the face. "Uh, never mind that."

They made camp in the early evening at the foot of a row of large hills just north of the bridge over the lilac clover field. On the horizon to the northeast, Fenn could see the snow capped peaks of the ice realm.

"We'll have to make our way valley to valley, dale to dale, until we reach the mountains. Then we have to find Kingdom Pass," Rogget said. "That'll take us right into the realm... eventually."

"We'll need warmer clothes," Sadie said.

Rogget slapped his forehead. "Ach, I forgot. We were to pass by the Gnome Eaters again."

"But they wouldn't have had time to get us clothes," Fenn said. "They went with us to fight the Wretched and now they have to defend themselves."

"You'd be surprised, I think," Rogget said. "Wiley sent a few out right away to sneak into the Ruud for extra blankets and such."

Fenn frowned. He didn't want to delay the trip any longer than necessary. But they had forgotten about the clothes. He shrugged. What else could they do?

"All right then," he grumbled. "We'll have to head back."

"No, no. That won't be necessary," Rogget said. "There'll be more encampments up this way. We can barter for supplies and warmer clothing from them."

"We don't have much to trade."

"I think stories and news of the Ruud will do," Rogget smiled.

"How will we find water in the frozen realm?" Grayson said.

"We could melt chunks of ice in our mugs over the fire," Sadie said.

They all turned to look at her and smiled.

"What?" she said. "Can't we?"

"That's exactly what we'll do," Rogget said.

Fenn turned to Grayson and saw his cheeks redden, suddenly realizing a newfound respect for Sadie.

They hiked to the edge of a small copse of trees and after collecting enough firewood, Rogget set to work digging out a fire pit amid a circle of large rocks, while Grayson and Sadie disappeared into the wood to find branches for making a lean-to. Fenn sat on a boulder watching Rogget.

"It'll be all right to have a fire at this distance, I think," Rogget said. "Might be a risk to keep it aflame through the night."

"You think they'll come looking for us?"

Rogget nodded. "The plan was, o' course, for the Gnome Eaters to throw them off. But they saw you. And likely Clutch won't want to let you get away with taking back your charm. It would make him look bad, I expect. I don't think the guard will be this far out yet, though."

Fenn nodded. Rogget had finished the pit and piled sticks into the middle of the hole and took out his flint. Darnit roared from the woods and Rogget dropped the flint and jumped up.

"Darnit," he called and the bear peered out from the trees. "Don't scare me like that." He turned back to the kindling and knelt, but his hands shook as he tried to light the flint. "Darn bear. If he don't stay hidden it won't be my fault if he ends up shot again."

He lit three flints but they all burnt out before the kindling caught the flame. Rogget fumed. "Darn bear." He shook his head, rose, and walked the few feet to the trees and talked to Darnit. "You have to stay hidden, there, I tell you."

Fenn found this behavior puzzling. Darnit was hidden, like he'd been told. Except for the one outburst of a roar, he seemed rather content at curling up against a tree on the cold ground. Rogget must have been very worried still. Fenn tried to curl up in his tunic for warmth but the impatience of waiting for the fire made him shake off the cold. He stood up, walked to the fire pit, squatted down beside it and pushed his arms out toward the kindling and flint sticks lying burnt atop it. A feeling of power rushed through his chest and a small flame caught the sticks and began to billow. He quickly added more kindling and waved his hand over it. Rogget turned from Darnit in the trees and came back to watch him build up the fire.

"Your last flint must have worked, after all," Fenn told him with a smile.

Rogget muttered, "About time," and added a log to the pile.

Grayson and Sadie returned, pulling a pile of branches and logs behind them on a blanket. They set them up and tied them with Rogget's rope, building a nice lean-to under which they could sleep.

"There'll only be room for two." Sadie looked at Fenn, worried. "But we'll take turns."

"It's all right," Fenn said. "You two built it. You should sleep in it."

"Maybe tomorrow we can find more wood and build another one. Unless we decide to move on."

"We should keep moving for a few days until we're sure the Wretched aren't following us," Rogget said.

Grayson looked dejected, but he nodded.

They ate and talked and sat around the fire, until Rogget told them to go to bed. "I'll put out the fire in an hour or so, so bundle up in your blankets."

Fenn curled up against a boulder away from the wind, facing the fire, his knapsack at his feet, and tried to sleep. He had his charm back and reached to his neck to hold it. It was warm and his blood pulsed in his finger tips as he touched it.

Lucas was standing in the cellar of the Path wissenry with the woolen blanket pulled back, exposing the tunnel, its door slung wide open. "Go on," he said. "Get in." A wicked smile formed on his face and Fenn stepped back away from him. "No."

"Aw, come on, look, there's nothing in there to fear."

Fenn peered into the dark hole and saw a faint glow; it grew brighter and brighter until out of the tunnel floated the burning tree of the Hass of Emorah and Lucas laughed and laughed.

And then his mother's voice surrounded him. "Don't be afraid," she said. "It's only a dream."

Suddenly he was startled awake by a yell and the sound of a gunshot.

"No, Darnit, run!" Rogget screamed.

Fenn scrambled to his feet, only to find them caught in the straps of his knapsack, bringing him tumbling to his knees. He was grabbed from behind and wrapped in rope before he realized what was happening. Sadie screamed; another gunshot rang out and he heard Rogget's muffled shouting.

"Little thief," Clutch seethed in his ear and dragged him to a horse. He lifted him effortlessly onto its back, and then climbed on behind him.

"Let's go!" he called out and the horse shot off into the darkness.

With the wind rushing in his ears, Fenn thought he heard a crowd of men screeching a war cry. He looked back and saw only shadowy figures in the dim light of the cloud-covered moon.

Chapter Thirty-eight

Welk paced in front of the hearth with Dunham nervously twitching and clicking his tongue a few steps away, mirroring his movements.

"Must you make all that noise?" Welk scolded.

Dunham made a shallow bow. "Your forgiveness, Sire."

Welk rolled his eyes and continued his pacing. It seemed hours since he'd received the crudely written note from the wide-eyed young guard. The boy had been on patrol, he'd said, at the border of the wasteland when he was approached in the early morning darkness by a gang of thieves. He looked as if he'd seen the devil. And where was Sorgood? How long ago had he been summoned?

All was working surprisingly in Welk's favor, with little or no effort on his part. He'd spent all the day before perfecting his plan to enter the hill country to gain support for something of an attack on the ice realm. It would allow him to meet with Clutch, to gain the loyalty of the folk of the hills, thus planting himself above the other kingdoms of the Ruud, and to begin the task of aiding the maiden and her loyal eis in their civil dispute. It was all so neatly packaged he was giddy with excitement to get started. Then he received the note. Clutch was, it seemed, right outside the Ruud. The days it would normally take to track him down were reduced to nothing. Now he only needed to get Sorgood out of the way.

Finally he heard the creak and boom of the old door to the lobby and Sorgood approached with his entourage, striding toward him with a look of power on his face that did not disappear until he reached Welk at the hearth.

Sorgood made a low bow and his guard followed suit. "You summoned, Sire?" he said.

Welk was sure he detected a faint hint of exasperation in Sorgood's voice, as if he fidgeted between showing loyalty to his king and dominance to his guard. But their faces remained stony and their eyes distant. If he was reading them correctly, the guard detested Sorgood as much as any other folk in the Ruud did.

Frieden, pale and blond, stood just beyond Sorgood, refusing to humble himself by hunching as the master of the guard tended to do. Welk forced himself not to look at the young felid folk. After meeting up with the boy outside the beast forest in Timber, he'd absentmindedly called his name out of surprise. The boy had eyed him suspiciously and took the first opportunity to dart away into the forest. But of course the wissenry hadn't told him of his connection to Welk. For all he knew, they hadn't bothered to tell the boy his real name.

Welk gave the chamberlain the note from the thieves and it was handed to Sorgood.

"This," he said, "came from the wasteland early this morning. Tell me what you make of it."

Sorgood took the paper to the wall, closer to the fire, and held it up in front of his face, studying it. Frieden followed and looked over Sorgood's shoulder. A slight, proud smile found its way to Welk's lips.

"Was it written by a child, Sire?"

"Read all of it." Welk watched Sorgood carefully.

"Ah." he walked back to Welk, with Frieden following like a

curious kitten. Sorgood handed the note to the chamberlain. "The Wretched. I'm surprised to find they have a writer in the group."

Welk nodded. It would be Goggle, if he still lived. He remembered Goggle fondly. Clutch's favorite, and like a puppy—very hard not to like.

"Well," Welk raised his voice. "What do you make of it?"

"It's a trap, Sire," Sorgood said. "They mean to rob you."

Welk paused, looking over Sorgood's face. "Yes," he said and nodded. "I thought as much. Why did it take you so long to arrive?"

"I was on my way to Cold Sea Port, Sire. To interrogate some pirates regarding our quarry."

"Very well, Sorgood. Continue with your plans. I won't expect to see you again for some time."

"Yes, Sire."

Sorgood hesitated, his brows creased just a bit as if he fought with doubt, before bowing low again. His guard also bowed to the king and then followed the little man out.

"We should reinstate the backward bowing out rule, Dunham."

"Sire?"

"It would prolong his agony in trying to hide his smirk from me."

Dunham smiled and looked toward the door after Sorgood. He chuckled. "I'm glad to hear the king is not taken in by his obeisance, Sire."

"Ah, so you've decided Sorgood is against the king?"

"Oh, no, Sire. I wouldn't go that far. But I think..." He paused.

"You may speak freely Dunham. I need at least one person to always speak freely to me."

"Well, Sire. I think Sorgood is mostly for himself, rather than against the king."

"But he is also for Emorah, is he not?"

Dunham nodded. "That would be my thinking, Sire."

"And you, Dunham. Be truthful with me. I will not punish one way of thinking or the other. Where do you stand with Emorah?"

"Sire, I would willingly take the punishment if my way of thinking offended you. I stand against Emorah. But I stand with you. If you tell me that Emorah also stands for the king. I will stand with it."

Welk tilted his head and let a small smile come to his lips.

"You would stand with it out of loyalty?"

Dunham smiled. "I would stand with it, Sire. But that does not mean I would believe in its teachings. You recall the list I was to make, of possible enemies of your father?"

Welk nodded.

"It would appear, after my spy's reports, that Sorgood tops the list."

Welk's brow rose. "What is the report?"

"That he follows the representatives of Hass, or that they follow him. And spies report many a time that Sorgood was alone with your father, King Evan."

"You are a good and faithful servant, Dunham. I thank you for your candor."

"Aye, Sire. Always your servant." He bowed low.

Welk watched Dunham's shoulders as he bowed and wondered if it were true or not. Could he trust Dunham? How to tell? He was suddenly struck with loss. If only his father had not died young. If only his father had not betrayed him. All those he trusted were lost to him. Rue the fair, taken so young in life. His father, her betrayer, the cause of her death. They were both gone to the ether leaving him without counsel. Clutch, the only other he could confide in, well...he could at least find him on occasion. But he would do well to have someone handy, like Dunham.

"Sire?" Dunham looked concerned.

Welk shook his head, waved his hand as if to bat away the emotion.

"We need a guard, Dunham. Twenty men. Can you find them?"

Dunham nodded.

"Alert me when Sorgood has passed the boundary of Timber. We will ride out then."

Welk handed the poorly written note to Dunham and listened to his deep, fatherly voice as he read aloud.

"We have that boy. Come to get him. In the waste land. We'll let him go or else. We want ten big doars and ten gold rings." He paused and looked to Welk. "Ten gold rings, Sire?"

Welk chuckled. "Goggle doesn't know how to spell many words, I'm afraid. You'd better bring a lot of doars and gold. If Clutch told him to write bigger numbers and he didn't, he'll drag him behind a horse."

"You know these folk, Sire?"

Welk nodded. "I do." He raised his eyebrows at Dunham's surprise. "Do you not remember more than ten years ago, when we were both younger men. I ran away to live the life of a vagabond?"

"Ah, yes Sire." Dunham smiled.

"I met up with the Wretched for a time."

"And they didn't kill you, Sire? You, a prince of the Ruud?"

"Clutch had his reasons. Besides, I believe I'd renounced the throne at the time."

"I do recall." He began the tsk-tskinng with his tongue again. "Sad times, Sire."

Welk frowned. "And not so sad. At least then there was adventure. And hope for another chance at happiness."

Dunham nodded. Welk reached out and patted him soundly on the shoulder. "Let us not dwell on the past, then, good man." And he did feel the weight of it finally begin to slide. He could not yet completely trust Dunham, but he could see now that there was something bigger than himself. Something more important than Rue-Anna and their love. It was just as his father had tried to tell him, after all. The Ruud was the thing. The Ruud was his heart. He could trust the Ruud.

Chapter Thirty-nine

Fenn woke to the smell of campfire and bitters and to the snorting of horses in the misty cold morning. He sat up and winced; his body ached from head to foot. The wild horse ride the night before, the rocky spot on which he was forced to sleep, and his hands tied behind his back, all served to give him pain.

Clutch, Goggle, and Crud, another of the Wretched, sat by the fire watching him. Beyond them, to the north, Fenn could see the towers of Steingefan rising in the hazy distance over the tall grass. He was back home; most of him feared being so near to the place he knew he must flee, but some small part of him was joyous and he gulped deep breaths of Ruud air, sniffed out the morning aromas, and listened for the sparrow song.

"Here." Clutch held out a mug of bitters.

"I don't drink bitters," Fenn said. "Even if I could take the cup."

Clutch put the mug down at the edge of the fire and came up behind Fenn, untying his hands.

"You won't get far if you try to run. You might as well have your hands to drink."

Clutch offered him the mug and Fenn saw his hemp rope

and gold charm dangling from the dirty man's neck as he took it from him. Instead of the stone the children of Path had carved for him, his mother's charm clinked up against a shard of amber rock.

"Where's the stone?" Fenn asked.

"Drink."

Fenn lifted the mug reluctantly and sniffed it. It smelled earthy, but he'd tasted it before and the name bitters didn't describe it well enough. He took a sip and grimaced.

"There was a stone charm on my rope. What did you do with it?"

"Ah," Clutch said. "Tossed it off somewhere."

Fenn's jaw set and he glared at Clutch. "Why are we here?"

"Border of Michelruud. Waiting on the king." Goggle smiled like he had a secret he couldn't wait to share. "I sent him a note about you."

"What if he doesn't come?"

Clutch smiled, then broke out in laughter. More horses approached from behind him and the straggling, tired Wretched joined them.

"Where are the rest?" Clutch said.

"Left behind," one said. "We was ambushed again, by the Gnome Eaters. They had the Scary Brutes with 'em and some others from round about."

Clutch growled and looked at Fenn. "This is your fault. We were all just fine, getting along, until you showed up."

"You didn't get along," Fenn said.

"We got along in our way."

Fenn chuckled. "If you want to call it that."

Clutch glared at him. "We'll be well rid of you soon enough."

Fenn realized they'd stolen his sack when he saw them digging jerky from it; at least they shared it with him and offered him a hard biscuit. He was forced to drink the bitters to moisten it. But his spirits woke shortly after and he felt alert, clear-headed, and energetic.

They heard horses and all turned to the south to see them approach.

"It's him, get up."

They moved forward, one of the men pushing Fenn along, to stand beyond the fire. It was the King of Michelruud, with ten horses behind him. Clutch smiled broadly as the horses slowed and formed a row some twenty yards away, in front of his men.

"Welk," Clutch called out gleefully. "I knew you couldn't resist an adventure. I got something you want."

Fenn looked over at the king, curious. He'd only seen the King of Michelruud, Evan at the time, in passing in Path or along the roads to the port. He'd certainly never been in conversation with a king before, and he was sure that Clutch was supposed to speak to him with more respect. He should say Sire and Highness and bow and all that. But maybe criminals didn't follow the rules of conduct the way regular folk did. Still, he would have thought a king would be angry at the insult of being called by name. But King Welk actually smiled and sat forward on his horse. With a light tap of his feet, the horse moved toward them.

Clutch and Goggle moved forward as well and met him halfway.

Fenn could hear some of their words. Money, ransom, evil bairn. And they laughed. The King of Michelruud was laughing with Clutch the crook. Fenn was stunned and looked around at the others who didn't seem to notice.

Clutch turned back to the group, whistled and waved his hand. One of the men tossed Fenn his knapsack, grabbed him by the scruff of his neck, and pushed him forward toward Clutch and the king. As he approached, Fenn kept his eyes on Welk of Michelruud. He didn't look half as mean as Clutch, though they both were dark of hair and eyes. King Welk peered curiously back at him.

"So," he said looking down at him from his horse, "you're the one causing all the trouble."

He didn't seem angry. "Yes, Sire," Fenn responded politely and the king laughed.

Welk looked him over, shaking his head. "We haven't decided what to do with you yet, but you're certainly worth a bounty." He raised his arm and signaled to his men and one of them approached with a large bag. Welk took it from him and held it out to Clutch. As Clutch stepped forward to take the bag, Fenn caught sight of something in the grasses to their right. Something prowled there, low to the ground, inching its way toward them.

"Hand over the boy first," Welk said with a sly smile at Clutch.

"I'll hand him over, but he's not to get on a horse until you toss the gold."

"Ah, Clutch, you don't trust me?"

Clutch laughed. "About as much as you trust me."

They both smiled, angering Fenn. Clutch grabbed at his knapsack and dragged him over to Welk who summoned one of his men to dismount and stand beside Fenn.

"Oh, and he had something of yours," Clutch said.

But just as Welk tossed the bag of ransom across to Clutch, one of his men screamed, "Felid!"

Fenn was startled and something or someone pushed him to the ground; horses reared and whinnied, men ran screaming this way and that. A shot rang out, whoops and hollers, almost gleeful, sailed through the air, and then Fenn heard the unmistakable growl of a bear.

He looked up in the panic and saw Clutch looking down at him with fierce rage on his face. Fenn reached up, grabbed his hemp rope from Clutch's neck and broke it off.

"You little—"

Clutch had Fenn by the throat, but suddenly the thief was pulled to the ground and dragged away.

Chapter Forty

In the chaos, Welk's horse reared up and tossed him into the grass. Pounding hooves and frantic whinnies echoed around him and the horses disappeared quickly, chased toward the Ruud, he assumed. He raised himself up to peer at the scene; felidae rounded up his and Clutch's men, pouncing on them and dragging them back toward the spot where they'd attacked. But Fenn Foster was left alone and running northward, flinging his knapsack onto his back. Welk crawled quickly, keeping as low as possible away from where the men were being captured and as soon as he felt his distance was enough, he stood and darted forward after the boy.

"Fenn, run!"

The other children sat on horses fifty yards away and Welk picked up his speed, but the boy was fast.

"Hurry," the innkeeper's son called. "Someone's coming."

But just as he'd reached his friends, the boy paused and bent forward to catch his breath and Welk sprinted to close in on him.

"Stop!"

Welk was almost at Fenn when he looked to one of the horses to see young Sadie Pratt, the stationer's daughter, had a firearm.

"Sadie, no," Fenn said. "It's the king."

"Get on the horse, Fenn," she demanded. The girl took a determined aim at Welk. The innkeeper's son sat with his mouth open and his eyes wide.

Welk turned to Fenn, who seemed confused. He looked at Welk, and then back to his friend. His eyes searched the meadow behind Welk for others but they still fought the felidae, and what looked like the Gnome Eaters, a hundred yards back.

"No one is coming to help you," Welk said. He must keep the boy on the ground long enough for his guard to arrive. But it sounded as if no reinforcement would come.

"I'm not the evil bairn. I'm not going to destroy the Ruud." The boy was desperate.

This was not the declaration Welk expected.

"The folk of the Ruud believe otherwise," he said.

"You can convince them. Tell them I mean no harm."

"It would change nothing."

"Fenn." Miss Pratt still aimed her firearm at Welk. "Get on the horse."

"If you were an adult," Welk said. "I'd have your head."

"Adults, you kill," the innkeeper's son responded, apparently his shock subsided. "Children are abandoned to Steingefan."

Welk smirked. Clever boy.

"You go on back to the battle," the girl said to him. "I don't want to shoot the king."

"No, I don't imagine your father would be pleased at the news."

"Does he get news in prison?"

Sarcasm. He never expected such from the daughter of the king's stationer. "Your father is a guest in the castle at Michelruud. He will be sorely disappointed to hear of your behavior."

"I don't believe you."

Welk shrugged and looked again at Fenn Foster of the

wissenry. "I will hunt you across the eastern realm until you are captured. There is nowhere for you to run. Nowhere to hide."

"There is no prophecy," the boy said, clearly angry. "I'm not the new bairn."

"The folk believe in a prophecy; they will not be dissuaded. But if you are not the bairn, why do the beast folk fight for you now?"

"Maybe the beast folk don't like kings who pick on little kids."

"You are more than a child. You have the mark."

"The mark has nothing to do with it," the innkeeper's son said.

"You know of this mark?" Welk asked him.

"He reads." The Pratt girl smirked and raised her firearm again to her cheek.

"Why are we talking about this?" Fenn said. "I'm not going to destroy the Ruud. I don't know what the mark is, but is has nothing to do with prophecy because there's no such thing."

"You are a fine representative of the wissenry," Welk said. "All logic and no heart. The faire eis are gearing up for battle. Those marked are needed now more than ever. You may be the bairn, if one exists, but you are certainly the hope of the beast. Either way you pose a danger to the Ruud."

"What are you talking about?"

Welk realized then for certain—Fenn Foster did not know who he was.

"Fenn, just get on the horse and let's get out of here," the innkeeper's boy said.

"Why do you hesitate to run?" Welk said. "What is it that you want?"

The boy paused as if thinking and Welk eyed him carefully. Finally, he seemed to have an answer ready.

"I want you to leave me alone," the boy said.

Welk sighed with anger, rolling his eyes. "Is that all?"

"No. I want the folk of the wasteland freed. I have a writ you signed to Forbes Billings twelve years ago. You swore that upon ascending to the throne you would pardon all those banished to the wastelands."

Welk sputtered and laughed, even as he felt the blood drain from his face. "You want...what?"

"I want you to honor your writ to Forbes Billings."

Welk creased his brow and peered at the boy. Perhaps Kirche was right. This was a boy who could be turned into a devotion for the folk most assuredly. How odd he was.

"I need a guarantee that you will leave the Ruud forever and I will not see you again unless I seek you out."

"I swear it."

"Then give me the writ."

Fenn dropped his backpack from his shoulders and pulled it open. He foraged through it until he found the paper and drew it carefully from the sack.

"I have it here, you see."

Welk held out his hand. "Bring it to me."

"No. You see that I have it. It stays with me. It's my guarantee that you will honor your promise and free them all."

Welk rolled his eyes and turned briefly to the still scuffling guard fifty yards behind him. "And then what of future criminals?"

"No more banishment."

Welk shook his head helplessly. He remembered the writ. The night he signed it was still clear in his mind despite his fill of drink. He'd wanted to sign it, thinking it would rile his father. But Forbes Billings didn't bring the writ to the king, as he'd hoped. The folk was smarter than that and Welk realized he was biding his time until Evan died. He should have known the writ would show up sooner or later.

"Very well," he said. "You will disappear. And I will proclaim the banished pardoned and end the punishment. But if you go against your word..." Welk stiffened his lips, forming his words carefully. "If you do not leave. I will have little choice but to have the folk of the wasteland executed even as they arrive home to meet their families."

"You wouldn't," Fenn whispered.

"Are you willing to test me?"

"Now will you get on the horse?" the innkeeper's boy pleaded and the young lad climbed on behind him. The Pratt girl lowered her firearm, looked off to the distance where felidae encircled Welk's men and Clutch's thieves, and then looked back at him with concern.

"Begging your greatest pardon, Sire," she said. "I'm just a stupid kid. I didn't mean any harm. But Fenn here's not like you say. He's not going to hurt anybody."

"You've staked your life on that, lass."

Welk clenched his fists in fury. Horseless, no sword, without arms at all. A gun aimed at him! He only wished he'd invited Sorgood along so he could have him whipped for the humility of it all. And worse, it was now clear that Fenn Foster of the wissenry had no knowledge of his own part in what was to come.

Chapter Forty-one

I am not the bairn," Fenn told the king sternly, trying one last time to reason with him before Sadie and Grayson forced the horses away. "There was never a prophecy. I don't want to destroy the Ruud. It's my home."

"Just because you feel that way now means little," King Welk said.

"I will leave as I promised. I was planning to leave anyway, to explore for the wissenry."

"There are more dangers outside the Ruud than in. If you come with me now, you may live your life in safety under guard."

"As a prisoner?" Grayson shook his head. "Come on, let's leave."

"What about my friends?"

"Never mind, Fenn," Sadie said. "He's stalling, waiting for help. We need to leave now."

"Would you let them and their parents go if I went with you?"

"Yes, of course. It's you we want."

"No, Fenn," Grayson said.

"I cannot guarantee your life or your safety if you run," the king said.

"But you just bargained with him to leave," Grayson said. "You promised to stop hunting him."

"That was not part of the agreement."

Horses galloped toward them. A herald called out, "The king!" Suddenly, Fenn heard small grouchy voices hissing at him.

"Run, you fool. Run."

Fenn looked around and saw several felidae crouching in the grass. One huddled there, in his folk form.

"We could not hold them forever. Run."

Before Fenn could decide what to do, Grayson kicked his horse and they turned and left the king of Michelruud standing alone in the meadow.

"Do you know where you're going?" Fenn asked Grayson over his shoulder.

"We're to meet Rogget in Banished."

"Did I see Gnome Eaters back there?"

"We have a story to tell you, for sure," Grayson said, but they were silent as the horses were driven hard, back toward the wasteland village.

At the first stop, to rest the horses at a stream, Fenn retrieved his hemp rope from the bottom of his knapsack. Holding it up, he laid the charm and shard of amber rock against the palm of his hand. The rock pulsated against his skin, much like his charm sometimes did, but the beats were harder, traveling deeper, up his arm and to his chest, beckoning Fenn to place it there. His first impulse was to close his hand around it and squeeze, but when he did so, both the charm and the shard dug into his skin and he was forced to relax his grip. Tying the rope around his neck, he sat for a moment watching the horses drink. Once the throbbing ceased and the charm and amber shard were at home against his skin, he begged Sadie and Grayson to tell him what they knew.

"Rogget would love to tell you all about it," Sadie said.

"I can't wait that long. What happened back at camp last

night?"

"You know just as well as we do. The Wretched came and got you. And the Gnome Eaters showed up and there was fighting like mad for hours."

"It wasn't hours." Grayson rolled his eyes with a smile. "But it did seem to go on for a time. First we were held by some of the Wretched."

"And then the Gnome Eaters came and bashed 'em and then they took us."

"And then some of the Wretched grabbed us back."

"It was crazy."

"But you escaped."

"Eventually the Gnome Eaters ran the Wretched off. A bunch of us followed along as scouts were sent out to find you; but we all figured where they were taking you."

"Where is Rogget, then? I heard Darnit roaring back at the attack."

"Rogget stayed behind," Grayson said. "He's hurt. But it's not bad. He's being tended by Pinta."

"Yeah, he's probably in a fit right now. We weren't supposed to leave."

"It's a good thing we did, though." He looked at Sadie with a big grin. "We rescued Fenn."

"Yeah, we did."

They looked very pleased with themselves.

"But Sadie, you can never go home now," Fenn said. "You threatened the king. And where did you get a gun?"

"Don't you dare tell another soul," she said. "It belongs to Pinta."

They were right about Rogget. He was beside himself, lying on a rag mat in Pinta's hut, yelling one second and wincing with pain the next.

"But it's all right now," Pinta soothed him. "Look, the children are fine and well and they've brought Fenn back to us. And your bear, Darnit, is over across the way waiting for you."

"We've got to move," Rogget said. "We've got to get away before they come for him."

"The Wretched won't be coming too quickly, Rogget," Fenn said. "If they come at all. Their horses are tired. And anyway, we can stay here for as long as we want. I promised the king I'd never go back home. He won't come after me now."

"You talked to the king?" Rogget sat up amazed.

Fenn nodded.

"And you promised to stay out of the Ruud?"

Fenn nodded again.

"And you think he believes you?"

Fenn shrugged. "Why wouldn't he believe me? Besides, I had something to bargain with."

"Bargain?"

Fenn pulled out Forbes' writ and smiled.

"Where'd you get that?"

"I stole it back from Clutch when I found my charm. King Welk says he'll honor it; he'll pardon them all. And, no more banishment."

"Ah, pash," Pinta said, shaking her head. "You're not going on about the writ now too, are you?"

"But King Welk promised."

"And you believed him? He's a king, boy. He doesn't have to honor his word to the likes of us."

Rogget shook his head. "I don't like it. Not one bit. Pinta's right. It's a ruse, I tell you. I think we need to move and soon."

"But Rogget," Sadie said. "You can't move yet."

"I can. You got those horses don't you?"

"They're not ours," Grayson said. "The Wretched will come after them soon enough."

"But we can take them as far as the borderlands north and then set them off."

"Rogget's right, Fenn. I get the feeling we need to go far

away," Grayson said.

"If you really think it's necessary," Fenn said. "But I don't want Rogget moving before he's ready."

"I'm ready," Rogget said.

Pinta nervously packed his things and Rogget climbed atop one of the horses while Sadie, Grayson, and Fenn climbed atop the other.

They sat around the fire a hundred miles out from Banished, long past the lilac clover range, wrapped in blankets, sheltered from the wind against huge white boulders. The sound of the great rushing river was dampened by its icy covering. Snow-capped mountains of the ice realm towered over them from the north as Grayson began to speak.

"Here is all I know," he said.

Fenn had cajoled him each day, every chance he had, during their trip north. He must tell what he knows of the history of the Ruud. If they were ever to figure out the mess they were in, they had to know everything they could. He was adamant at first that he would not share his information. It was forbidden; it was against the law. And any talk of the Hass of Emorah would only upset Sadie.

"Take a look around," Fenn had told him. "We're not in the Ruud anymore. We're outcast. There are no laws here and no Hass. Not to mention the fact that our lives may depend on what's in your head."

Finally, after days of persuading, he'd agreed and now sat bundled in a woolen, hooded overcoat bartered from a nomadic tribe just south, and covered in a blanket, in front of the fire. Rogget sat, as wide-eyed and curious as Sadie, waiting for him to begin the story that Fenn said he'd tell.

"A true story," he'd said, "that few other folk know."

"It was hundreds of years ago. Michelruud, the first king, was once a great wissende in the Kingdom of Ruhm."

"A wissende?" Sadie said. "Michelruud was a wissende?"

"A great wissende," Grayson said. "And the Kingdom of Ruhm is a great kingdom. The Ruud is nothing compared with it."

"How would you know?"

"Just let him tell us, Sadie," Fenn said, impatient.

"It's described in the history of the Ruud. The real history of the Ruud."

"What do you mean, the real history?"

"That's what Fenn wants me to tell you. There are two histories. One is the big book that sits out in the front room at the inn."

"And we have a copy at the stationer's," Sadie said.

"Yes," Grayson said. "Anyone can read it, if they can read. But that's not the real history."

"How do you know?"

"Because it said so in *The Book of Katze*. Katze said his was the original history."

"Let him finish the story," Rogget barked. Sadie flinched and hunkered deeper under her blanket.

"Michelruud was a great wissende. The wissenry in the Kingdom of Ruhm was not exactly like the wissenry here. They were scientists and learned folk. They studied the world. They didn't counsel folk and help them. That was the job of the Hass. Only, according to the history, they weren't always called the Hass. First they were the House of the Spirit. They studied philosophy."

"What's philosophy?" Sadie murmured.

"If the wissenry studied *how* things were, the Hass tried to say *why* they were."

Sadie shook her head.

"I don't really understand either," Fenn said.

"For instance, according to the history, there was a terrible plague in the Great West. The wissenry figured out that the disease was carried by tiny insects that fly around sucking the blood of eleshags and then laying eggs in folks' cured meat."

"That's gross."

"But the Hass would say that the plague was brought by Rett to punish the folk for misbehaving."

"Who is Rett?"

Grayson sighed. "This is going to be hard."

"Well, go on, just talk then. We'll listen."

"The Hass of Emorah tells folk how to behave and how to live. Rett is their devotion, the spirit being they follow. He used to live thousands of years ago, but the folk became angry with him when he told them that they should live in peace with the beasts. For that, they had him put to death. But later, realizing that they'd done wrong, they declared him a son of Mutterede and now they worship him. They say that Rett's spirit returned from the dead to create the Hass of Emorah, his representatives on Kell. Their job is to tell the folk how they are supposed to live and why Rett allows things happen. The wissenry was about facts and studies and things and they just told folk the truth."

"Okay. So what happened? Why did Michelruud leave?"

"The Hass of Emorah kept the folk in fear all the time over all sorts of things. But when the wissenry insisted that the beast folk and main folk are related, like brothers, the Hass didn't like it."

"Is that true?" Fenn said. "Are beast folk and main folk the same?"

"Related."

"I can see why the Hass wouldn't like to hear that," Rogget said. "Seeing as how they hate the beast."

"The Hass claimed that main folk were better than beast folk," Grayson said. "But the beast folk have greater power than the folk. The Hass said it was because they'd made a bargain with Mutterede's sister Horatia. They said the beasts were evil and wanted only to destroy the mortal folk."

"But I thought there were no beast folk in the west?" Sadie

said.

"There were in the beginning. But as time went on, the folk pushed them off their lands. According to the book, there weren't many beast folk left after a few hundred years and the Hass made up stories about them raiding folk villages and causing all sorts of mayhem. And when the wissenry insisted that the beast were just like folk and not to be feared—that they were sentient, like folk—the Hass started saying that the wissenry was evil—in league with the beast folk and trying to destroy the Kingdom of Ruhm."

"So, Michelruud left?"

Grayson nodded. "He foresaw a great purge—a great killing. He believed their lives were in danger. But not all of the wissendes left."

"So, he wasn't a prince or anything?" Sadie asked, disappointed.

Grayson shook his head. "Just a wissende."

"So, that's why you were afraid when you saw the Hass in Cold Sea Port," Fenn said.

"No, not really," Grayson said. "This is only history. It was all long ago."

"We're afraid of the Hass because they're mean." Sadie stared intently into the fire and slowly shook her head.

"Did they do something to you?" Fenn asked her.

"My brother."

"I didn't know you had a brother."

"I'm sorry, Sadie," Grayson said. "I was hoping you wouldn't have to remember."

She wiped tears from her face and smiled weakly. "It's not something you ever forget, Grayson. You know that."

He nodded. "You're right. But it stays in the back of your mind, and deep in your heart. No need to bring it to the fore if you aren't ready."

"What are you talking about?" Fenn looked back and forth

266

between them.

"My mother," Grayson said. "And Sadie's older brother."

"What happened?"

"Don't let's talk it out now," Rogget said. "If you're not up to it."

"I don't mind," Grayson said. "But I don't know how Sadie feels about it."

"You go ahead."

Grayson stared at Sadie for a few silent moments before nodding.

"My ma was fading away," he said. "She'd just given birth to my little sister Matilda. My grandmother said she would bleed to death without a dose of some special wissende medicine. My da tried to leave the inn to get some, but the Hass wouldn't let him pass. They'd been in the square, whipping children and one of their horses trampled Sadie's brother. There were folk outside the doors to the inn, front and back, enraged, calling out the Hass. Folk were screaming."

Grayson was suddenly far away, in his own memory and his eyes were wet with tears. Fenn wanted to make him stop, but didn't know if it was better to end it, or better to let him continue. Finally, Grayson spoke again.

"When Father Treacher arrived, he tended to Odom, but he died quickly. He couldn't get into the inn to see my ma until the next day when the crowd had calmed down and the Hass managed to leave. It was too late."

They were all silent for some time. The fire crackled and spit and a light wind washed them with smoke and then lifted it off them. Darnit whined and buried his nose under a paw.

"I'm sorry," Fenn said.

"Odom was seven years old," Sadie said. "I really don't remember much about it. Just that there was shouting and running and horses and my mother was screaming. And then they told me he was dead."

"We were both only about four years old at the time," Grayson said.

"Haven't you ever seen the Hass in Path?" Sadie said.

Fenn shook his head. "Never."

"The wissenry knows, like the rest of us, when they're due," Rogget said. "They keep their young fosters inside for the duration."

"Why do they come every year?" Fenn said.

"Tribute."

"Aye," Rogget said. "The Hass helped dispel the beast long ago and ever since they've demanded tribute."

"But what about the stone?" Grayson said. "Maybe they're looking to get it back."

"You mean the kell stone?" Fenn said. "From the prophecy?"

Grayson nodded. "The stone was a symbol of unity and power for the beast and the Hass stole it and hid it from them shortly after they came to the west. According to the history, Michelruud stole it back and returned it here. But later, he had to give it back to the Hass."

"Why?" Sadie said.

"You knew about the kell stone all along?" Fenn said.

Grayson nodded.

"We had a pact," Sadie said. "No more secrets, remember?"

Grayson looked to the fire and sighed. "It's forbidden to know these things. I couldn't tell anyone."

"How is it forbidden?" Sadie said. "And how would you even know that? I've never even heard of any of it."

"It says so on the very first page of the original history in *The Book of Katze*," Grayson said. "Roarn commissioned a rewriting of the history. The original history was destroyed and banned. Anyone caught with a copy would be put to death. You think I'm going to go around talking about it?"

"Now, come on," Rogget said. "We can't always know what's important to say and when. Grayson didn't mean us any harm by keeping quiet about this."

Grayson shrugged.

"It doesn't really make any sense," Fenn said.

"I didn't really read all of that part, about the stone, anyway," Grayson said. "It didn't seem important at the time. I thought it was legend."

Fenn rubbed his palms against his eyes and then stared into the fire. "I'm too tired to try to understand any of it."

"It's grown-up stuff," Sadie said. "We shouldn't have to understand it."

Grayson looked at her, tired and defeated.

"I'm just saying," Sadie said. "We shouldn't have to. That doesn't mean we don't have to."

"I feel out of place, too," he said.

"I didn't say I felt out of place."

"But you are. We all are. We don't belong here."

"But here we are." Fenn sighed. "I need to sleep. I think if I could sleep, I could figure some of it out."

"I won't argue with sleep," Grayson said.

"It's too early," Sadie complained. Her mouth fell open in a gaping yawn.

"As we go," Rogget said. "T'will get colder and colder. But we ought to find villages and encampments along the way where we'll get food and warmth, in exchange for this news of the Ruud."

"You mean you want to tell the history? We can't do that?"

Rogget shook his head. "It may be the only thing we have worth anything."

They nodded and bundled up for a spell of rest. But sleeping in the face of a journey into the ice realm would be hard fought, Fenn realized. And he lay watching the clouds in the darkening sky, listening to the crackling fire for hours.

When horses approached, they all darted up, and Rogget struggled to douse the embers left in the fire pit.

Chapter Forty-two

Leah sat in the front room of the inn in Path watching the small village square and the occasional passer-by. Soon they would be leaving for a rustic journey north to the caverns of the eastern continent, and into the hill country. A group of folk had arrived from Ruhm—spelunkers—to join them in what she assumed would be an adventure hunting the kell stone. Yet, she couldn't find any enthusiasm for the trip. She held her journal on her lap and looked at it. She could write as if speaking to her mother, but she found it difficult to stay away from topics that should not be broached. At some point, she realized she was not alone and flinched. Looking up, she saw Prenalin take a seat on a bench next to the window opposite her.

"You have not been yourself, of late," he said. "You are changed since..."

"Since the forest?"

He shook his head. "Before. Since the hunt."

She nodded. "Yes."

"It was not my idea that you would be taken on as aide so shortly before this trip. I felt it wasn't a proper introduction to the position."

She couldn't help chuckling. "No, I would say not."

"Kirche insisted. As soon as you graduated from the Hass school, he said, you were to be hired on."

Leah tilted her head and peered at him.

"What is it?" he said.

"I thought *you* chose me."

"No. You were Kirche's choice."

Her brow furrowed. She distinctly remembered the day in Aaronland, when Kirche had asked her to go up to his room and bring him the ledger and notes from his desk. And there, slightly hidden under a short stack of books, was a note he was writing to his brother back home in Ruhm. He'd said that Prenalin had selected her. He wondered why Prenalin would choose such a pretty girl for his aide.

"Is something wrong?"

"Nothing," she shook her head. More lies. Would they never end?

"I don't mean to speak out of turn, Leah." He leaned forward, putting his elbows on his thighs. "But I would like to offer you some advice."

"I am always happy to take advice from you, Pren."

"You know that I understand your feelings, with respect to the beasts."

She nodded.

"But I told you that you must not speak them. And I can see now that you are struggling with upsetting notions. Doubts have a way of eating away at us."

"You would simply have me not speak them."

"No, more than that. It's not enough to merely not say what is on our minds. We must examine our doubts, our fears, and any thoughts that do not ally with the Hass. And then we must accept that there will always be problems with our thinking. The goal is, and ought to be, to learn not to trust our own doubts and insecurities and instead learn to trust only the Hass."

Leah stared out the window for a time pondering what he'd

said. She thought of the flaming tree in the beast forest and considered telling him about it. Would he believe her? Somehow she knew that he would find a way to disregard her find. It was only the Hass for Prenalin. Only the Hass had the answers, and to question Emorah was to question truth.

"But, what if our doubts regard matters of morality?" she said.

He shook his head when she turned to him, hopeful.

"The Hass is the arbiter of morality. It is well enough to think we have it right. But we must allow that the Hass controls the truth. The Hass determines what is good."

"I think I understand," she said. "If my view differs from that of the Hass, my view is wrong."

"Exactly. No matter how much you may feel otherwise."

Prenalin left her there at the window, more confused than before. There had been a short time during which she thought he could be made an ally in her fears. He seemed to think like she did, but was wise enough not to speak his mind where Kirche could hear him. But now she realized she would not be able to share her real feelings with him.

Rubbing her hands together atop her journal in her lap, Leah struggled to come to terms with her lies. She was guilty—she was in debt to so many—the beast lord, Lucas, Pren, and Kirche. How could she think herself moral when she had lied, and continued to lie, to so many folk?

She should tell all, at least to Prenalin and Kirche. She should tell them, at least, what she knew of the kell stone and that she was kin to Dakenruud. What difference would it make, really? And she should tell them how she escaped the beast forest—what she'd promised to the beast lord. But would Kirche send her home to look for the stone? Perhaps he would. She could have a new position within the Hass—she could be the one to find the kell stone. That was it. That was the answer. She must find the kell stone. It was the only way for her to atone—to save her dignity.

She would not be a liar if she did so...well, not so much.

Kirche and Prenalin came into the lobby with the porters, Gretchen and Zelda. Xavier, the youngest porter had now been promoted to bodyguard to replace Alphonse and stood small and timid next to Kipling and Redd.

"Shall we make an evening tour of Path, before our trip north tomorrow?" Kirche beamed with excitement; he was already robed in purple and held his mitre under his arm. "Your face is healing quite nicely. You might not need your scarf after today."

"Lord Kirche." Leah stood, cupping her journal at her chest.

"Of course," Kirche said. "You may put away your journal first. Have you done much writing? Have you pieced together any information about the kell stone? Do you know where it might be?"

She froze, stunned, her mouth open, a slight shock on her face. Why would he ask that? Did he know about her lies? How could he? Out of the corner of her eye she saw Prenalin turn his face away from her.

"I..." She paused, her heart pounding in her chest. Even as she knew deep within her soul it was wrong to lie and to keep secrets, that very same conscience told Leah she must not trust in Kirche. Even that thought caused her pain and she winced.

"Are you ill?" Kirche said.

"Forgive me, Lord Kirche. I must tell you something. Something of great importance."

Prenalin turned to look at her, his face drawn and pale.

Chapter Forty-three

You're going to have to stop disappearing," Phil told Lucas as they hiked with the king's guard north through the woods toward the hill country. "We're supposed to be guarding you."

"I was with Sorgood, on an errand."

"Aye, you were with the master of the guard at that time. But where did you disappear to before that?"

"I'm not a member of the guard. I'm a citizen volunteer. I come and go as I please."

"Oh, yeah?" Brinkley said. "Then how come we were told to guard you?"

"You were just supposed to watch me and make sure I don't get into any trouble. You know, get hold of a firearm or something."

Tildon Weeks and Edgar Wolf had rejoined the guard and were happy to have Lucas' company for their tour of duty. They were assigned a perimeter guard north of the Waverly wissenry in Aaronland as Sorgood said that was the most likely reentry point for Fenn Foster and his traitorous abettors. But Lucas wondered how long it would be before they were ordered into the hill country to hunt the kids down and return them by force to Michelruud. He knew the folk would never let King Welk rest until they were certain that the evil bairn was under lock and key...or worse.

Lucas sat at the campfire while the guards marched their perimeter. Movement in a nearby shrub caught his eye.

"Psst there," a small brownie called to him. "I have news."

The brownie waved Lucas over. Knowing the creature would never want to be seen out in the open by the others, he left his cup of bitters by the fire and followed him into the wood.

"You asked that you be brought news of the Hass girl."

"And you are?"

"Pardons." The brownie bowed slightly. "I am Eerf today."

Lucas knelt on the ground and shook the small folk's hand.

"The girl did as she promised and returned the head of Zeelif, who will now be Zeelif forever." He frowned.

"It is a fine name for a memorial."

"We keep watch on Kirche. But there is little we can do should he decide to harm another. Many of the larger beast have come out of the forest to patrol. It is not good."

"No, it is not. But perhaps it is time to take this chance."

The brownie bowed again and trod off into the woods leaving Lucas to concentrate on Quarn, whose scent he'd caught as soon as he'd left the fire. He turned and watched as Quarn emerged from the wood and took his folk form to speak.

"Why do you continue to harass me? Even now that Dag Voorspeld knows of your treachery."

"Voorspeld's opinion doesn't change who you are. As your uncle—"

"Yes, yes, I know. You think being my uncle gives you the right to supercede my parents' wishes. It does not."

"I am your closest kin."

"You are no longer my kin. You have lost your honor with the felidae."

Quarn's face scowled in fury. Without a word, he fell into

his felid form and leapt at Lucas knocking him to the ground.

"Och wen mudeh en," he growled.

"You will be outcast." Lucas struggled to keep the cat's drooling jaw from getting to his throat.

Suddenly Quarn roared and Lucas saw an arrow bouncing at his shoulder. The cat leapt off him; Lucas sat up to see the eis assassin pulling another arrow from his quiver.

"You attack my prey," the eis said to Quarn and raised his bow to aim.

"No!" Lucas dove in front of Quarn and the assassin lowered his bow.

"You would protect him?"

"I would protect anyone from senseless murder."

Quarn limped into the woods and Lucas heard his padded feet break into a slow run. He turned to the eis again, who smirked at him. But just as the assassin moved to take aim once more, this time at Lucas, Footman Wolf's voice echoed around them.

"Wissende warrior? Where have you gone to now?" He laughed at his own joke.

"I told you he was always running off," Phil said.

The eis lowered his bow and returned his arrow to the quiver.

"Another day perhaps," he said.

"I would know your name."

"Of course. It is well you should know the name of the eis who will kill you. I am called Na-Atten-tu."

"Why do you take such pleasure in the kill, Atten? You would risk the tenuous peace between our folk."

He laughed. "Perhaps that is the reason."

The guardsmen's footsteps tramped through the wood and Atten smiled at Lucas.

"One day soon, you will be my prize."

He turned and fled into the woods just as Edgar and Phil came upon Lucas.

Chapter Forty-four

Welk paced the library in his heavy robe and slippers. The castle was quiet this evening, no one stirred, not even Dunham. But Welk couldn't stop his thoughts enough to let him read or sleep. He could still see himself turning, stomping in a fury back to his men, Fenn Foster riding off to the east behind him. He'd fumed and shouted orders at his guard like a madman. Where were the horses? Where were their firearms? Why had they done nothing to stop the felidae?

It was only Clutch who could calm him. He'd called to him from where his men gathered up the remains of their dignity and supplies.

"It is done," he'd said. "There is nothing to be gained by rage. The boy is away once more."

Welk sucked in a heavy breath. "He is a sly one, isn't he?"

Clutch nodded and his men began to call to him to leave. They none of them liked being too near a king who could punish them. And so they had parted company.

He'd done as he'd promised Forbes Billings years ago. Welk had sent out the commands to Arnot and Ricker. They would allow the banished to return home and replace all property they could. From that point on, banishment was no longer a punishment to be used against a folk of the Ruud. And if the other kings refused, it would mean war. War, he'd said. The stationer sat at his writing desk frozen.

"War, Sire? You mean me to use that very word?"

Yes, he'd meant it. No more talking. No more pandering, trying to reason, and arguing over who controlled which borders and whose folk took whose sheep. The Ruud could not function as three kingdoms.

And as yet, he'd heard no grumbling against his commands from either Aaronland or Damon Wall. He would soon have the kingdoms of the Ruud united as one.

"We must call a meeting of all the representatives in the hills and the Ruud," he'd told Clutch before his men could drag him away. "Will you spread the word?"

"I will. What will be the purpose?"

"We will decide our rights to the hill country, and approach the eis with our demands."

Clutch had balked, but he smiled. "It was good to see you again."

"And you."

Welk turned back to his men, but Clutch had called out once more. "The girl," he'd said. "What will you do about her threat?"

"Nothing."

"But she aimed a gun at the king."

He laughed. And he could still hear himself say it. Where had it come from? And wasn't it true?

"I am no more a king than you are."

Chapter Forty-five

In the dim light of early evening, the kids scrambled behind the boulders and listened as horses approached. Rogget put an arm across the rock as if to hold them back from jumping out and betraying their position. The horses came into their tiny encampment and Fenn couldn't help but peer out at the intruders.

"Oi there'n," Wiley Arbus called out. "T'is that you, Rogget and company?"

Almost laughing in relief, they came out of hiding but the fierce roar of a large brown bear had them frozen.

"Oh, come now, Petunia," Wiley said. He dismounted and walked up to the bear, giving her a hesitant pat on the shoulder.

"That's not Darnit," Grayson mumbled.

"Indeed, no," Bruck said. "That there's Petunia. As fine a bear scout as we ever met."

Wiley laughed. "We wouldn't have rightly known what she was, if we hadn't met with your bear Darnit. Oh, look, she finally smelt him out."

Darnit had let out a grumble and Petunia lumbered toward him. Rogget and the others shook themselves out of their stunned silence and watched as Darnit and Petunia sniffed, nudged shoulders, and got to know each other.

"I think you got a story for me," Rogget said and built up the fire again to warm their guests. Wiley and Bruck Lerned sat with them around the pit rubbing their hands together over the flames.

"Like to thought we'd never find you, at first. And then, what you knows? A bear. And she seemed eager to make her way northeast," Wiley said.

"Aye," Bruck said. "She's got the smell o' Rogget's bear, I told him."

"That weren't your idea. It was mine."

"Nonsense. I said it first."

"And what coincidence. We needed to find you."

"But...another bear?" Sadie said.

Bruck slapped at his leg and fell slightly backward, laughing. "It were the Wretched again. Grindelwell was run off with a few doars he stole off Clutch—to the port. Everybody reckoned he would try to find a boat off to the south as he owed every other folk, and then some, more money than he could count."

"Aye, but instead, he took Clutch's doars and gambled himself into a fine fortune. Paid off his debtors and brought back Petunia. He thought she was all willing to be his partner in crime, but when he stopped walking, she didn't."

"Nope," Bruck said. "She kept right on, through every camp in the hills rooting out jerky, apples, and berries."

"It were Grindelwell what gave us the news."

"News?" Rogget said.

"Aye, we bring big news," Wiley said. "And we thought, what better way to find you than to follow a girlie bear obviously in search of a boy to run off with."

They all turned to watch Darnit and Petunia push their way into the shrubbery and disappear into the night.

"We may never see him back again," Rogget said.

"Amazing news," Bruck said.

"Right." Rogget turned back to the fire. "Let's have it."

"King Welk sent word through the Ruud that he is honoring a writ he signed some twelve years ago."

Rogget gasped. "You don't say?"

"It's true," Bruck said. "Forbes Billings' writ will be honored."

"All the banished are pardoned."

"And what's more, all their property what can be returned to them, will be."

"And how did he get Arnot and Ricker to agree to that?" Rogget said.

"He plain as out ordered them to accept it, as we heard tell it from Grindelwell."

"And Clutch confirmed it."

"You've spoken to him?" Fenn was suddenly nervous.

"Indeed. All the hills are in truce over the news. You never saw so much amity among fighting folk. Here tell a big meetin' is in the works."

"Did you tell them you were coming to find us?" Grayson said.

"Oh, no son," Bruck said. "But I don't think you need to worry yourselves about them."

"Not for another week or so, anyway," Wiley said. "There's going to be much to do about the hills with these changes."

"Aye," Bruck said. "Some of the hill folk are banished. They might up and head home to take on what you call normal lives."

Wiley laughed loud and Bruck joined him.

"Well, that is good news," Sadie said.

Rogget eyed Fenn warily. Fenn knew what he was thinking. Just because King Welk had honored the writ didn't mean he would stop hunting Fenn. As much as Fenn wanted to believe Welk's promise to leave him alone, he trusted Rogget's judgement more.

He, Grayson, and Sadie sat at the fire listening to the three folk talk of freedom and their days of youth until long into the wee hours of the morning when Fenn found himself nodding off to sleep, his hemp rope and charm pulsating warmth across his chest. The amber shard of crystal that Clutch had added to the rope was warmer than his charm and he often thought it throbbed and filled him with a sense of strength. But Father Treacher had once told him about the odd sensations of growing up and he surmised it wasn't the stone at all, but that he was becoming, finally, an adult.

Fenn was awakened by Lucas' screams in his head. And in that place between sleep and awake, he could see him, running forward toward him, screaming, "No!" Lucas reached out to him, to stop his floating away. But Fenn realized, gradually, that he was not floating away. He was being carried.

"Fenn!" Rogget called after him. "Fenn! No!"

Fenn woke, but couldn't move. He was cradled in the arms of a luminous being, shining so bright in the darkness he had to blink. He felt no arms holding him up; it was if he lay on a pillow of air. He tried to feel concerned about this situation, but he was almost giddy as he said to himself, "Kidnapped again." Still he thought he ought to be frightened, or angry. Instead, he was warm; he felt as if all was set to right again. No worries. He was going home.

As he was carried away into the cold darkness of the night sky, he heard Wiley Arbus' terrified scream.

"Angel!"

Books by this author

Fantasy by Dana Trantham
Children of Path: The Kell Stone Prophecy Book One
The Wretched: The Kell Stone Prophecy Book Two
Mark of the Faire: The Kell Stone Prophecy Book Three
The Kell Stone Prophecy: Complete Trilogy

Story Runners: Awakening

Women's, Literary, Romantic Comedy, and Young Adult
by Dianna Dann

Camelia
Always Magnolia
Bookish Meets Boy

Paranormal Humor by by D.D. Charles
Zombie Revolution

Children's fiction by Dana Trantham
Zombie Cats (middle grades)
Wayward Cat Finds a Home (children's chapter book)

www.waywardcatpublishing.com
Dianna Dann   Dana Trantham   D.D. Charles

Now available from Wayward Cat Publishing

Mark of the Faire

The Kell Stone Prophecy Book Three

An excerpt

L eah Hallowsing cowered in the darkness, sobbing once again. She couldn't be sure how long she'd been lost, but it seemed weeks. She had little food left, and feared she could not fight off the cave rats again. They followed her as she crawled along the cavern floor, feeling her way, sure she'd plunge off a cliff to her death if she dared to walk; they scurried around her, occasionally nipping and pulling at her skirt. Several times now, one landed on her pack and, screaming, she battled him off. The time would come when it would be more than one. At some point, they'd have her pack and she'd have to consign herself to starving alone in the caves of the east, far from home.

She could crawl no more, she decided; she must rest. Every time she tried to sleep her mind brought her images she couldn't force away. Her father in his closet office, sitting across from her, the shadow of candle flame dancing on his face. "You are kin to the apostates," he kept saying. "What do you think of that?"

And Kirche, smirking. Watching her. She couldn't stop remembering the day she'd nearly told him about her father, about the journal of Dakenruud, about the kell stone.

"I must tell you," she heard herself say over and over again. "Something of great importance." Kirche had stared at her, almost as if he knew what she would say. And she stumbled. "I..." She could no longer remember why she'd thought to tell him the truth—could not recall what had stopped her. Was it the look on his face, the deadness in his eyes? "I'm frightened of the caves," she'd told him. It was a lie...then.

In her moments of hope, which were few of late, she'd see Prenalin—the horror in his eyes as he reached for her other hand, just as the one slipped from his grasp. She could still hear his screams. "Leah! Leah!"

"Oh, Pren," she whispered.

They'd gathered their gear in Path, and rode hard northeast with Kirche's spelunkers, Wivel and Pike. Wivel reminded Leah of the shepherds and cowmen she'd met on school field trips. Thick with strength and tanned, he had the sharp, dark features of a man who lived for physical exertion. And his wife, Pike, as lean and wiry as an acrobat, always a thin straight line of a smile on her lips. They were eager to tour the caverns of the eastern continent and Kirche was only glad to make a quick journey of it.

He'd heard tell of a meeting in the hills between King Welk and the land pirates and deserters of Ruhm who made the place their home. He wanted to get the spelunkers to work, enjoy a bit of cave hunting himself, and then move on, leaving them to search for his kell stone while he and his entourage traveled south to find out what they could of Welk's planned meeting with the eis.

The caverns of the eastern continent rose like a giant collection of sloping ant hills, rocky and brown, surrounded by forest. They'd lost track of the spelunkers within hours, but nobody worried; they were tasked with the find and would meet Kirche back in Ruhm.

"Keep to this path here," Wivel had told them. "It circles back around. Don't go off it or you could find yourselves lost."

And so she, Prenalin, and Kirche hiked in the dim light of the upper level near their campsite, up natural steps and down, in and out of pure rock, sometimes stopping to peer up at slits of sunlight highlighting enormous boulders resting uneasily against one another above their heads.

It happened so quickly, the slip, the tiny misstep that had Leah clinging to the rock, kicking her feet in search of something beneath them to support her. Prenalin reached out and grabbed at her fingers just as she lost her grip. They stared at each other, frozen in time. All sound was muted but for her breath in her ears. Her hand pulled from his grasp like thick sap from a tree and though it seemed to take hours, she knew she only glimpsed his face and it was gone—she slid into the darkness, tumbled deep into the rock, tripping, falling, until the ground leveled beneath her. Prenalin's voice echoed far away, calling her name.

"Pren," she screamed.

He was no more than muffled noise and moving away, falling deeper into silence. She tried to climb out. For what seemed days she tried, until her fingertips and palms were bloodied and raw. She cried out; no one answered but herself.

At some point, she couldn't know how much time had passed, she feared they'd give up on her. It was then she began to move, determined to find a way out. And in her head, her own words did little to comfort her. "I'm frightened of caves."

Frightened. Leah pressed her hands against the sides of her head, forcing the sight of Prenalin's fear away. It wasn't true, she wanted to say. It was a lie. I'm not afraid. They must be searching for her, she promised herself. Prenalin wouldn't leave her to die in the dark.